MURDER IN THE SUPREME COURT

CHAPTER

1

*"Oyez! Oyez! Oyez! All persons having business be-
fore the Honorable, the Supreme Court of the United
States, are admonished to draw near and give their
attention, for the Court is now sitting. God save the
United States and this Honorable Court."*

AS THE MARSHAL CHANTED THE OPENING RITUAL, NINE
black-robed justices stepped through heavy burgundy drapes
behind a winged Honduras mahogany bench and took their
seats. Attorneys who would present the first set of oral
arguments sat at a long counsel table in front of, and below,
the bench. Before them were twenty ten-inch quill pens
carefully crossed on writing pads, a tradition from the Court's

earliest days. An older attorney wore a morning coat; the rest were in dark, vested business suits.

"Let's begin," said Jonathan Poulson, Chief Justice, who sat in the middle of the bench. Bald except for tufts of white hair around the lower perimeter of his head, wire spectacles perched low on an aquiline nose, a long slender index finger pressed against his cheek, he listened as attorneys seeking admission to the Court were introduced.

"Admission granted," Poulson said. The clerk administered the oath. "Welcome, ladies and gentlemen," Poulson said. "Let's get on with the first case, *Nidel* v. *Illinois*."

A young attorney walked to the podium, cranked it higher, arranged long yellow legal sheets on it. His hair was thick and dark, and he had a sallow, slightly pockmarked face. "Mr. Chief Justice, and may it please the Court," he said in a strong voice, "two years ago, in the spring, the plaintiff sought to seek an abortion in her home state of Illinois . . ."

Poulson leaned back in his black leather chair and listened to the attorney's introductory remarks while looking out over the huge, majestic courtroom. It never failed to impress him, the dignity and beauty of it, walls and columns of white marble from Spain and Italy contrasting with carpet and drapes as red as blood. Directly in front of him, high on the west wall, was one of four thirty-six-foot marble Weinman friezes. Poulson absently identified each of the symbolic figures; the winged female figure of Divine Inspiration flanked by Wisdom and Truth. To the left stood the Powers of Good: Security, Harmony, Peace, Charity and Defense of Virtue. Evil was represented on the other side; Corruption, Slander, Deceit and Despotic Power.

The room was filled with spectators, as it usually was when a controversial issue was being argued. Those with special interest gathered in front of a gleaming brass rail. The press was in a designated section to the left. Behind the rail sat the general public. Every seat was occupied, and the line outside was long.

The Chief noticed a small boy looking up at the ceiling, a vast expanse of gold-leaf lotus blossoms, symbolizing Endurance, set against brightly lighted red and blue squares.

He returned his full attention to the attorney's words. He hadn't missed any of them despite his mental wandering. Years on the bench had honed that skill, first as an appellate judge in the Ninth Circuit, then with the U.S. Court of Claims until being nominated a little more than a year ago for Chief Justice by President Randolph Jorgens.

Jorgens, a conservative, had been swept into office on a nation's disenchantment with previous liberal, permissive administrations. He could have tapped an existing justice for the Chief's job but honored the tradition of not doing that for fear of upsetting the delicate balance that existed on the Court. Instead, he reached out to his old friend Jonathan Poulson, who, like the new president, espoused conservative ideology, a hard-nosed Constitutionalist, fiscally sound and overtly disdainful of changes that challenged time-proven American traditions.

The attorney was interrupted by the Court's only female justice, Marjorie Tilling-Masters, an attractive and brilliant woman who, besides bringing a moderate, reasoned philosophy to the bench, had been responsible, simply by virtue of being female, for changing the tradition of addressing justices as, "*Mr*. Justice Poulson," or "*Mr*. Justice Brown." Since her arrival, the *Mr*. had been dropped, although an occasional slip of the tongue still occurred.

The justice to Poulson's immediate right, Temple Conover, leaned close and said, "The attorney has a lisp."

Poulson smiled. As the oldest justice and the one with the most tenure on the Court, Conover took advantage of his seniority to display irreverence at times Poulson considered inappropriate. Conover had become a media char-

3

acter, irascible and argumentative, brilliant, foppish in his dress, flamboyant in his life-style. He'd recently married for the fourth time. His new wife was twenty-six; he was eighty-two. He was a devout liberal.

The justice to Poulson's left, Morgan Childs, leaned toward his microphone and said to the attorney, "Mr. Manecke, it's my understanding from your affidavits that the original appeal was based upon the refusal of the state to finance the plaintiff's abortion. That strikes me as vastly different from the argument you're presenting here today, that it is a woman's right to determine the fate of her own body."

The attorney looked up from his prepared statement and said, "Justice Childs, the issue is broader than simply one of fiscal decision making. That's why this case has reached this level. We're dealing with a basic issue of individual rights within a free society. To reduce it to . . ."

Childs waved his hand and shook his head. "That's my point, Mr. Manecke. I simply wish to keep things straight. Either we're arguing a woman's rights or the balancing of a checkbook."

A few of the spectators in the audience chuckled. Chief Justice Poulson looked up, which ended the momentary mirth.

Childs pressed, "We're being called upon to decide a national issue, Mr. Manecke. It would help if we knew what that issue was."

The attorney tried to get back to his prepared statement but another justice asked a question.

Poulson turned to his chief clerk, Clarence Sutherland, who sat behind him, and asked, "What is the substantive issue here?"

Sutherland smiled and shrugged. "Sex, I suppose."

Poulson drew a deep breath and returned his attention to the attorney's comments. Clarence disappeared through the curtains, found a book he was looking for in a library housed behind the bench, returned and handed it to Poulson. "Page eleven, sir. It has relevance."

When the plaintiff's attorney had completed his hour, the older attorney in the morning coat stepped to the podium. He represented the state of Illinois. Poulson knew him well. They'd been classmates in law school.

"Mr. Chief Justice, and may it please the Court," he said, "I stand before you today as a representative of a confused and troubled American electorate. Concepts that have withstood the test of time are being rewritten by those with special, self-serving motives. The values that have provided the linchpin of the American dream, the fabric from which the American cloth has been woven, are being placed in deliberate jeopardy. In the case that has been brought here today . . ."

Justice Marjorie Tilling-Masters picked a piece of lint from her black robe. A security guard politely asked a spectator to remove his arm from the brass rail as the ancient Justice Conover mumbled to no one in particular, "The point, get to the point."

Chief clerk Clarence Sutherland walked behind the justices and handed a note to another clerk, Laurie Rawls. She read it, looked up and pouted. The note said he couldn't keep their dinner date. He shrugged and was about to return to his chair when a sharp, clear report crackled through the heavy silence of the room.

"Get down!" the marshal shouted.

All nine justices, robes awry, got down beneath the bench. Spectators looked around, and fell to the floor. Armed guards wearing white shirts and black ties ran to the bench. Clarence Sutherland had dropped to his knees next to Laurie Rawls. They looked at each other in shock.

"Stay low," a guard yelled.

Clarence poked his head up above the bench and saw a

security man walk into the courtroom carrying an unidentified object. He was smiling. "A lightbulb," he said in a loud voice. "Just a lightbulb that fell out of its socket."

"A lightbulb," Clarence said to Laurie as he helped her to her feet.

"It sounded like a gun," she said. "God, what a scare." She slumped in her chair and blew a strand of hair from her forehead.

Clarence leaned close to her ear. "Sorry about tonight but something came up."

"Who is it this time?"

"Come on . . ."

"Have a nice night." Her words were formed of ice.

Order was restored in the room. The old attorney stepped to the podium, tugged on his formal coat, cleared his throat and said, "Mr. Chief Justice, and may it please the Court, as I was saying . . ."

CHAPTER
2

JONATHAN POULSON SAT IN HIS CHAMBERS ON FRIDAY morning, three days after the lightbulb incident. "Where's Clarence?" he asked his other clerks.

"I don't know," one of them said. "Traffic, I suppose."

"Yes." Sutherland was often late, which always upset the Chief Justice. He believed in punctuality, felt those who didn't were attention-seeking bores.

A buzzer sounded at 9:25, five minutes before the Friday conference was to begin. Of all the rituals of the Court, the Friday conference meant the most to Poulson. Thousands of potential cases were presented to the Supreme Court each year under the concept of the Court granting a writ of cer-tiorari, from the Latin *certiorari volumus*, meaning, "We wish to be informed." Most cases were dismissed by a clerk's written evaluation. Of those that survived a clerk's analysis, the Friday conference was crucial. Final decisions were made during it.

The nine justices gathered in a foyer off the main conference room where they engaged in the ceremonial act of helping each other on with their robes before shaking hands and entering the largest of four such conference rooms. Richly paneled in American quartered white oak, it contained a large conference table with a black leather inlay that was piled high with notebooks, memos and briefs. Poulson sat at the east end of the table, his customary place. Temple Conover, the senior associate justice, sat at the west end, again tradition. The junior associate justice, Morgan Childs, took his place nearest the door, where he would act as doorman and messenger, sending out for and receiving reference material.

"Good morning ladies and gentlemen," Poulson said. "The first matter we are to consider is . . ."

At ten minutes before ten there was a knock at the door. Poulson looked at the junior justice and raised his eyebrows. It was unheard of for anyone to intrude on the sanctity of the Friday conference. Temple Conover summed up everyone's feelings when he snapped, "Who the hell is that?"

"We'll see," Morgan Childs said.

The junior justice opened the door. Standing there was one of Conover's clerks, Laurie Rawls. "It had better be important," the Chief Justice said.

"It is, sir. It's . . ." She began to cry.

"What *is* it?" Poulson said, standing and going to the door.

"It's awful—"

"*What* is awful?" Poulson said. The eyes of the other justices were now on her.

"He's . . . oh, my God, he's dead . . ."

"Who's dead?" Childs put in quickly.

8

"Clarence . . ."

"Clarence Sutherland?"

"Yes . . . he's been . . ." And she broke down and collapsed against Poulson's chest.

He held her for a moment, then released her and moved into the hall, followed by the others. "Where is he?"

"In the Court."

Poulson briskly led the group down a broad hallway. They passed through the Great Hall's vast expanse of Alabama marble and rows of monolithic columns, collective footsteps ricocheting off the hard floor, black robes flowing behind them. A security guard snapped to attention. He'd never seen all nine of them walking as a group through a public area before.

They passed through huge double doors leading into the courtroom. The doors closed behind them with a heavy sigh. They rose and looked toward the bench, then tentatively moved up one of two interior aisles. There, seated in the Chief Justice's chair, was Clarence Sutherland. His head was cocked to one side, which caused wavy blond hair to droop in that direction. He appeared to be smiling, although it was more of a grimace. He was dressed in the same slate gray suit Poulson remembered him as having worn the previous day, green paisley tie neatly knotted against his Adam's apple, pale blue lisle button-down shirt curving to the contour of his vest. The only thing unusual was his forehead. In the center of it was a small, crusted hole from which blood had erupted over his right eye and down to his upper lip, where the beginnings of a moustache had trapped it and kept it from flowing further.

"He's dead," Morgan Childs said, stepping closer and craning his neck to get a better look.

"Murdered," Temple Conover said.

"In the Supreme Court," Chief Justice Jonathan Poulson added, like a judgment.

9

CHAPTER
3

LIEUTENANT MARTIN TELLER OF THE WASHINGTON MET-
ropolitan Police Department took a bite of prune Danish.
His phone hadn't stopped ringing since Clarence Sutherland's body was discovered. He'd just hung up on the head
of security for the Supreme Court, who had cleared him for
twenty-four-hour unlimited access to the court building until
the investigation was over. Now, he was talking to a reporter
from the Washington *Post*. "You know more than I do at
this stage," he said. "Yeah, that's right, it was a .22 and
he was sitting in the Chief Justice's chair when it happened.
Other than that . . . what? Who told you that? . . . Your sources
are privileged? Wonderful, so are mine. Sure, I'll get back
to you the minute we come up with something." How many
times over the years had he said *that*?

He hung up the phone and finished the Danish, washing it down with the cold remains of a container of coffee. He opened a file folder on his desk marked SUTHERLAND, C. HOMICIDE, and read the only two pieces of paper in it, then closed it and lighted a clove cigarette. He'd discovered cloves six months earlier while trying to quit smoking, his rationalization being that they tasted so bad he'd be reluctant to light one up. It hadn't worked. He was now a two-pack-a-day clove cigarette smoker.

The phone rang. "Detective Teller," he said.

"Good morning," a pleasant female voice said. "This is Susanna Pinscher at the Justice Department. I'm calling about the Sutherland matter."

"Matter?" he muttered to himself. At Justice even a murder was a legal "matter." "What can I do for you?"

"Well, I've been assigned to the case over here at Justice. I was told you'd be handling it at MPD and thought we should touch base."

Touch base . . . boy, she had all the lines. Still, it made sense. "Okay."

"Look, Lieutenant Teller, could we get together this afternoon? I'd like to set up a system to pool information."

"Do you have any?"

"Any what?"

"Information. I'm afraid I don't."

"Just background on the deceased, the circumstances of his being found, how he was killed."

"We're even."

Her sigh wasn't lost on him. He'd try to be more cooperative. "It's been a tough morning, Miss Pinscher. Sorry if I seem short. Sure, let's get together."

"How about three this afternoon?"

"No good for me. I'm interviewing Sutherland's family then." He silently debated it, then asked, "Want to come with me?"

11

"Well, I . . . yes, thank you, I appreciate the offer."

"I'll meet you in front of Sutherland's house at three. Know where it is?"

"I have the address. What kind of car should I look for?"

"Forget the car. You'll know me immediately."

"Really? How?"

"I'm the handsomest detective on the force, a cross between Paul Newman and Walter Matthau."

"And modest as all get out."

"Yeah, that's me. See you at three."

He hung up, stood, stretched and looked out his window over a blustery October Washington day. "Almost winter," he muttered as he rolled down his shirt sleeves. The right cuff flapped open. He'd noticed the missing button while dressing that morning but was running late. Besides, all his other shirts were missing buttons too. He slipped on his suit jacket and went to a small cracked mirror hanging crookedly near the door. Some days he felt younger than his forty-six years, but this wasn't one of them. His reflection in the cracked glass didn't help. He'd put on weight and was developing jowls beneath prominent pink cheeks. Loss of thin, brown, straight hair had advanced enough to cause him to start parting it lower so that the long strands could be combed up over the balding spot. "Moonface," he'd been called in high school. He smiled as he turned to retrieve the Sutherland folder from his desk. No matter what age had done to him, he looked better now than when he was in high school. At least the acne was gone.

Five minutes later he was seated around a small, scarred conference table with his superior, Dorian Mars, four years younger and possessing a master's degree in criminology and a Ph.D. in psychology. Also at the table were four other detectives assigned to the Sutherland case.

"This is the most important case in my career in law enforcement," Mars said, puffing on a pipe. He looked at

Teller. "It'll be a pressure cooker until it's solved, Martin. They're already talking bottom line. Which means our collective neck if we don't handle things well . . ."

Teller nodded solemnly and adjusted the buttonless cuff beneath his jacket sleeve. He opened the Sutherland folder and said, "We'll stay in the kitchen, Dorian, no matter how hot it gets," wishing he was able to curb a recent tendency to mimic his boss's penchant for the well-worn phrase.

HE WAS late getting to the Sutherland house, a huge and sprawling white stucco and red brick home set back on four acres in Chevy Chase. The original house had reflected the federal style of architecture popular during its construction in 1810. Numerous additions and wings had transformed it into a more eclectic dwelling.

Parked in front of a long, winding driveway was an MPD squad car. Two uniformed officers stood next to it. Another car was parked twenty feet further up the road. Teller pulled his unmarked blue Buick Regal behind the second vehicle. The door opened and Susanna Pinscher stepped out, a nicely turned pair of legs leading the way. Teller was immediately aware of her beauty. He judged her to be about five feet four inches tall but she carried herself taller. Clean, thick, black, gently wavy hair with errant single strands of gray fluttered in the breeze. Her face was definite and strong, each individual component prominent yet in sync with the others. She was fair, with full, sensuous lips etched in red, large expressive green eyes defined by an appropriate amount of mascara, rouge so expertly applied to her cheeks that the color seemed to emanate from within.

She extended her hand and smiled. He took it and said, "Sorry I'm late."

"It's okay. I just got here. You are Martin Teller?"

"You didn't know me right off?"

13

She cocked her head and narrowed her eyes. "Definitely Paul Newman. I don't see the Matthau, though."

"I think we can work together, Miss Pinscher. Come on."

They walked up the driveway. He allowed her to get ahead of him and took in her figure. A subtle pleated plaid skirt swung easily from her hips. She wore a blue blazer over a white blouse. She suddenly stopped, looked over her shoulder and asked, "Coming?"

"I'm with you." So far.

They told a uniformed black maid who they were, and she asked them to wait in the foyer. Teller looked around and whistled softly. "It's bigger than my whole apartment."

"He's a successful psychiatrist," Susanna said.

"There are poor ones?"

The maid returned and led them across a vast expanse of study and through another door, then along a corridor until reaching a separate wing. She knocked on heavy sliding doors. They opened and the maid stepped back to allow them to enter.

"Good morning, I'm Vera Jones, Dr. Sutherland's secretary. I hope you don't mind waiting. This dreadful thing has taken a toll on everyone, especially the immediate family."

"Of course," Susanna said.

The patient-reception area, which was also her office, was decorated in subtle earth tones, spacious and strikingly neat. Two sharpened pencils were lined up perfectly parallel to each other on top of a yellow legal pad on her polished desk. A large leather appointment book was squared with the corner of the desk.

Everything in order, like the woman, Teller told himself.

Vera Jones appeared the last word in a dedicated, organized secretary. Fortyish, tall and slender, her clothing was like her hair, matter-of-fact, nondescript, functional and

14

not likely to detract from whatever business was at hand. She held herself erect and moved through the office like a blind person who knows her surroundings so intimately that a stranger would assume she was sighted. Her face was a series of sharp angles. Her mouth, wide and thin, was undoubtedly capable of being drawn even thinner under pressure.

Still, Teller thought, this could well be a sensuous woman. He'd come to the conclusion after his divorce that sexuality had nothing to do with sexiness. The overtly sexual female wearing provocative clothing, flirting, leading conversations into sexual innuendo was likely to be deceptive. He'd come to appreciate and trust subtlety, respond to it. He glanced at Susanna, who'd taken a leather wing chair next to Vera's desk, and wondered at her style.

Vera sat behind her desk and checked the pencils' alignment. She sighed; her breasts rose beneath a forest green sweater. Teller noticed their fullness. He took a matching chair across from Susanna and asked, "How long have you worked for Dr. Sutherland, Miss Jones?"

The turn of her head was abrupt, as though the question had startled her. "Twenty-two years," she said.

"That's a long time."

"Yes, it is." She paused, looked down at the desk top. "Is there any possibility of postponing this interview?"

"Why?" Teller asked.

"It seems so . . . so unnecessary considering the personal tragedy the family must face. The boy hasn't even been buried yet."

"That's tomorrow, isn't it?"

"Yes."

Teller looked at Susanna before saying, "I don't like it either, Miss Jones, but I don't make the rules."

A faint light came to life on a compact telephone console

on her desk, accompanied by a gentle bell. "Excuse me," she said. She got up and disappeared through a door.

"What do you know about him?" Teller asked Susanna.

"The doctor? Probably the most famous psychiatrist in Washington, confidant to the rich and powerful, a special advisor to the former administration on mental health issues, very rich and powerful, a world figure in his profession."

"What about his kid?"

"Clarence? Very little except that he's dead, murdered in the Supreme Court, of all places. He graduated from law school with honors and probably had a prestigious law career ahead of him."

"What else?"

She shrugged.

"I understand he was considered one of Washington's most eligible bachelors."

"That's natural in a city with more women than men."

Vera returned and said in a soft voice, "Dr. Sutherland will see you now."

His office was surprisingly small, considering the dimensions of the rest of the house. A glass coffee table in front of a beige couch served as his desk. Two orange club chairs faced the table. A comfortable brown leather recliner was in front of a draped window immediately to the couch's left. On the wall behind the club chairs was an ornate dark leather couch, its headrest curving up like a swan's neck.

"A relic," Dr. Sutherland said coldly from behind the glass table as he noticed Teller's interest in the couch. He hadn't stood when they'd entered.

Teller smiled. "You don't use it?"

"Seldom, only when a patient insists. Most don't. Please sit down. *You* can use that couch if you'd like."

Teller looked at the leather couch, turned to Sutherland and said, "Thanks, I think I will." He sat on it and extended a leg along its length. Susanna sat in one of the club chairs.

Dr. Sutherland leaned back on his couch and took in his visitors with restless eyes beneath bushy salt-and-pepper eyebrows. He had a full head of white hair that threatened to erupt any moment into disarray. He was deeply tanned —sunlamp or Caribbean vacations? Teller wondered. His dress was studied casualness, sharply creased twill riding pants, boots shined to a mirror finish, a blue button-down shirt and pale yellow cardigan sweater. He evidently was aware that he was being scrutinized because he said, "I've canceled all professional obligations since this tragedy with my son."

"Of course," Susanna said.

"My condolences," Teller said.

"Thank you."

"It was good of you to see us," Susanna said.

"I didn't expect both of you. Mr. Teller had made the appointment. Might I ask what official connection you have in this matter?"

"Oh, I'm sorry. I'm Susanna Pinscher. I'm with the Justice Department. Naturally, when something of this magnitude occurs, we're brought into it."

"The world is brought into it," he said, removing glasses that changed tint with the light, and rubbing his eyes. "Have either of you ever lost a child?" he asked.

"No," Teller said. "It must be tough. I have a couple of kids..."

Sutherland replaced his glasses on his nose and looked at Susanna. "Do you have children, Mrs. Pinscher?"

"Miss Pinscher. Yes, I have three. They live with my former husband."

"Very modern."

"It was best for both of us."

"Undoubtedly. It's a trend."

"Pardon?"

"Children being with the male partner. Biology has taken second place to social . . . progress."

Teller knew the tenor of the conversation was making Susanna uncomfortable. He sat up and said, "This is just the beginning, Dr. Sutherland. Nobody likes probing into a family in times of tragedy, but that's what's going to be happening until we get to the bottom line."

"Bottom line?"

"A cliché. I work for someone who uses those terms. Look, I'm not sure there's a hell of a lot to discuss today. It was important that we make contact because—"

"Because along with many other people, I am a suspect in my son's murder."

Teller nodded.

"I understand that, Mr. Teller."

"How about Mrs. Sutherland? Will she understand it?"

"To the extent she needs to. I didn't kill my son."

"I don't doubt it. Who else is in the family?"

"My daughter. She's in California working on her doctorate in English literature."

Teller asked, "Will she be here for the funeral?"

"There are some logistical problems with that, Mr. Teller." Sutherland stood and his height surprised his visitors. His posture on the couch indicated a shorter man, but he'd unraveled himself into over six feet. He extended his hand and said, "You will excuse me."

Teller asked as he shook hands, "What about Mrs. Sutherland, doctor? When can we see her?"

"Obviously not for quite a while. She's under heavy sedation. Perhaps later in the week."

"Of course," Teller said. "Well, thanks for your time. We'll be in touch."

"I suppose you will." He left through a door to the rear of his office.

Teller and Susanna went to where Vera Jones sat ramrod straight behind her desk, her hands crossed on the legal pad.

"Thank you for your time," Susanna said as she headed for the sliding doors.

Teller didn't follow her. He walked to a row of built-in bookcases and perused the books. "Has he read all of these?" he asked.

"I would imagine so," Vera said.

"I have a lot of respect for doctors, especially ones with Dr. Sutherland's reputation." He openly admired a large landscape that hung behind her. "That's a Sutherland, isn't it?" he asked.

"Yes."

"Graham Sutherland. I always liked his landscapes better than his etchings. Any relation to the family?"

"Distant." She led them to an outside door used by patients.

"Thanks for your time, Miss Jones," Teller said. "By the way, where were you the night Clarence was murdered?"

"Here with Dr. Sutherland. We were working on a paper he'd written for a psychiatric journal . . . he's widely published."

"I'm sure he is. Have a nice day."

Teller escorted Susanna to her car. Before getting in she looked back at the house, bit her lip and said, "Strange."

"Did you ever know a shrink who wasn't?"

"It's her. She bothers me. I feel sorry for her."

"Why?"

"I don't know, a type, a sadness in her eyes."

"I know what you mean. Say, how are you fixed for dinner tonight?"

He couldn't tell whether she legitimately wasn't sure of her plans or was groping for an excuse. She said, "I'm busy."

"Well, maybe another time. Let's keep in touch."

He watched her drive away, then drove back to MPD headquarters. At six he went to his apartment in Georgetown, where he fed his two cats, a male named Beauty, a female named the Beast, put a TV dinner in the oven and settled into his favorite reclining chair. Two paperback books were on a table next to him, a historical novel by Stephanie Blake and a collection of Camus's writings. He chose Camus, promptly fell asleep and awoke only when the odor of a charred TV dinner was strong enough to get through to him.

ACROSS TOWN in a large and tastefully decorated cooperative apartment, Susanna Pinscher said into the telephone in her bedroom, "I love you, too, honey. I'll see you this weekend. Okay. Pleasant dreams. Let me speak to daddy."

Her former husband came on the line. Their three children lived with him by mutual agreement, although Susanna visited freely and had taken them for the entire previous summer. The decision to give her husband custody had been a wrenching one but was, she continued to tell herself, the right one.

"Everything okay?" she asked.

"No problems. How about you?"

"Exhausted. They've assigned me to the Sutherland case."

"A biggie. That's all everyone talks about these days."

"I don't wonder. Murder in the Supreme Court. A first."

"Take care of yourself, Susanna. You'll be out this weekend?"

"Yes. Good night."

She prowled through the apartment, ending up in the kitchen, where she made herself an English muffin and coffee. She hadn't had dinner, had come straight home from the office, her briefcase bulging. She'd changed into a nightgown and robe and read until calling the kids.

She finished the muffin and went to the bedroom, where

she took an art book from a shelf. She climbed into bed and found an entry on the British artist Graham Sutherland. She read it, closed the book and turned out the light, wondering as she did why a detective from the MPD would know anything about a relatively obscure British artist.

What was law and order coming to?...

CHAPTER
4

SUPREME COURT JUSTICE TEMPLE CONOVER SAT IN THE sunny breakfast room of his home in Bethesda. He wore a pale blue flannel robe, blue terry-cloth slippers and a red wool scarf around his neck. Next to him was an aluminum Canadian crutch he'd used since his last stroke. The final draft of an article he'd written for *Harper's* magazine on the growing perils of censorship was on a place mat.

A grandfather clock in the dining room chimed out the time, 7:00 A.M. Conover poured what was left of coffee made for him by the housekeeper and looked out a window over formal Japanese gardens, a gift to his second wife, who was Japanese.

"Good morning, Temp," his current wife said from the doorway. Long blond hair flowed down over the shoulders of a delicate pink dressing gown secured at the waist by two buttons. A childlike, oval face was puffy with sleep. She leaned against the open archway, the toes of one foot curled over the top of the other, the bottom of the robe gaping open and revealing smooth white thighs.

"Hello, Cecily," Conover said. "Do you want coffee?"

She came to the table, saw that the glass carafe was empty. "I'll get more."

"Call Carla."

"I'd rather get it myself."

She returned ten minutes later with a fresh carafe, poured herself a cup and sat across from him, one shapely leg dangling over the other. He coughed. "How do you feel this morning?" she asked.

"Well. The article is finished." He slid it across the table. She glanced down at it, then sipped from her cup.

"How was the concert?" he asked.

"Boring."

"Where did you go after?"

"To Peggy's house for a nightcap."

"More than one. You didn't come home until almost two."

"We talked. Okay?"

"You might have called." He started coughing again. His eyes teared up and he gulped water. She started toward him but he waved her away. When he stopped coughing he asked, "Why didn't you call? I worry, you know."

"I didn't want to wake you."

"Who was there?"

"The usual group. Temp, I'm tired of the questions, of the suspicion every time I go out."

"Is it so without cause, Cecily?"

She exhaled a burst of air and returned her cup to the table with enough force to send its contents slopping over

23

the rim. "*Please* don't start on that again. One single incident doesn't—"

She was interrupted by the self-conscious clearing of a male throat. Standing in the doorway was a tall dark man of about thirty whose name was Karl. He wore tight jeans and a gray tee shirt stretched by heavily muscled arms and shoulders. A helmet of black curls surrounded a face full of thick features, heavy eyelids, a full sensuous mouth and a nose worthy of a prizefighter. He'd been hired six months earlier as a general handyman, gardener, and occasional chauffeur to Justice Conover. He lived in one of three garage apartments at the rear of the property.

"Sorry to barge in," he said with a trace of a German accent, "but I wondered if you needed me today to drive. You said yesterday that the Court limo might not be available."

Temple looked at the young man, whose attention was fixed on Cecily. "In an hour," he said. "I'll be ready in an hour."

"Yes, sir." Karl vanished from the doorway.

"What happened to your Court limo, Temp?"

"Maintenance, I think, or being used for the funeral."

"You're not going?" she asked.

"Of course not."

"You should. He was chief clerk."

He tried to control the trembling in his right arm but couldn't, and it quickly spread throughout his body. The crutch crashed to the floor and his hand hit the carafe.

"Are you all right, Temp?"

"Look at you."

"What do you mean?"

"Can't you at least have the decency to cover up when a man enters the room?"

She looked down, then up at him. "I'm wearing a *robe*, for God's sake."

24

"It has snaps, why don't you use them—?"

"This is ridiculous," she said as she pulled the hem of the robe over her bare legs and tugged the upper portion of it across her chest. "Excuse me, I have to get dressed for the funeral."

He placed the palms of his hands on the table and slowly pushed himself to his feet. She came around, picked up his crutch and handed it to him.

"Why do you have to go to that bastard's funeral, Cecily?"

"Because I think it's right—"

"Sutherland was a disgusting—"

"I don't want to discuss it, Temp." She left the room. He followed, his steps slow, labored, the rubber-tipped crutch preceding his right leg as he dragged it across the floor. He reached her bedroom, opened the door and said, "You insult me by going to Sutherland's funeral."

She tossed her robe on the bed and entered her private bathroom.

"You slut," he said just loud enough for her to hear.

She'd been leaning over the sink and peering at herself in the mirror. She straightened, turned and said, "And you, Mr. Justice, have the gall to talk about insulting someone?"

He tottered and grabbed the door for support. The trembling increased. It appeared he would topple over at any moment. She ran across the room and gripped his arm.

"Don't touch me," he said in a strong voice. She stepped back. He raised the crutch as though to strike her, lowered it. "All right, damn you, go to his funeral, Cecily, and *celebrate* his death for me."

CHAPTER
5

THE EPISCOPAL PRIEST CONDUCTING THE GRAVESIDE SER-
vice for Clarence Sutherland glanced at the thirty people
who'd come to pay their final respects. Clarence's mother
was near collapse and leaned against her husband. Their
daughter, Jill, who'd arrived on an overnight flight from
California, stood with her arm about her mother's shoulders.

A delegation from the Supreme Court headed by Associate Justice Morgan Childs stood together. Childs looked
up into an angry gray sky and blinked as the first drops of
rain fell. Next to him was Clarence's clerk colleague, Laurie
Rawls, who was crying.

Martin Teller turned up the collar of a Burberry trench-
coat. He'd awakened with the beginnings of a head cold.
He glanced at Dr. Sutherland's secretary, Vera Jones, who

stood behind the Sutherland family. She was the only person there, he realized, who'd dressed appropriately for the weather, right down to ankle-length Totes covering her shoes.

The corpulent, ruddy-faced priest still seemed to be catching his breath after the walk from the limousine. He looked down at *The Book of Common Prayer* he held in his beefy hands. "*Unto Almighty God we commend the soul of our brother departed, Clarence, and we commit his body to the ground...*"

Dr. Sutherland stepped forward, scooped up a handful of soil and sprinkled it over the coffin as cemetery workmen lowered it on straps. The rain fell harder and the priest held a hand over his head. He spoke faster.

Teller sneezed loudly, momentarily distracting attention from the grave site of three security men assigned by the Treasury Department to Justice Childs.

"*The Lord be with you,*" said the priest.
"*And with thy spirit,*" a few responded.
"*Let us pray. Lord have mercy upon us.*"
"*Christ have mercy upon us,*" was the reply.
"*Lord have mercy upon us.*"

Teller watched the mourners return to their limousines. When they were gone, he approached the grave and looked down at the coffin. Who did you in, kid?

"Everybody has to leave," a workman said.

"Oh, yeah, right. Sorry."

There were several phone messages waiting for him when he returned to MPD headquarters, including one from Susanna Pinscher. He called her first.

"You were at the funeral?" she asked.

"Yeah. Very touching. And wet. I caught cold."

"So fast?"

27

"If it gets serious I can claim workman's comp. You know, Miss Pinscher, I was thinking about you last night."

"You were?" Her voice had a smile in it.

"Yes, I was. I finally figured out who you look like."

"And?"

"Candice Bergen."

"That's very flattering coming from Paul Newman."

"Definitely Candy Bergen."

"Do you always decide who people look like?"

"It's a hobby. How about dinner this week?"

"It might be hard. I—"

"To discuss the case. I have some thoughts."

"I'd like to hear them. Tell you what, Detective Teller, let's make it Saturday night. I have an appointment Saturday morning with Justice Childs. I might also be speaking with some of the other justices during the week. I'll be able to fill you in on those interviews."

"Sold. I'll pick you up at seven. Where do you live?"

There was a long pause. "Do you like Indian food?" she asked.

"No."

"How about Hungarian?"

"Of course I like Hungarian food, as long as I don't have to steal the chicken. I am Hungarian, at least half of me. My mother was a stoic Swede."

"Well, I have a favorite Hungarian restaurant, Csiko's, on Connecticut Avenue, Northwest. It's in the Broadmoor Apartment Building. How about meeting there at seven? I'll make a reservation."

"See you then, but give me a call if anything breaks sooner."

"I will. Talk to you soon."

It was true that Martin Teller was part Hungarian. It was

not true that he liked Hungarian food, especially goulash, or anything with paprika in it. As far as he was concerned, cooking Hungarian food for his father, and having to eat it, had sent his Nordic mother to an early grave.

CHAPTER
6

"What about Sutherland's friends? Have they been contacted?" Dorian Mars asked Teller.

"We're doing it now," Teller said.

"Not fast enough. The commissioner called. He's up in arms."

You sure turn a phrase, Dorian. Well, not to be outdone . . . "What does he expect, miracles?" Teller lighted a clove.

"I wish you wouldn't smoke those things in here, Marty. They're offensive."

"Not to me."

"Please."

"Okay." He carefully extinguished it, saving its expensive remains.

"Let's go over it," Mars said. "Everybody in the Court has been interviewed?"

Teller shook his head and eyed the cold cigarette. "Of course not, Dorian. Setting up interviews with people in the Supreme Court takes time."

"I understand that. What about the family?"

"Still working on it. The father, the shrink, is sort of impressive, strange but sure of himself, arrogant as hell, dresses good. The sister is getting her Ph.D. in California."

"California what? California politics, California geography?"

"California, Dorian. That's where she goes to school. She's studying literature."

"Classical? English?"

"Hungarian."

"A Ph.D. in Hungarian literature?"

"Something like that. I haven't met the deceased's mother yet."

"Why? Procrastination is the thief of time."

"Because her only son has been shot dead in the Supreme Court, which tends to give a mother headaches."

"Talk to her. Talk to anybody, but get something going fast. I'm under a hell of a lot of pressure from up top."

"I understand," Teller said.

"Are you coordinating with Justice?"

"Sure. We're in touch every day."

"Good. Marty, give me a gut feeling about this case. Who do you think?"

Teller shrugged. "It's wide open. I wish I had even a solid hunch to give you, but I don't. The only thing I will say is that it might be a woman."

"Why?"

"His life-style. The kid was handsome, smart, a dedicated swinger, broads all over the place, probably lots of them mad at him. I'm going over after this meeting to check out his bachelor pad in Georgetown. I had it sealed off the minute we heard he was dead."

"A woman, huh?"

"Maybe, maybe not. Sometimes it makes sense to me, but then it comes off too much like a dime novel, a woman coming into the Supreme Court in the middle of the night and putting a bullet in his head while he sits in the Chief Justice's chair. When I look at it that way, I end up leaning toward somebody who works in the Court. His coworkers didn't like him much, either."

"Why?"

"Power. He was on a power trip, from what I hear. Maybe he caught a justice in the john doing something he shouldn't be doing and held it over his head, if you'll pardon the visual.

"Don't be ridiculous."

"It's not ridiculous. Supreme Court justices are human, just like you and me. They go to the bathroom and—"

"I know, I know. Let's get back to family and friends. The father, you say he's strange. Is he strange enough to have killed his own son? And if so, why?"

Teller picked up his cigarette from the ashtray and put it between his lips.

"Don't, Marty."

"I won't light it. The father? What father kills his only son?"

"It happens. Life's a stage, and we're all players on it."

"You're so right, boss . . . Look, Dorian, too many could have killed Clarence Sutherland. There seem to be as many motives as there are alibis. I'll keep plugging. By the way, I ordered a wall chart for my office."

"A chart?"

"Yeah, a flow chart, it's called. I was getting confused with the Sutherland case so I thought I'd put it all on a chart. This chart has arrows and stars and even glitter letters to highlight things. It might not mean much to you but I wanted it. It was cheap."

"How cheap?"

"A hundred. I billed the Sutherland case number."

"A hundred?" Mars sighed. "I wish you'd cleared it with me first."

"Sorry."

"I'll approve it. I'll approve anything to see things move."

"Things'll move, believe me, Dorian."

"I want to meet every morning here at nine until the Sutherland case is wrapped up."

"Sure, bank on it, Dorian. Nine, right here, every morning."

"Good."

TELLER DROVE to Clarence Sutherland's Georgetown town house. A uniformed patrolman stood in front. Yellow tape had been strung across the entrance, and a sign on the door read NO ENTRANCE.

"How's things?" Teller asked the patrolman.

"Not bad, Lieutenant. How's with you?"

"Not bad. Anybody been around?"

"People from your division, that's about it. Say, Lieutenant Teller, if you're planning to be here for a little bit, how about letting me go for coffee?"

"Sure. Make it a half-hour. That's all the time I've got."

He entered a small foyer. To the left was a door leading to Sutherland's apartment. A staircase to the right led to another apartment upstairs. Teller fished out a key, opened Clarence's door and stepped inside.

The living room was large, lavishly decorated. A conversation pit formed by persimmon couches dominated the room. A large projection screen hovered over everything. Teller went to it and saw that it was linked to an elaborate television system that included a videotape recorder. Next to it was a long bookcase on which dozens of videotape cartridges were neatly stacked.

He went to the bedroom. It was the same size as the living room. A circular king-sized bed was made to appear even larger by a mirror that spanned the wall behind it. There was a television projection screen in that room too, as well as an expensive stereo system within arm's reach of the bed.

"What the hell is that?" he asked himself as he approached a panel of buttons and dials next to the bed. He pressed one button, and a small chandelier made of tiny pieces of mirror rotated above the bed. He turned one of the dials. A magenta spotlight came on. It was aimed at the chandelier, and its beam flashed off the mirror chips, creating a mosaic of twinkling light in every corner of the room.

"Lord," Teller muttered as he played with the other dials and knobs. Soon, he had the room spinning in multicolored light, reds and blues, even a strobe effect that caught everything, including the hand he injected into its field, in stop-motion.

He shut off the lights and opened a drawer in a table next to the bed. He didn't expect to find much. The initial search of the apartment had turned up an array of so-called recreational drugs, nothing of the hard variety but enough to send the kid to jail had it gone that way. A telephone book had been taken from the apartment and delivered to Teller at headquarters. He'd turned it over to another detective with instructions to contact every person listed in it.

He picked up the only item in the drawer, a diary of sorts. In it were dates and names, first names only, with initials following. What intrigued him were symbols next to each name. They'd been carefully drawn with a variety of colored pens, stars and circles, exclamation points, question marks, and an occasional "Dynamite . . . Dull . . . Promising . . ."

"A busy boy," Teller muttered to himself as he put the book in his raincoat pocket. In the good old days he'd have been called a cad.

He looked about the rest of the apartment, then returned to the living room, where he took a closer look at the videotapes on the bookcase. There were a few old movies, but most of them were disgusting corn porn. The label on a homegrown one read CINDY AND ME, APRIL. Touching stuff.

"Excuse me," a voice said from the front door that Teller had failed to close behind him.

"Yeah?"

"Are you a detective?"

"Who are you?"

"Wally Plum. I live upstairs."

"What can I do for you?"

"You can call off those goons outside. I live here, and I resent being stopped every time I come home."

"Oh, I'm sorry. They let you in, don't they?"

"That isn't the point."

Teller took a closer look at Wally Plum. He was thin and what was called good-looking, like many other young men around Washington. His features were angular, his skin surprisingly dark considering his blond hair and eyebrows. He'd begun balding prematurely; his hair was carefully arranged to maximize what he had. He wore a too-tight doublebreasted charcoal gray suit, and a blue shirt with a white collar that was pinched together by a thin gold bar beneath a solid maroon tie.

"Mr. Plum," Teller said, "I'm sorry for any inconvenience, but a murder has been committed—"

"I know that. Clarence was my friend."

"Yeah? How close were you?"

. Plum laughed. "If I tell you, will that make me a suspect?"

"Could be."

"We were good friends. I rented my apartment from him."

"He owned this place?"

"Yes."

"Not bad on a law clerk's salary."

"He had help."

"Family?"

"Yes."

"Nice apartment. I was noticing his collection of tapes."

Another laugh. "He had some good stuff."

"What about this one?" He pulled CINDY AND ME, APRIL, from the shelf and handed it to Plum.

"Oh, that. We used to kid around sometimes."

"What'd you do, take movies of yourselves?"

"Sure."

Teller took the cartridge from Plum and returned it to the shelf. "The bedroom," he said. "It looks like a setup."

"It worked well for Clarence."

Teller shook his head and crossed the living room to the couch. He pushed on a cushion with his fingertips, then sat on it. "You know, Mr. Plum, I do believe the world has passed me by."

"How so?"

"All this sort of stuff. I don't understand any of it."

"Generation gap. Things change."

"I know." He lit a cigarette. "I have two daughters, and most of their talk is all Greek to me. Well, so long as you're here, tell me about Clarence Sutherland."

Plum sat in a chair near the door, crossed his legs. "What would you like to know?"

"Anything you can tell me. Start with what he especially liked to do."

"You've seen the apartment."

"I mean besides that."

"There was nothing besides that."

"Come on, he must have had hobbies, interests aside from chasing girls. Where did he like to hang out?"

"A lot of places."

"Did you hang around with him in those places? Were you drinking buddies?"

"Clarence didn't drink, maybe an occasional glass of wine."

"Drugs?"

"No."

"They found lots here in the apartment."

"I wouldn't know about that."

"I wish you did. I might be more inclined to cross you off as a potential suspect." And if he believed that, he'd believe in the tooth fairy. Hell, maybe Mr. Plum did...

Plum raised his eyebrows. "Oh, that's the way it is. Did Clarence use drugs? No, just soft stuff that everybody's into—"

"Like what? Pot?"

"Yes."

"Coke?"

"Once in a while. You *drink*. There's that generation gap again."

"I'm not in the mood to debate it with you," Teller said.

"Good. Anything else I can tell you about Clarence?"

"Other friends. Who'd he hang out with besides you?"

"We didn't hang out, Lieutenant."

"Whatever you want to call it."

"Clarence had many friends. Despite his prestigious family his friends included many sorts. Sometimes he enjoyed the low life. Clarence liked to get involved with strange types."

"Give me some of them."

"Names?"

"If you know them."

"I don't remember names. There were parties. He'd invite them, or meet them in a bar and—"

"Male, female?"

"Mostly female."

"Mostly? Was he—?"

"Gay? No. Bisexual? No. Clarence was straight."

"But sort of kinky."

"Depends on your point of view. Look, Lieutenant, Clarence in *my* view was a normal, healthy American male, having a good time before it was time to settle down."

"Did he have a steady girl friend? Somebody he saw regularly. Was he, forgive the expression, in love with anybody?"

"Not that I know of."

"Do you know any woman who might have wanted to take a shot at him?"

"No."

"Do you know any women who were in love with him?"

"Sure, a few. Clarence had charm to burn."

"Name one."

"Laurie Rawls."

"From the Court?"

"Right. She drove him crazy, calling at odd hours, showing up when he was with somebody else and making scenes. That lady has a problem. She played the game, but deep down all she wanted was to have a brood of kids and keep the apple pies coming out of the oven."

"Sounds like a nice girl."

"If you're into that."

"Clarence wasn't, I take it."

"You take it right. I already told you—"

"What else can you tell me?"

"Nothing really. Sometimes he saw older women. It's a

trend. Older women are into younger men these days. It makes them feel young."

"I'd think it'd make them feel older."

"Doesn't seem to work that way. At any rate, he saw a few from time to time."

"Names."

"Don't know them. Sorry."

Teller stood and took another look around the room. "Well, Mr. Plum, thanks for your time and talk. Very enlightening."

"My pleasure. You will talk to the men outside."

"Sure. By the way, they're not goons. They're police officers doing their job. End of speech."

"Don't take offense, it was just a phrase."

"Yeah, I know. By the way, what were you doing the night Clarence was killed?"

"I was in bed."

"Alone?"

"Of course not."

"An older woman? Sorry . . ."

"I'm not sure *how* old she was."

"Do you remember her name?"

"I . . . frankly I'm not sure . . . do you really have to know?"

"Not if you don't. Thanks again."

TELLER STAYED in his office until seven, then went home, where he put a frozen dinner in the oven and played a recording of *Der Rosenkavalier*. As waltz melodies drifted from his speakers he danced across the living room with an imaginary partner, who of course was Susanna Pinscher. "You look lovely tonight, my dear." She looked up into his eyes. "And you are the most attractive man I've ever known—"

Beast, his female cat, startled by a sound from outside, leaped from the couch and landed on the turntable. The needle dug into the vinyl record as it skated across the grooves, sending a cacophony of scratch and hiss into the room.

"Damn you," Teller yelled at her. She escaped the swing of his hand and scurried beneath a chair. He took a bottle of gin from the kitchen, poured himself a drink, sat in his recliner and offered a toast to the empty center of the room. "Here's to you, Miss Pinscher, wherever you are, and to you, Clarence Sutherland, whoever you were." He downed half the contents of his glass and added, "Generation gap, my ass."

CHAPTER
7

DAWN BROKE CRISP AND CLEAR THE FOLLOWING SATURday. Susanna was up early. She did twenty minutes of exercises, took a hot shower with the adjustable shower head set at maximum pulsating pressure, dressed in a taupe wool gabardine jumpsuit over a claret turtleneck sweater, slipped into a pair of boots and got her car from the garage. She had plenty of time to make her appointment with Justice Childs, so she stopped in a neighborhood luncheonette, bought the Washington *Post* and read it over coffee and honeydew melon.

A half-hour later she exited the George Washington Memorial Highway at a sign that read NATIONAL AIRPORT and found a road leading to the general aviation section of that complex.

Morgan Childs's aviation background was well known to millions of Americans, and Susanna had boned up on the media reports that had created such public awareness. Childs was the most public of the nine Supreme Court justices. He'd been a combat ace in Korea, had been shot down and captured, escaping after six months of captivity. The dramatic details of his escape and subsequent heroism had captured the media's and public's attention. His picture had been on the cover of *Time*. Television crews followed him throughout Korea, sending back vivid images of that war's reigning hero. He'd returned to the United States much decorated, admired and in demand as a speaker and talk show guest. Eventually, public interest waned and he resumed private life as an attorney, then became a district court judge and, finally, was appointed to the highest court of the land, the youngest person ever to receive such an honor.

Susanna parked in a visitor's area and walked along a row of small aircraft. At the end was a hangar. Its door was open and she went inside. A young man in a three-piece suit stepped out of interior shadows and asked politely, "May I help you, ma'am?"

Her initial reaction was to question his authority but she reasoned that Justice Childs had probably been assigned security and that the young man represented it. "I'm Susanna Pinscher, I have an appointment with Justice Childs."

"Oh, yes, Miss Pinscher, the justice told me you'd be coming."

She looked in the direction of his finger. In a corner of the hangar and wearing olive green coveralls was Morgan Childs. His head and shoulders were lost inside the engine cowling of a 1964 vintage, fabric-covered, single-engine Piper Colt. He heard her approach, straightened up and smiled, which lit up a square, tanned, and rugged face. "Hi," he said. "I'd shake hands but no sense in two of us

42

being covered with grease." His hands were black, and one cheek was smeared.

Susanna smiled. "You do your own repairs?"

"That's right. I always packed my own chute too. Besides, I like tinkering with this animal."

She touched the fabric on a wing. "It's yours?"

"Yes. I've had it a long time. I hope you don't mind meeting me out here, Miss Pinscher. I thought it would be less hectic and more private than the Court. Excuse me. I don't want to forget to replace this." He leaned into the engine and tightened something with a torque wrench.

Susanna leaned closer and watched him work. His fingers were thick and blunt, a workingman's hands. Like her father, she thought. She then realized how much Childs and her father had in common. Both had gray crewcuts, an anachronism. Her father, who'd retired to St. Helena, California, in the wine country north of San Francisco, had been an airline pilot with Pan Am for years. He too liked tinkering with mechanical things; nothing was beyond his ability to fix.

Childs straightened up, leaned against the plane and wiped his hands on a greasy rag. "Well, Miss Pinscher, let's talk. What do I know about Clarence Sutherland's murder? Not nearly as much as you do, I'm sure. I was with the other justices when the body was discovered, had the same shocked reaction, couldn't believe that not only had a Supreme Court clerk been murdered, but that he was sitting in the Chief Justice's chair, in the courtroom, when it happened."

"I would assume shock is an understatement."

"Yes, I suppose it is. I represented the other justices at his funeral."

"I read that and wondered why they all didn't attend."

"Too much pressing business in the Court."

She hesitated, then asked, "Were any of the justices . . . well, how shall I say it? . . . Were any of them . . ."

43

"Unwilling to attend the funeral because of animosity toward Sutherland? I doubt it."

"Why were you chosen, Justice Childs? Were you and Clarence Sutherland particularly close? I know he clerked for Chief Justice Poulson."

Childs shrugged and tossed the rag on a tool-laden table next to him. "R.H.I.P., Miss Pinscher."

"R.H.I.P?"

"Rank Has Its Privilege. I'm the junior justice. They asked for a volunteer and chose me."

"Like the military."

"Exactly."

"What about Clarence?" she asked. "I'm trying to piece together some sort of picture of him."

"Clarence Sutherland? Well, drawing an accurate picture of him isn't so easy. He was a rather enigmatic young man." A strong gust of chilled October air whistled through the open hangar doors and blew a set of engine specs for the Colt from the table to the floor. Childs picked them up, folded them carefully and put them into his coverall pocket. He looked toward the open hangar door and said, "I'd intended to get in an hour of flying this morning, Miss Pinscher. I'm afraid that's all the time I have, another hour. How about continuing this discussion up in the air?"

"In that?" she asked, pointing to the Colt.

"Yes. It's a fine airplane, stable, airworthy. Up to you."

"I'd love it . . . I think . . ."

They flew north at seven thousand feet. Childs talked a good deal about the aircraft—it had a Lycoming engine, a cruising range of 325 miles, a top speed of 120 mph and a service ceiling of twelve thousand feet.

Susanna had taken flying lessons years earlier but had stopped short of receiving her license. Flying with Childs brought back all the memories of those days, the intense feeling of freedom from earth's bonds, the exhilaration . . . She looked down at houses that seemed plastic symbols on a Monopoly board, tiny automobiles following slotted highways, racetracks that would fit into the palm of her hand.

"Enjoying it?" Childs asked.

"Very much," she said over the roar of the Lycoming.

"I'm happiest up here, Miss Pinscher. Things up here make more sense."

"I understand, but I have to make sense out of Clarence Sutherland's death."

"Of course. Fire away."

"Who didn't like him?"

Childs laughed and banked the aircraft into a tight left turn. "Time to head back," he said.

"Because of what I asked?"

"No, because of time. I have an appointment." He squinted as he scrutinized the instruments. "Who didn't like him? Lots of people, I'd say."

"Including you?"

"Yes, including me, I'm afraid. Clarence was . . . well, he was a bit of a spoiled brat. He had the attitude that he was born to the good life, and I suppose he was. Lots of money, family support, a good mind and a handsome face. Women fell in love with his boyish good looks, the vulnerable little boy in a man's body. He was a charmer, that's for sure, Miss Pinscher."

"Did you resent him for that?" Susanna asked.

Childs looked at her in surprise. "Resent him? Why would I do that? I didn't like him, but I didn't resent him. I think I felt more sorry for him than anything."

"Why, sir?"

"Because he was like so many young men today, Miss Pinscher. Put them in a tough situation and they can't figure out how to blow their own noses. They've been coddled, protected, sheltered. They never become men, although they

45

think they do because they wear suits and bed down a string of women." He pointed out the window. "There's the airport . . . Them's my sentiments, Miss Pinscher, they're children when they should be men. Too damn soft for my taste, however unjudicial that may sound."

Susanna watched as Childs set up the Colt for a landing, coordinating his approach with the ground controllers, flying parallel to the runway, then turning onto his base leg and, with a smoothly executed left turn, lining up with the long, wide strip of concrete.

"It was a nice ride," she said after they'd come to a stop at his tie-down spot. "Thank you."

"Glad you enjoyed it." He walked her to her car. "Can I give you an unsolicited opinion? We justices love to give opinions."

"I'd very much appreciate it."

"Clarence was very probably killed by a woman. It may be attractive to the media, but I'm afraid you'd be wasting your time investigating any man, including those on the Court. God knows we're not perfect, to put it mildly, but Clarence was a man who treated women badly. Common knowledge, I'm afraid. I've no evidence, no suspects for you, but it seems likely that one of his women got mad enough to seek her revenge."

"But you have nobody particular in mind?"

"No. As I understand it, you couldn't tell the victims without a scorecard."

She shook his hand and thanked him again for the flight.

"Please come back again, Miss Pinscher. I enjoyed having you aboard."

CHAPTER
8

"PRETTY FANCY FOR A HUNGARIAN JOINT," MARTIN TELLER
said after joining Susanna at a table in Csiko's. "I feel like
a prince."

She laughed. "It is a little overdone but I like it. Wait'll
the gypsy violins start in."

They ordered drinks, a Bloody Mary for her, gin—*not*
vodka—on the rocks for him. He settled back in an armchair
and took in his surroundings; Austrian shades and draperies,
burnished brass and polished wood, high ceilings with ro-
coco plastering, a single red carnation on each table. "Very
nice," he said, sipping his drink. "Are you Hungarian?"

"I'm a mixed bag, a little of this, a little of that, including
a dash of Hungarian."

A waiter brought menus. "How did your interview with Childs go this morning?" he asked.

She put down the menu, glanced up over half-glasses. "Strange, maybe, but I find most people strange these days."

"Why is Childs strange?"

"Hard to say. He's very nice, friendly, open. He took me for a ride in his plane."

Teller put on a leer and wiggled an imaginary cigar in his fingers. "In his plane, huh? I thought he was married, four kids, nice quiet suburban life."

She removed her glasses. "Don't be silly. He was pressed for time and I got to ask a lot of questions while we were up in the air."

Teller waved his hands. "Don't mind me. I'm a little upset. I had to take Beauty to the vet today."

"Your dog?"

"Cat, one of two. He has hair balls."

"Oh." She replaced her glasses on her nose and returned to the menu.

He chose roast duck that was billed as a specialty of the house. "Careful of the red cabbage," she said, "it tastes like it's fermented." She ordered *szekely gulyas*, a pork and sauerkraut stew sprinkled with paprika and cooked with sour cream.

"So, Miss Pinscher, tell me about the rest of your week. Did you get to interview any of the other justices?"

"No, just Childs. He thinks a woman killed Clarence Sutherland, that he was a womanizer and evidently made at least one of them mad enough to kill him."

"I talked with a few employees at the Court and got the same picture."

She sat back. "A woman just walks into the main chamber of the United States Supreme Court and kills the chief clerk?"

"You can never figure women, Miss Pinscher. No offense. Can I call you Susanna?"

"Sure. Unless you prefer Candy."

"As the poet said, Candy's dandy but liquor's quicker."

"So true . . . Look, Lieutenant, I hate to be a party-pooper but a man is stone dead by hands other than his own. Maybe we ought to get back to cases."

He nodded gravely, but pleaded for a reprieve until they'd finished off apple strudel and coffee served in glasses resting in silver filigree holders.

"All right," he said, patting his stomach, "what do *you* think? Is Childs right about the perpetrator, as my boss would say? Did a woman do in young Sutherland?"

"—Certainly seems reasonable."

"What did Childs personally think of Sutherland?"

"Didn't like him, called him one of the soft generation."

"That wouldn't sit well with Childs. I did some reading up on him this week. A real hard-nose, military all the way. I never realized he came out of a poor background. Somehow I always assume people in his position were born right."

"Give him credit. He's a classic American success story."

"Yeah. I got a hold of that series *Life* did on him, the one written by Dan Brazier. It was good."

She nodded. "I read that series too. That was an interesting story in itself, the relationship between Childs and Brazier," she said, referring to a close friendship that had developed between the two men.

Brazier had been a UPI reporter assigned to Korea. Like Childs, he'd been captured by the North Koreans while covering a front-line skirmish, and they'd ended up in the same prisoner-of-war camp. The escape masterminded by Childs included five other prisoners, Brazier among them. They became inseparable after that, and Brazier had what amounted to an exclusive pipeline to the war's leading hero, the *Life* series representing only one of several rewards for that closeness.

After the war, Brazier ran into serious medical problems

directly linked to his captivity. One of his legs was amputated. A year later his other leg had to come off and he retired from journalism. As far as Susanna knew, he lived in obscurity in San Francisco.

"Does Childs still support him?" Teller asked.

"I don't know. The last I heard he did." Morgan Childs had sent a check to Dan Brazier every month for years. He'd tried to do it anonymously, but the press learned of it and reported on his generosity, which only added to his public image of a heroic, loyal and dedicated human being.

"An after-dinner drink?" Teller asked.

"Thank you, no. I really should get home. I was supposed to spend the weekend with my kids but this morning's meeting with Justice Childs threw a monkey wrench into my plans. I want to get out to see them first thing tomorrow."

"I don't see much of my kids. Two daughters, both in college. They come through once in a while, but most of their free time is spent with their mother in Paris."

Her eyes widened. "Paris, France?"

"Paris, Kentucky. She married some guy from there. Nice guy, takes good care of her, which got me off the alimony hook . . . By the way, I don't know what you like to do when you aren't working, but I've got two tickets to Cav-Pag at Kennedy Center next weekend."

"Cav-Pag?"

"Two one-act operas, *Cavalleria Rusticana* and *Pagliacci*. They usually play them together and call it Cav-Pag. Do you like opera?"

"I take it you do."

"Love it. I'm a hell of a tenor in the shower."

"Can I let you know later in the week?"

"Sure."

Her car was parked a short distance from the restaurant. He walked her to it.

50

"Thank you for a lovely dinner," she said. "I didn't intend for you to pay, especially since I chose the restaurant."

"You chose good. Besides, it was worth every penny. I like talking to you."

"Thank you. I don't know much about opera, but I'd like to go to . . . what's it called?"

"Cav-Pag. That's great. I'll talk to you during the week."

He watched her drive off, then got in his own car and drove to M Street, Northwest, in Georgetown. He parked illegally even though the new police commissioner had called for a crackdown on cops taking advantage of their position, walked a block and turned into Club Julie.

It was dark, smoky and crowded. The room was long and narrow, and a bar ran half its length on the right. In the center of the left wall was a tiny bandstand. Seated on it was the Julie of Club Julie, surrounded by keyboard instruments, an organ, acoustic and electric pianos and an electronic rhythm machine that duplicated the sound of percussion instruments.

"Hello, Marty," Julie said as Teller sat at the only empty stool at the piano bar. There were ten stools, seven of them occupied by middle-aged women, all of whom knew him. A waitress brought him gin on the rocks without being asked, and Julie launched into a medley of old sing-along tunes—"If You Wore a Tulip," "Down by the Riverside," "Ain't She Sweet," . . . Teller sang along with the others. One hour and four gins later, he was holding a microphone and doing his best Frank Sinatra act, pulling notes up from the heart, closing his eyes and belting them out to the delight of the crowd.

"Good night, Marty," Julie said as Teller stood unsteadily and waved to hangers-on as he headed for the door.

"Sing 'My Way,'" a drunk at the bar muttered.

51

"Next time," Teller said. He took deep breaths of chilled night air, found his car and went home, singing "My Way" all the way to the front door.

"Generation gap, my ass."

CHAPTER
9

"LET'S GO OVER IT," TELLER SAID TO DETECTIVES GATH-ered in his office. A sizable contingent of them had de-scended on the Supreme Court and had taken preliminary statements from almost everyone, including the nine jus-tices.

"I felt like a fool asking a Supreme Court judge for his whereabouts the night of the murder," one of them said.

"What did he say?" Teller asked.

"It wasn't a he, it was a she, Justice Tilling-Masters."

"What did she say?"

"That she was at a party with her family."

"Did it check out?"

"Yup."

"Who else?" Teller asked.

They ran down a list. Of the nine justices, six had alibis that could be confirmed.

"Whose alibi has holes?" Teller asked.

"Conover, Poulson and Childs."

"They lied?"

"No, but they aren't solid," a hefty detective named Vasilone said. "For instance, Marty, Poulson was supposed to be at a party too, but I talked to somebody else who was there and he puts Poulson's departure at a different time than what Poulson told me. I'm still trying to get hold of other people who were there."

"What about Conover?"

"Says he was home alone working on a manuscript."

"Wife?"

"Out at a party, at least that's what her husband says. I asked him about household help and he told me he gave them all the night off."

Teller twisted a little finger in his ear. "How about Childs?"

Another detective reported on Childs. "He says he was tinkering with his airplane at the airport that night."

"At that hour?"

"That's what I said, Marty, but he told me it's the only time he can get away."

"Any corroboration?"

"An airport guard says he saw him earlier in the evening but doesn't know what time he left."

"Okay, that takes care of the top. What about everybody else in the Court?" He was handed a list of people who could not definitively account for their activities.

"There's lots more to interview," Vasilone said. "You can only do so much."

"I know," Teller said. "Keep plugging. I want daily reports."

When they were gone from his office he sat back, feet

on the desk, and closed his eyes for a moment. When he opened them he looked at framed photographs of his daughters on his desk. "If you knew what I had to do for a living you wouldn't be so quick to ask for money." Which reminded him that they were due their monthly allotment. He wrote each of them a check, included a note in the envelopes which he signed "Love, Dad," and mailed them in a box just outside MPD.

He hoped they appreciated him.

CHAPTER
10

CHIEF JUSTICE POULSON WALKED BRISKLY THROUGH HIS
reception area, nodding to secretaries and clerks as he passed.
He entered his main chamber, tossed a stack of files on the
desk and looked at a clock-barometer on a shelf behind his
chair. The meeting of the judicial conference had run a half
hour longer than planned, and everything else that afternoon
would be affected, pressured, compressed.

Poulson hated the administrative aspect of being Chief
Justice. He'd thought about it when offered the position
by President Jorgens. There were many advantages to being
an associate rather than the Chief. The other eight justices
concerned themselves only with law, but the administrative
details of running the Court fell to him, all the bureaucratic
nitty-gritty. He was also expected to preside over such

organizations as the judicial conference, which in reality was nothing more than a lobby of federal judges.

On the other hand, he thought as he opened a small walnut-faced refrigerator and took out a bottle of Bailey's Irish Cream, there were compensating factors. Because he was Chief, the Court was known as the "Poulson Court." He officially ranked third in federal government protocol, although there were those who felt that because of the vice-president's political impotency, the chief justice was actually second in power only to the president.

Then again, he told himself as he poured a small portion of the liqueur into a glass and replaced the bottle in the refrigerator, there was a price to be paid for that power. The other justices were relatively anonymous, could live their private lives without gawkers and autograph seekers, all except Marjorie Tilling-Masters, of course, whose appointment to the Court had garnered wide media attention.

There was a knock on his door. "Come in," he said.

A secretary entered carrying a yellow legal pad. She came around behind him and placed the pad on the desk. "Justice Poulson, these are the phone calls that came in while you were gone."

"Thank you," he said. He glanced at the names on the paper. "Pinscher? She called again?"

"Yes, sir."

"All right."

"And Mr. Smithers is waiting."

"What's that about?"

"The film, sir."

"Oh, right. Give me a minute, then send him in."

"Yes, sir."

He waited until she was gone before draining the glass. He took a tissue from a desk drawer and wiped the glass clean, then placed it in its customary spot on the shelf behind him, where the cleaning crew would find it. He rubbed a flat area of his right thumb with his other fingers. His wife, Clara, referred to his right thumb as his built-in worry stone. He massaged his nose where his glasses had left their mark, told his secretary, "Send him in."

Walter Smithers came through the door. Tall, and carrying the leather attaché case, he represented the American Bar Association.

"Mr. Smithers," Poulson said, standing and offering his hand.

"It's a pleasure, Mr. Chief Justice. It's good of you to find time for me."

"I'm afraid I don't have much of that commodity this afternoon. I try to keep to a tight timetable, but things can sometimes get out of hand."

Smithers sat and opened his case. He handed a set of papers to Poulson and said, "I think this accurately sets forth our proposal, Mr. Chief Justice. When I heard that you were interested in having the visitor film replaced, I immediately took it up with our public-information people. There was unanimous agreement that the new film should reflect the Court as it is today. After all, it no longer is the Burger Court. It's now the Poulson Court."

Poulson glanced at the proposal. "Mr. Smithers," he said, "the cooperation and support of the ABA is gratifying. I've been at the receiving end of some good-natured kidding about replacing the film. A few of my colleagues, in their more whimsical moments, accuse me of what seems to be called ego-tripping. My goal is to present to the American people the most accurate and up-to-date portrait of the nation's highest court. The Supreme Court has changed dramatically, not only in its faces but in its philosophy, a philosophy which, I might add, accurately reflects the sense of the American people, as I believe it should. Since assuming office I've brought about a number of changes within the Court that reflect this new philosophy, and I feel the visitor film should too. However, I have a reservation."

"What is that, sir?"

"It seems to me inappropriate for the American Bar Association to finance this new film. Even though a conflict of interest obviously does not exist, certain factions might take exception. That's why I expressed the idea to you on the phone of having the ABA work with the Supreme Court Historical Society in producing a new and more up-to-date motion picture. I'd prefer that the society receive credit for having produced it."

"We have no problem with that, Mr. Chief Justice."

"Good. I'm anxious to see the project get underway, and I assure you the full cooperation of the Court."

Smithers realized Poulson had effectively ended the meeting. He rose, shook hands and promised to get back shortly with a more detailed schedule. After he left the chambers, Poulson took a toothbrush and toothpaste from a cabinet and went to a private lavatory, where he enthusiastically brushed his teeth. He returned to his chambers, checked his appearance in a mirror and buzzed his outer office. "Please have the Court limousine wait in the basement for me," he said.

"Yes, sir."

Minutes later he climbed into the back seat. "The Treasury Department," he told the uniformed driver.

A young man met them, and Poulson followed him to an elevator leading to Treasury's basement. The young man led him along a dimly lit steam tunnel until reaching the White House. They rode an elevator to a higher floor and stood in front of the Oval Office.

"Please wait, sir," the young man said as he crossed a large carpeted area and spoke in hushed tones to a woman behind a desk. He returned to the Chief and said, "He'll see you in a moment, sir."

A few minutes later the woman said, "Please follow me." She opened the doors and he stepped into the Oval Office.

President Jorgens was behind his desk. He smiled, stood and came around to shake Poulson's hand. "Good to see you, Mr. Chief Justice. I appreciate your taking time out from a busy schedule."

"Any time, Mr. President. How have you been?"

"Splendid. The sharks may proliferate but I still know how to swim. Sit down, make yourself comfortable."

"Thank you."

Jorgens touched an American flag as he passed it, settled in a large leather chair and propped his feet on the desk. "Jonathan, what's happening with the abortion case?"

The directness of the question took Poulson aback. He shifted his legs and squeezed the tip of his nose. After a few moments he said, "It's very close, Mr. President. No one, on the Court or in public life, is *for* abortion. But there is a legal issue here as defined by *Nidel* v. *Illinois*. Individual philosophies are rendered mute—"

"Lawyer talk. Legalese, Jonathan. I campaigned on a promise of righting wrongs in society, of returning to basic values. We had a president who was supposed to do that and didn't. I thought you understood all that."

"I do, of course, Mr. President, but the individuals on the Court carry with them their own views of the law. I talked with Justice Childs this morning. I'd assumed he'd be in favor of Illinois, but after our conference I realized that the legal question bothers him. Unlike Congress, one cannot depend upon a man's predisposition to a given issue on the Court."

"Or a woman's?"

"Yes, but I think Justice Tilling-Masters will support the state's position. That's my reading of her, at least."

"I hope so."

The President put his hands behind his head and stretched.

Poulson noticed the beginnings of wear in the sole of his shoe. He considered mentioning it, then thought better of it. After all, that was the late Adlai Stevenson's trademark, and the association would hardly, he thought, amuse the President. Instead, he said, "I've ordered a new visitor film be produced."

"Film?"

"The one visitors watch in the Court's small theater. I'm having it updated."

"That's nice, Jonathan. Let's get back to the abortion question. Is there anything that I can do, or my people, to help shape a rational decision in *Nidel* v. *Illinois*?"

Poulson searched the President's face as he formulated a reply. Randolph Jorgens was a self-assured man. He stood well over six feet and kept himself in good physical condition in the White House gym. Leathery, lined, tan skin testified to his Arizona heritage. His smile was wide and appealing, always at the ready. His cool gray eyes missed little while building a vast industrial empire, or after having entered the political arena. *Smart*, was the operative word around Washington—smart, and hard, and shrewd.

"I don't know of anything that might come from the executive branch, Mr. President, that would especially help in this matter." What Poulson wanted to say was that the entire conversation was inappropriate. The Court was supposed to be sacrosanct, a bastion of independent thought and judgment without influence from any other part of government, including the President of the United States.

Poulson's appointment by Jorgens to the Chief Justice's chair had been energetically debated during confirmation proceedings. An exhaustive FBI investigation, along with the Senate's own probe, had been nerve-racking for the entire family. Poulson was aware that the President had ordered his own secret investigation utilizing the IRS and, it was rumored, certain CIA personnel. There had also been long, in-depth conversations between the two men before Jorgens announced his choice. Those conversations had concentrated on relative political and social positions. Poulson had evidently satisfied the President's perception of what the new Chief Justice should believe in and espouse from the bench.

Questioning during the Senate Judiciary Committee's confirmation hearings had been spirited and, at times, hostile, depending on the questioner. One liberal senator had expressed his concern over the extent to which Poulson could function independently of the new administration, to which Poulson had replied, "I am, after all, Senator, a human being. I am subject to all the foibles of other human beings, including distinguished members of the United States Senate. I am, at the same time, a man who has devoted his life to the law. I believe in law above all else. Without law we cease to function as a civilized society. There have been many times in my career when my personal beliefs were placed in direct conflict with the larger issue of jurisprudence. In each of those instances law prevailed, just as it will should I be confirmed Chief Justice of the United States Supreme Court."

He'd meant every word of it.

"I'd like to be kept informed on a daily basis," Jorgens said.

"Of course, Mr. President."

"What about Conover, Jonathan? I assume he'll vote in favor of the plaintiff."

"It's likely, Mr. President."

"Damned old fool."

Poulson said nothing. As much as he disliked Temple Conover's life-style and persistent, in his view, misguided, liberalism, he did respect the senior justice for his rock-solid adherence to his convictions.

"Is there anything else, Mr. President?"

"This Sutherland matter, Jonathan. Where does it stand?"

"I just don't know. All we can do is to cooperate fully with the investigative agencies assigned to the case—"

"I don't like what I've heard about it."

"Such as, Mr. President?"

"The bastard's success in compromising people before he was killed."

"That was unfortunate, as we all know. I certainly was never in favor of accepting him as one of my clerks to begin with."

"Then why did you?"

Poulson winced against the question. The President knew why he had, and to ask the question was provocative. Still, Poulson felt compelled to answer. "As you know, his father was instrumental in that decision. Besides, no matter what Clarence Sutherland was personally, he was a brilliant young man. I don't think there's ever been a clerk here, during my term, with his skill at writing briefs. But of course if I had known about his other side . . ."

"Hindsight is a waste of time, Jonathan. I just wish you had been a little quicker to see what was happening beneath your eyes, in your own chambers. By the time you did, and reported it to me, the barn door had been open one hell of a long time."

"It seems to me, sir, that—"

"There are serious questions of governmental operations and even national security involved up in this mess, damn it." His face reddened. "Our highest intelligence echelons may have been compromised, at least potentially, by his actions, as has this very office. I had a briefing this morning by the CIA, and the threat of his knowledge . . . through his father . . . is a real one."

He suddenly stood and smiled, came around the desk and slapped Poulson on the back. It was all there again, the infectious grin, the warmth, the sense of being your best friend. "Let's keep on top of it, Jonathan, really on top of it."

"Of course. Thank you, Mr. President."

"Thank *you*, Jonathan. Please give my best to Mrs. Poulson."

"I certainly will, sir, and the same to the First Lady."

Poulson retraced his steps through the steam tunnel to the Treasury Building, where his car was waiting. "The Court, sir?" asked the driver.

"No, home, please. I'm tired, very tired." He leaned back and closed his eyes, his shirt clammy and cold against his skin.

VERA JONES knocked on Dr. Chester Sutherland's office door. He told her to enter. He was with a patient, a high-level administrator in the Department of Agriculture. "I'm sorry to disturb you, doctor, but Mr. L. is on the phone. He says it's urgent."

Sutherland looked at his patient, said, "Excuse me, please." He went through the door at the rear of his office and picked up a phone on which there were three buttons, one of which was lighted. "Hello, Mr. L.," he said.

"Hello, Dr. Sutherland. There's a meeting at ten tomorrow morning."

"Of course, I'll be there. Thank you for calling."

The man who'd placed the call gently hung up his phone, left his office and walked down a long, carpeted corridor until reaching the Oval Office's oak doors. He knocked, was told to enter.

"The meeting is set, sir," he said.

"Thank you, Craig."

Craig departed. President Randolph Jorgens stood, scratched his belly through his shirt and ran his hand over a leather horse on his desk. "I need a vacation," he said.

CHAPTER
11

SUSANNA PINSCHER WAS WITH MATT MITCHELL, HER SU-
perior at the Justice Department. Large drops of rain splat-
tered against the window in his office; a cold front had
invaded the city from the north. It was three o'clock in the
afternoon but was dark enough outside to be night.

"Are you sure you don't want some tea, Susanna," Mitchell asked. "You're soaked. You'll catch pneumonia."

"Okay, some tea."

"And put this on." He dropped a beige wool cardigan
sweater in her lap as he passed. "I keep it around for when
I get all wet. Which is too much of the time." Brief smile.

She draped the sweater over her shoulders and shivered.
She'd gotten caught in the storm while walking back from
a meeting in Chief Justice Poulson's chambers. She'd used

an underground tunnel as far as it extended down Constitution Avenue, but was exposed the rest of the way.

Mitchell returned carrying a steaming cup of tea. He handed it to her, looked down at her feet and said, "You're making puddles on my floor."

"I can't help it."

He laughed. "Puddles beat waves."

The hot cup felt good in her hands. She inhaled the tea's aroma, sipped it.

"So, Susanna, how did it go with Poulson?"

"He's pleasant enough, seems anxious to cooperate. The only sticky point is where the interrogations should be conducted."

"I take it he doesn't want them held in the Court."

"He feels the Court has been violated enough and questions why follow-up investigations can't be held outside the building."

"He has a point. The first thing Poulson did after becoming Chief was to slap an even tighter lid on everything that happens inside the Court. Any clerk who's even seen talking to a reporter is fired, no excuses, no explanations. They can't even say no comment. Opening up the Court to a full-scale MPD investigation is like inviting every reporter in town to a public meeting. Cops are biologically incapable of keeping their mouths shut."

"Matt, I realize the Supreme Court is a special place, but a murder happened there. My training has always said that you investigate where the crime occurred."

"This is different, Susanna. In the first place, we don't get involved in murders very often. In the second place, the MPD has already interviewed everyone in the Court and did it inside the building. The place has been gone over with the old fine-toothed comb, and if the President decides to go ahead with appointing a special prosecutor, there'll be that much more disruption to the Court's activities." He sat on the edge of his desk. "There's another aspect to all this, Susanna, and maybe you haven't considered it. If a Supreme Court justice had been murdered it would make sense. The fact is that a clerk was killed, and if he'd been shot anyplace else other than the Supreme Court it would be just another routine MPD investigation."

"If."

"Okay, but the fact remains that there are more important considerations than Clarence Sutherland's murder. There's the law of the land to preside over. That's the Court's job, after all."

"What about if a murderer is sitting on the Supreme Court, presiding over the law of the land?"

He started to respond, pulled back, shook his head, stood and went to the window. "Miserable day." He turned and said to her, "You don't really believe that, do you?"

"That Clarence Sutherland's murderer might be one of nine justices? I don't like to believe it but it's a real possibility, isn't it?"

"No."

"Then who?"

He returned to the desk and leaned close to her. "Susanna, you go around spouting theories like that and your days in this city, and on this job, are numbered."

She placed the empty teacup on the desk and closed the gap between them. "I thought the name of the game was to solve Sutherland's murder, Matt, no matter where or what."

"That's true, but let's not go beyond Justice's scope. We're at least partly in this for show . . . I spoke with the assistant attorney general this morning and he—"

"*Show*? I quit."

"Quit? That's ridiculous."

"Like hell . . . not only am I told by my superior that my assignment is a kind of sham, I'm told that this big, won-

67

derful Department of Justice that I broke my buns to join is in show business."

"Calm down."

"Then say something to help me."

"Keep working on the Sutherland case. Go after it full steam ahead, but also please don't lose perspective. There are other things that share parity with Sutherland's death."

"I'll try." She handed him his sweater, picked up her water-soaked pumps and went to the door. "Matt," she said, "I don't mean to be a pain in the neck, I really don't, but I have to feel that what I'm doing is important."

"It is. I was shorthanding the situation, Susanna. Ignore it."

She'd try.

CHAPTER
12

SUSANNA PINSCHER AND MARTIN TELLER STOOD IN THE Grand Foyer of the Kennedy Center's Opera House, one of three large theaters contained in the vast and sprawling arts complex. The performance of *Cavalleria Rusticana* was over and it was intermission.

"Did you enjoy it?" Teller asked.

"Very much."

"It's some theater, isn't it?"

"I've been here before."

"To see an opera?"

"No. Chinese acrobats. I had the same impression of the place then that I have tonight. It's big, formal and sort of stuffy."

"Opera buffs seem to like it that way. Makes them feel

elegant or something. But every time that chandelier dims I get goose bumps. How about a drink?"

"It's so crowded," she said, pointing to a mob surrounding a small bar.

"Don't worry about that," he said. "I belong to the Golden Circle society."

"What in God's name is that?"

"A bunch of people who pay a *thousand* bucks a year for the privilege of not standing in line for a drink during intermission. You wouldn't think a cop could manage it, but I wash my own socks and make out with the finer things."

"I'm impressed, socks or no socks."

They were served cognac in snifters. They clicked rims and he said, "Here's to indulgence."

She smiled. "Tell me, Detective Teller, why does a man who spends his working days dealing with the low life lay out a thousand dollars a year to rub shoulders with opera buffs?"

"You have it wrong." He leaned close to her ear. "I can't stand these people. The fact is that dealing with what I deal with every day makes me sort of crazy for a change. What I get out of opera is a beautiful change. Fantasy after eight hours of reality. Makes sense?"

"It does." She clicked her glass to his and drank.

The second half of the evening, *Pagliacci*, was less inspiring than the first.

"I believe they call this kind of writing *verismo*," Teller said as they left the ornate red theater and headed for his car. "It means 'realism' but it doesn't work as well as traditional opera. Puccini trumped all of them, including his fellow Italians."

"You're a very interesting...man," she said as they drove from the parking garage.

"You were about to say character."

"No, I wasn't, but I guess it would fit."

"I also get my shoes shined instead of doing them myself, and I send my laundry out."

"A typical bachelor."

"Typical?"

"No, I'm sorry. I enjoyed tonight. Very much. Thank you."

"Where to now?"

"Home."

"Hungry?"

"No."

"Feel like singing?"

"After hearing those wonderful voices?"

"They weren't so great. I have V-discs that are better."

"I wouldn't know from better, I'm afraid. Damn little opera in my upbringing."

"Ditto. I got the taste for it late in life . . . Look, I know a nice place in Georgetown. A bunch of crazies hang out there but they're basically nice people, just like to sit around and drink and sing. The owner and I are friends. He plays the piano. He made a million in frozen French fries and then dumped the whole business to open a club. I don't know whether you'd like the place or not but they serve steak sandwiches on garlic bread until closing, and sometimes the music is good and—"

"Do they serve French fries?"

"The best in D.C."

"Let's go."

Instead of sitting at the piano bar, Teller took her to a corner far from the bandstand. They said little to each other as she observed the Saturday night crowd.

"Well, what do you think?" he asked after their drinks and sandwich platters had been served.

"I don't know yet, I haven't tasted it."

"I mean the place. Nice atmosphere, huh?"

71

"Yes, it's—"

"What's the matter?"

"It's sort of sad, seeing people in a singles bar—"

"Singles bar? This isn't a singles bar. If it were I wouldn't come here."

"Don't be touchy. It's just that I wish those women sitting around the piano bar were *with* someone..."

"But that's what's nice about Club Julie, Susanna. It's *like* a club, no hassles like in real singles bars. Women can come here and feel safe."

"I suppose you're right. Funny, but it makes me think of Dr. Sutherland's secretary... Vera Jones."

Teller sliced into his steak and took a bite. "Good. Don't let it get cold."

"Do you think she's ever been married?"

"Vera Jones? Most people have been, although she does come off like one of those who hasn't. But I don't figure her for the singles'-bar scene. Not her style—"

"What is her style?"

"Quiet, a one-on-one type, maybe a twenty-year affair with a married man."

"Dr. Sutherland?"

"Not likely, but you never know. I do think she's loyal and discreet enough to be a twenty-year mistress, don't you?"

"Yes. Do you find her attractive?"

"Yes, in a cold sort of way."

"Hidden passion, as they say in the purple romances?"

"Could be."

"A legitimate suspect?"

"Everybody is at this point."

"Including the nine justices?"

"Including the nine justices. Do you know who interests me?"

"I'm afraid to ask."

He grinned. "That court clerk, Laurie Rawls. She was at the funeral and bawled all through it. I figure there was more to her relationship with Sutherland than just a co-worker."

"*Cherchez la femme . . .*"

"Huh?"

"Justice Childs's advice to me. Look for the woman. Have you interviewed Laurie Rawls?"

"One of my people did. Uneventful. She said she liked Clarence, enjoyed working with him. Her alibi is shaky, but so are a lot of other people's."

"If you'd like, I'll talk to her. She might open up to another woman."

"Could be. I understand she's been temporarily assigned to the Chief Justice. She'd worked for the old man, Con-over."

"I'll call her Monday morning."

Julie, the owner, came to the table and asked Teller if he wanted to sing. Teller shook his head, but Susanna insisted. "I've never heard a singing detective before."

"You still won't have," he said as he went to the band-stand, and picked up a microphone while Julie played an introduction to "As Time Goes By."

"*You must remember this, a kiss is still a kiss,*
A sigh is just a sigh.
The fundamental things apply, as time goes by."

He smiled at Susanna as he ventured into the second stanza. She nodded her approval and leaned her chair back against the wall, her thoughts divided between attention to his resonant voice and the thing that had led them to spend the evening together—Clarence Sutherland's murder. She felt overwhelmed. The number of suspects and the complication of it having happened in the United States Supreme Court.

The smell of garlic filled her nostrils, and chatter at adjoining tables deafened her. She closed her eyes against a pain that had started at the back of her neck and was now creeping up over her head and toward her forehead. She opened her eyes and saw a blurry Martin Teller.

> "...the world will always welcome lovers,
> As time goes by."

He held the last note and Julie rolled off a rich chord. Applause, applause. Teller put the microphone on top of the piano and made his way to the table.

"I warned you."

"It was terrific."

He sat down and looked at her closely. "You don't look so good, do you feel sick?"

"I . . . it's a migraine coming on, damn it. I get them once in a while."

"I'm sorry. Let's go, I'll take you home."

"I'm sorry to ruin the evening."

They pulled up in front of her building. Teller put his hand on the ignition key but didn't turn off the engine. "I'll walk you in."

"No, please don't. I'll be fine. Thank you for a really wonderful evening."

"I just wish you felt better." He turned, leaned close. "I'd like to kiss you."

"Well, then, Lieutenant, for God's sake *do* it."

CHAPTER
13

TEMPLE CONOVER SAT IN HIS CHAMBERS WEARING AN OLD, loose, nubby gray sweater. He'd changed from black shoes to worn carpet slippers as soon as he arrived that morning. It was almost noon. He was to attend a luncheon at the British Embassy on Massachusetts Avenue, known as Washington's "Embassy Row," at which he was to receive a plaque from England's equivalent of the American Bar Association for his years of "dedication to upholding the principles of freedom and justice." Cecily would join him there, and after lunch she was to drive him to the airport for a flight to Dallas, where he would address the Texas Bar Association's annual formal dinner.

He turned to his typewriter and quickly wrote a memo to Chief Justice Poulson.

75

Jonathan—Despite my consistent harping that we have too many clerks as it is, taking Miss Rawls from me at the peak time of cert petitions is intolerable. I know you lost Sutherland, but I'd appreciate your reconsideration of the transfer, as "temporary" as it might be.—Temple C.

He called out the open door to his senior secretary, a heavy, middle-aged woman named Joan who'd been with him for six years. She stepped into his chambers.

"Have this envelope delivered right away to the chief." He handed it to her. "Where's Bill and Marisa?" he asked, referring to two of three remaining clerks on his staff.

"In the library."

"Get them down here right away."

"Yes, sir."

They arrived minutes later and took seats across the desk from him. He waved a hand over piles of petitions for certiorari, requests to the Supreme Court to review decisions handed down by lower courts. Of five thousand such requests received each year, only about two hundred were accepted for review. Each justice was expected to analyze the five thousand petitions, then vote on which of them to accept. A minimum of four out of the nine justices was necessary for a cert to be granted.

Shortly after becoming Chief, Poulson had attempted to establish a cert pool, ostensibly to relieve the workload on each justice, but he'd been voted down, with Conover leading the opposition. The senior justice felt it had been a move on Poulson's part to gain additional control of the Court, something he felt had been happening with regularity.

In reality, it was the clerks who reviewed most petitions for cert and condensed them to one- or two-page summaries for their justices.

Conover picked up a thick file of cert reviews his clerks

76

felt warranted his special consideration. "I've read these and agree with your views, but what good are they if we can't get three of the others to go along with us?"

"I think we can, sir, on the job discrimination and ecology petitions," Bill said. "I spoke this morning with Justice Tilling-Masters's clerks, and they feel she'll be in favor of accepting them this term. We know the Chief's position. Justice Childs won't bend, but..."

The other clerk added, "Peg O'Malley, who works for Justice Sims, told me that he might go along with us on the job discrimination case if it's narrowed to the pension issue and doesn't include sexual discrimination."

Conover twisted in his high-backed leather chair and groaned as a sharp pain shot from his hip to his shoulder. "I don't see how that's possible," he said, his voice mirroring his discomfort.

"I'll keep working on her," Marisa said.

"Don't bother. I'd rather press on the ecology issue and the two petitions on church and state."

"Yes, sir."

Fifteen minutes later, and after Bill's help with his shoes and jacket, Conover stood by Joan's desk while she assisted him on with his overcoat. "Would you like me to walk down with you?" she asked.

"No."

She handed him his crutch and he slipped his forearm into its metal sleeve. "I want those opinions ready to be circulated when I come back."

Another of his secretaries, Helen, wished him a safe and pleasant trip. He thanked her, then said, "Mrs. Conover will be coming by to pick up theater tickets that are being sent over this afternoon. Please see that she gets them."

"Of course, sir."

Both secretaries watched him slowly and painfully leave the room.

"Poor man," Joan said aloud.

"It's awful to see him in such pain," Helen said.

"I sometimes think of Justice Douglas when I see him," Joan said.

"I do, too, especially when his wife comes in."

Joan shook a finger in the air and said emphatically, "The *only* thing they have in common as far as *that's* concerned is that they ended up with young wives. Justice Douglas's wife was a lady, a tremendous and loyal help to him before he died. I wish I could say the same for Mrs. Conover."

Helen started to say something but Joan cut her off. "Enough of this. Justice Conover's personal life is his own business. I just hope this dreadful thing with Mr. Sutherland doesn't open up that can of worms. Come on, let's get going on those opinions. If they're not on his desk when he gets back from Dallas we'll all be looking for jobs at Foggy Bottom."

CHAPTER
14

"I'M DELIGHTED YOU COULD GET FREE FOR LUNCH," Susanna Pinscher said to Laurie Rawls after they'd met inside the front door of the American Cafe's Capitol Hill branch on Massachusetts Avenue. Susanna had called Laurie to set up an interview and suggested lunch. The clerk declined lunch, then called back the following day and accepted.

They were seated at a blond wooden table in a corner. Susanna settled into her chair and looked across at her young luncheon guest. She'd liked Laurie Rawls from the moment they met. There was an openness and brightness about her, a wide-eyed inquisitiveness. She wore no makeup to mask her translucent, fair skin that gave off the same healthy glow as her short, straight brown hair. She was dressed in a pleated gray flannel skirt, a dusty rose blouse that buttoned to the neck and a blue blazer with the crest of her alma mater, George Washington University.

"I was surprised when you called back and agreed to lunch," Susanna said after ordering a white wine for herself and a kir for Laurie.

"Why? Because I'm a suspect? The fact is, Miss Pinscher, I'm interested in you. You've obviously succeeded in a field I'd like to get into. I thought lunch might be helpful for *me*."

Susanna liked her candor. "Well, the Justice Department isn't very glamorous, but it does have its interesting moments . . ."

"I'm sure."

"As I assume the Supreme Court does for you."

"I love clerking there. Some of my friends are clerking other places, but being in the nation's highest court is . . . well, it's kind of awesome."

"I understand you've been assigned to Chief Justice Poulson since Clarence's murder. It must have been tough . . . I mean losing someone you've worked closely with, and in such a violent way . . ."

"Yes." She took a long, deliberate drink, put down her glass, picked up a menu. "I'm famished. What do you recommend?"

"Some days the meat pies are good, and—"

"I think I'll have a California salad."

"I'll stick with turkey. Another drink?"

"Thank you, no, but you go ahead."

Susanna ordered another wine, and said to Laurie, "How well did you know Clarence Sutherland?"

Laurie hesitated a beat before saying, "About as well as anyone else on the Court, I guess." It was delivered too offhandedly, Susanna thought. Laurie added, "Clarence could be . . . difficult."

"How so?"

"He worked for Chief Poulson, he was chief clerk. Sometimes he made the other clerks pretty mad. Some of them thought he was cruel—"

"I see..." And rather obviously, Susanna thought, Laurie was one of them. She decided to pursue that sideways..."I've seen pictures of Clarence Sutherland. He certainly was a handsome man."

Laurie's face had seemed to sag, her buoyancy flatten out.

Their lunch was served. Susanna chatted about her job at the Justice Department, about her background and the events that led her to Washington and to her present position. Finally, almost abruptly, she decided it was time... "Laurie, were you in love with Clarence Sutherland?"

It was as though she had kicked her. Laurie's face turned to stone, she looked abstractedly around the crowded restaurant.

"Shouldn't I have asked?"

"You can *ask* anything you wish. You're investigating a murder and I understand I'm a suspect. I also know you know I haven't an alibi. I was caught in the traffic at what I'm told was the approximate time of the murder. I was by myself."

"Yes, I do know that, and it's true you, *along with many others*, are a suspect. But I also want you to know that I'm not interested in hurting people in the process of helping to solve this thing—"

"I'm sure... All right, you've asked a question... as one lawyer to another, I'll tell you our relationship was more than professional."

"As one woman to another," Susanna said, "was he in love with you?"

She grimaced. "Clarence was immune from such weakness, vulnerability..."

"I'm told Clarence was a womanizer."

81

"How quaint, old-fashioned..."

"Choose your own poison."

"Immature might be closer."

Susanna smiled. "Yes... well, he was young—"

"He's a dead young man now." Laurie's voice was cold, her face ice. "If it's all right with you, I think I've had enough discussion about Clarence Sutherland."

"I'm sorry if I've pried too much into your personal relationship."

"I realize full well your job, but..." Laurie stared at the tabletop, then looked up, a smile applied like makeup now on her face. "Look, Miss Pinscher, I'm sorry... I'm a grown lady... I've got degrees that say so, and I am a clerk of a Supreme Court judge. Fire away, ask anything you want. I'll try to be as truthful as I know how."

Susanna took the check from the waiter. "All right, Laurie. Did you kill Clarence?"

She started to answer, lost the words, then said with a short laugh, "Of course not."

"Good. Any notion who did?"

"None."

"Possibilities? I mean at least in theory?"

"Do we have time?"

"He was that disliked—?"

"Hated, I'm afraid, would be more accurate."

"But not by you."

"They say the two emotions are close—sometimes indistinguishable."

"Laurie, do you think a woman killed him, a woman who'd been hurt by him as you obviously have been?"

"I don't know. There were so damn many. But there were plenty of men who hated Clarence's guts too."

"Husbands?"

"I guess, but I wasn't thinking about them especially

82

. . .Frankly—" her tone became more confident, and confidential—"It was a mystery that Clarence was even able to stay on as chief clerk."

"Oh? My understanding was that, whatever else, he was brilliant, competent and knowledgeable."

"He was all those, one of the brightest people I'd ever met. He had a sadistic side that set others against him. The things . . . he could be cruel for no reason . . . even toward his superiors . . . The other clerks constantly expected Chief Justice Poulson to fire him, but of course it never happened—"

"Why not?"

She hesitated. "Justice Poulson is a gentleman, a decent human being. But, in confidence, he's also weak. Some said that Clarence played on his weaknesses to keep his job."

"What weaknesses?"

Laurie shrugged. "Clarence knew things about Justice Poulson that evidently could have proved embarrassing to him. What they were I don't know." She was not being entirely truthful with Susanna. Her thoughts went back to the night in the Court when she and Clarence were together in her office. She'd just finished reading an analysis of a case he'd written . . .

"I envy you," she'd said.

"Why?"

"Your ability to take something as complex as this case, dissect it so quickly and put it all on paper in such a cogent, literate way."

He laughed. "Just a combination of genes, superior intellect, sensitivity, native talent and inherent survival instincts."

"Justice Conover feels differently about you," Laurie said, rolling her chair closer to him so that she could see what he was reading. It was one of many briefs filed in the *Nidel* v. *Illinois* abortion case.

"What else is new?" he asked, not looking up.

"He said you were ruthless and unprincipled."

Clarence looked at her and smiled. "What do you care what that senile old creep says?"

He leaned back in his chair and slowly shook his head. "These justices . . . They get their butts plopped down in a lifetime job because they spent their careers attending the right political functions, meeting the right people and saying the right things. Then they put on their black robes and make laws, at least when they're not fighting with their wives or playing footsie with some senator or seeing their shrink."

"Like your father—"

"Yes, like dear old dad, analyst to stars, confidant of the powerful, stroking their egos to make them feel worthy of their exalted positions . . . Do you know what, Laurie? These same people can be made to squirm when you push the right buttons." He turned to her and cupped her chin in his hand. "Give us a kiss."

"Not here."

"Nobody's around. Come on."

He tried to fondle her. She pushed him off. "Clarence, take it easy . . . later . . ."

"Why, because we're in these hallowed halls? Listen, Laurie, let me tell you a secret. Poulson's got a closetful of skeletons. I know which closet they're in and what they look like. He came down hard on me this afternoon and I reminded him, nicely of course, about one of them. He backed down. Oh, he kept his dignity. After all, Chief Justice Jonathan Poulson is, if nothing else, dignified. I loved it. And you can tell that old fool you work for that if he says anything else about me I'll broadcast his wife's top-secret erogenous zones."

Laurie stood, smoothed her dress and said she had to leave.

Clarence looked at his watch. "I have an hour." He stood and put his arms around her. "Plenty of time for us to—"

She slipped away from him, even though she was tempted in spite of herself, opened the door and went out, trying to shut out the sound of his laughter that trailed her down the corridor. . . .

Susanna put cash on the check, picked up her handbag from the floor. "What about the other justices, the other clerks? Did any of them feel strongly enough about Clarence to . . ."

It seems inconceivable . . . Clarence was provocative, difficult, but that a justice would . . . she shook her head.

They parted on the sidewalk and promised to keep in touch.

Susanna returned to her office, where she made notes of what had been said during lunch.

Further down Constitution Avenue Laurie Rawls closed the door behind her in Chief Justice Jonathan Poulson's chambers and sat herself in a chair. Poulson was behind his desk. He smiled warmly. "Well, how did it go at lunch?"

"Fine, sir. She's very nice, very bright, and doing her job."

"Yes, well, I hope you don't mind my encouraging you to accept the luncheon date with Miss Pinscher. When you mentioned it to me, my initial reaction was to counsel against it. After all, there's a limit to what people should be put through, murder or no murder. But it seemed a good chance to find out just what progress Justice and the MPD were making. I want this matter cleared up as soon as possible so that the Court can get back to normal. What did she have to say about the investigation?"

"Not too much, really, but it was evident to me, Justice

Poulson, that little progress has been made. Apparently the suspect list is as wide open as it was the first day."

"I see . . . well, sorry to hear that."

"Would you mind if I left early, sir? I'm not feeling so well."

"Of course."

She gathered her things from her office and walked down the back stairs to the Great Hall, impressive in its marble splendor. A frieze decorated with medallion profiles of lawgivers and heraldic devices looked down on her as she approached the courtroom. Two members of the Court's special security force stood at the doorway. "Hello, Miss Rawls," one of them said.

"Hello," she answered vaguely as she stood a few feet away and peered into the vast, empty arena where so many of a nation's great legal battles had been fought. She wanted to leave, but her feet felt as though they were set in the marble floor. She started to tremble, or feel as though she were, and her eyes filled with tears in spite of all her resolutions *not* to let that happen.

An abrupt sound rang out behind her.

"Sorry," one of the security men said as he bent over to pick up a clipboard he'd dropped. "You really jumped, Miss Rawls."

"Yes, I'm on edge these days. I suppose we all are."

CHAPTER
15

He heard her footsteps on the stairs, the fumbling in her purse, a key being inserted into the lock. The door swung open and she stepped into the small, cluttered apartment.

"Where have you been?" Dan Brazier asked. He was in his wheelchair near a window. Outside, on Broadway, in San Francisco's North Beach district, the transition from day to night was in progress and day's final warm glow bathed everything in yellow. It was the time of day when the dirt on the windows was most evident, years of accumulation on the outside, a murky brown film of tar and nicotine on the inside.

Sheryl Figgs, who lived with Brazier, placed a bag of

groceries on a butcher block table in the middle of the living room and handed him the mail.

"Where have you been?" Brazier repeated as he flipped through the envelopes.

"I bought food on the way home from work. How are you feeling?" She noticed that a bottle of gin she'd bought yesterday was almost empty.

Brazier ripped open an envelope and looked at a check from Supreme Court Justice Morgan Childs. As usual, it had been drawn on his personal account in Maryland, and the envelope contained only a box number as a return address.

"You got your disability check," Sheryl said.

Brazier opened that envelope, too, then dropped both checks to a threadbare, imitation Oriental rug.

"I asked you how you were feeling," she said, kicking off her shoes and pulling a purple sweater over her head. She was not an unattractive woman, although an almost perpetual downturn to her mouth created a sad moue. Her hair was blond and seemingly unkempt; no matter how often she washed it, it appeared to be dullish. Her face was thin, pinched, and very pale. Remnants of teenage acne had left a tiny cluster of scars on both cheeks, which she covered with makeup. She was tall and slender. White skin on her arms, legs and belly was soft and loose, like that of an older person. "Damn stretch marks," she often said when they were in bed. "That's what having four kids will do to you."

Once when she'd said it, Brazier had reacted angrily. "You're complaining about marks on your belly. I don't have any legs." He seldom mentioned his disability, and she felt guilty for days about provoking him to bring it up.

She fetched him more ice and he poured the remains of the gin into his glass. She made herself a bourbon and water and sat at the table. "I brought the newspaper," she said.

"You read it." He continued to stare out the window, the gin and ice cubes shimmering in light from outside.

She unfolded the paper on the table and started to read. "Hey," she said, "there's a whole story here about your buddy Childs."

Brazier turned, grimaced. "What's it say?"

She read in silence for a few moments. "Well, it's not really about him. It's about that Sutherland murder case. Listen to this. The woman who's investigating the murder for the Justice Department—her name is Pinscher, Susanna Pinscher—interviewed him up in his airplane."

Brazier grunted.

"Nobody'll make any public comments, it says here, but the reporter claims to have an inside source. He says the investigation is narrowing down to the women in Sutherland's life...he was a real swinger."

"What else does it say about Childs?"

"Nothing. Oh, it does say that all the justices are trying to keep a lid on the investigation inside the Court." She lowered the paper and looked at Brazier. "I don't blame them. Who wants people snooping around the Supreme Court—?"

"Let me see it," Brazier said. She gave him the paper and he read the article, then dropped the paper on top of the checks and wheeled himself to the table. "What's for dinner?"

"I thought I'd make a meat loaf. Do you want a salad?"

"No. I'm going out for a little while. How long does a meat loaf take?"

"I don't know. I'll look it up in the cookbook. About an hour, I guess. Where are you going?"

"Around the corner for a drink. I'll be back. Help me downstairs."

She knew it was useless to argue. She would have liked him to stay while she prepared dinner. Sometimes, when he hadn't had too much to drink, they'd be together in the tiny kitchen and talk. She loved talking to Don Brazier when he was sober. He was the smartest man she'd ever met, and even though she knew he didn't mean it, he often made her feel like an intellectual equal, someone he respected and listened to. When he was sober.

She took a red-and-black flannel jacket from a closet and helped him on with it, then wheeled him through the door to the top of a short, straight and narrow set of steps leading one flight down to the street. She watched as he pulled himself out of the chair and, using banisters on either side, literally walked down them with his hands. She followed with the chair, avoiding the scene with her eyes and keeping up a conversation to make his difficult journey go faster. "Mr. Valente talked to me today," she said. "He told me that they're going to rewrite all the software manuals and that he'd be interested in talking to you about doing some of the work. He remembers the things you wrote in magazines and says he'd like to meet you. I told him I'd see about having you come by someday for lunch and—"

He reached the bottom and she hurriedly slipped the chair beneath him. "If I wanted to write again I'd get a damn agent, Sheryl. I don't need you hustling for me, and you can tell your friend Valente to mind his own business. What are you doing, coming on with him?"

"Oh, for God's sake, Dan, he's my boss. He's married and—"

"Open the door."

She did, and he wheeled himself out to the street.

"An hour," she said.

"Yeah, an hour."

She prepared the meat loaf, kneading the bread crumbs, onions and seasoning into the meat, topping it with two strips of bacon and putting it in the oven. She placed two lettuce wedges on plates and brought them to the butcher block table, carefully folded two paper napkins next to the plates and placed silverware on them. Satisfied that she'd done all she could until the meat loaf was done, she sat in the living room and turned on local news on a black-and-white television set. She watched for a few minutes before her attention wandered, first to the flashing, garish red-and-green neon light on the window from a topless club two doors down the street, then to a row of framed photographs lined up on a small table next to her chair. She picked up one of the photos, held it close. Two men were in the picture, Dan Brazier and Morgan Childs, the latter now a Supreme Court justice. It had been taken in Korea shortly after they'd returned from their captivity. Both were grinning broadly. Their arms were around each other and Childs held two fingers in the air, forming a *V*-for-victory sign. "How handsome," Sheryl thought, meaning both of them. Brazier was still handsome, she felt, maybe even more so than when the picture was taken. They looked somewhat alike, Brazier and Childs, rugged, masculine, square faces and strong, forceful chins, clear eyes that saw through you, muscular bodies belonging to men of action, sort of like cowboys, it sometimes occurred to her.

Brazier's upper body had increased in strength since the loss of his legs. He refused to wear any type of prosthesis: "I don't want phony legs," although she knew that when he lived in Washington following the war he had gone to a hospital and tried a set. He never talked much about those years, and she knew not to ask many questions. He could become explosive when pressed for answers, which was why she hadn't asked about Dr. Chester Sutherland, father of the murdered law clerk.

Once, while rummaging through a dresser drawer, she'd come across old, pocket-size appointment books. One of them went back to Brazier's Washington days, and in it was written Dr. Chester Sutherland's name, address and phone number. On subsequent pages the entry "Dr. S." appeared next to times of the day. It had meant nothing to her when she'd first read the books. Brazier had seen a myriad of doctors in an attempt to save his legs. But after reading about the murder of Clarence Sutherland in the local paper, she'd returned to the dresser drawer and confirmed what she'd remembered.

The newscaster introduced a story about a love triangle in the Bay area that had resulted in one of the lovers being bludgeoned to death. It made her think of Brazier's comment about her boss, Mr. Valente. He often accused her of seeing other men, although it wasn't true. She understood, though. A man without legs felt only partially a man. He was wrong, though. Dan Brazier was more of a man than anyone else she'd ever known in her life ... strong and wise, a sensitive and pleasing lover ... When he was sober.

The aroma of meat loaf drifted from the kitchen and she felt good. Sheryl liked to cook, especially for Dan. She went to the kitchen, opened the oven and peered in at the bubbling loaf. "Looks pretty good." Then, in a markedly sadder voice ... "Please come on home, Dan. Please don't make me eat this alone."

As she had too many meals too many times before.

CHAPTER
16

IT WAS THE SORT OF BLEAK, COLD DAY THAT PRESAGED winter. The last leaves had fallen from the trees, and things formerly hidden by them were now visible.

Dr. Chester Sutherland looked through a tinted window in a limousine that had picked him up at his house. He watched Georgetown University's spires slowly glide by, the Potomac patterned by a cold, gray chop. Ahead, through skeletal branches of bare trees, a stark white, neocolossal building surrounded by miles of twelve-foot-high chain link fence came into view. A large sign on the George Washington Parkway identified it—CENTRAL INTELLIGENCE AGENCY. Until 1973 the sign had read FAIRBANK HIGHWAY RESEARCH STATION. But then, ironically, President Nixon, in the spirit of more open government, had ordered signs telling it like it was, and, some said, the CIA has never been the same.

The limousine was met at a gate by a team of General Service Administration guards. Credentials were scrutinized before it was allowed to proceed to the next checkpoint. Eventually the long black vehicle entered an underground garage where Sutherland was greeted by a dour young man in a blue suit who wore his ID badge on a chain around his neck. They went upstairs, their route taking them past unmarked doors until reaching a dining room that overlooked the woods of Langley, Virginia. A table covered with pale blue linen and set with expensive silver and china was prepared to seat four people. Sutherland's guide, who'd mentioned that he was with the agency's public-affairs office, excused himself and quietly left the room. Moments later another door opened and a tall man in his fifties entered, moved across plush, thick royal blue carpet and extended his hand. "Roland McCaw, Dr. Sutherland, deputy director of science and technology."

Sutherland shook his hand. "Yes, Mr. McCaw, Bill Stalk mentioned you to me. He said you'd come over from the navy."

"That's right. I'm still trying to get my land legs here at the Company. Drink?"

Sutherland shook his head.

McCaw went to a rolling liquor cabinet and poured himself a stiff shot of rye and a glass of club soda on the side. Sutherland observed him. He carried himself like a military man, held himself a little too erect, which would account for the way his suit fit him, like a garment on a rack instead of on a body.

"Bill will be joining us shortly, doctor. Please have a seat." He indicated the chair he wanted Sutherland to take. Sutherland sat and crossed his legs, careful to preserve a precise crease in his gray flannel trousers, topped by a straw-colored cashmere sport jacket, a blue button-down Oxford cloth shirt and a maroon knit tie. It was Saturday, and he resisted a suit on the weekend. Besides, he knew the people he'd be meeting with would all wear suits. He wanted to stand a bit apart.

William Stalk, director of the CIA's science and technology division, came through the door, "Sit, Chester," he said as Sutherland started to get up. "Hello, Roland. I see you got the jump on us." He went to the liquor cabinet and poured a vodka and tonic. "Terrible tragedy about your boy, Chester. I am so sorry."

"Thank you."

The fourth man at lunch was a small, thin Indian with thick glasses, Dr. Zoltar Kalmani. Sutherland knew of his work through professional and technical journals. His primary recognition was in the field of behavior modification using pharmacological agents, including drugs. He drank white wine and smoked thin brown Sherman cigaretellos, which, he commented in a high-pitched, singsong voice, did not contain saltpeter and thus did not interfere with his sexual life. His laugh was more a giggle.

The conversation stayed on everyday topics while two white-jacketed waiters served shrimp cocktails, a choice of filet of sole almondine or London broil, a bib lettuce salad with vinaigrette dressing, tiny boiled potatoes, coffee, and lemon or raspberry sherbet. (The CIA prided itself on gentlemen's manners—if not always substance.)

Once the table had been cleared Bill Stalk went to the door and locked it. "Cognac?" he asked. McCaw took him up on the offer, the others did not.

Stalk returned to the table, took a small note pad from his breast pocket and opened to a page on which six terse lines were written, each of them numbered. He removed a mechanical pencil from the same pocket, clicked a button on its tube and said, "Item One. Dr. Kalmani has been continuing with some of the research that came out of MKULTRA, a lot of which can be directly credited to your work, Chester."

Sutherland reversed his legs, nodded. "I believe I will have some cognac."

Stalk served the drink, then returned to his note pad. "Naturally, we've had to narrow our focus where experimentation is concerned, but that's probably all to the good. The public scrutiny the program came under prompted a closer evaluation of certain of its elements. Much of what we did was wasted, which, I might add, is no criticism of your work, Chester."

"I understand."

"It was a time when every avenue of interest had to be explored. It would have been a shame to ignore a potential area of legitimate research. But now that public probing has lessened, we would be derelict in not pushing ahead with the valid findings that came out of those previous efforts. Wouldn't you agree, Chester?"

He nodded.

What Sutherland really was thinking was that he wished he weren't there. He didn't understand why he'd been summoned to the meeting in the first place. He'd met with President Jorgens a week ago, and the matter of proceeding with the research had been thoroughly discussed. It was no longer his concern. He'd been out of CIA research for six years.

At the time of his recruitment it had made sense to him. His orientation in medicine had followed the same route as most of his colleagues—research. That was where the action was, and the scramble for funding was an ongoing one. He'd been flattered when the CIA had approached him, and for eight years he'd devoted a portion of his time to the project known as MKULTRA, a top-secret program in which drugs and hypnosis were utilized in a search for effective mind-and-behavior control. Hypnosis had been his specialty, although he'd taken part in many of the pharmacological studies as well. He'd been given carte blanche in the study; money was no object. National security was at stake, or so he'd been told.

But then newspaper probes uncovered the use of drugs on unwitting subjects. Books were written that further laid it open to the public. The families of subjects, some of whom had been killed by the experiments, brought suits against the government. The program was hastily scrapped, and those physicians involved with it quietly returned to their private practices, their names deleted from records released under the Freedom of Information Act.

Sutherland had been relieved when it happened. As much as he believed in the research, he'd found its demands an increasing intrusion into his practice and personal life. Above all, he did not want public knowledge of his involvement in government research. National security aside, there was still something inherently unsavory about it, he'd decided.

Bill Stalk moved to the second item in his note pad. Sutherland listened patiently, forcing his mind to focus on what the director of the agency's most secret division was saying. Eventually, he covered all six items.

"It sounds as though you've developed a solid research program based on the past," Sutherland said. "I wish you well."

"Thanks to you, Chester, and others like you, we have the foundation to build on. The dead ends identified themselves, which leaves us free to pursue more fruitful avenues of inquiry."

"People do not understand the necessity of such research," Dr. Kalmani said. "The future of a free world depends upon being in the forefront of controlling human behavior."

Stalk told a joke which was met with polite laughter.

McCaw lighted a cigar and puffed contentedly. Sutherland checked his watch. It was time to leave.

"Anyone for a little skeet shooting?" Stalk asked. "I reserved the range at three."

"I have to get back," Sutherland said. "I have weekend patients later in the day."

"You work too hard, Chester."

"The curse of my WASP heritage. If there's nothing more to discuss, I'll be leaving. Thank you for filling me in on future plans. They have no direct bearing on me, but as an old hand in the project it's gratifying to be kept informed. Dr. Kalmani, it was a pleasure."

"For me, too, Dr. Sutherland. I trust we shall see more of each other in the future."

Bill Stalk stood, shook Sutherland's hand and said in a lowered voice, "Chester, would you mind coming to my office for a few moments?"

Sutherland glanced at the others. He did not want to linger, yet couldn't deny the director his wish. "Yes, of course," he said.

Stalk's office was in a corner of the building. It was austere; the desk was bare, and a single set of bookshelves contained only leather-bound volumes of literary classics.

"I really have to get back," Sutherland said.

"I know, Chester, but asking you out here had very little to do with what we discussed at lunch."

"I gathered that."

"I'm sure you did. Of all the people of your professional caliber in the program, you're the one whose instincts I most trust."

"That's flattering, Bill, but to be frank with you I'm damn glad to be out of it. Why did you ask me back? Is there a problem that involves me?" He knew what the answer was but didn't want to acknowledge it.

"Security, Chester, that's the question. The continuation

of the research depends on security. Naturally, we released what we could of the files under the Freedom of Information Act. Hell, we had no choice, and we sanitized them as best we could. I've received information from . . . well, let's just say very high and reliable sources that there might be a weak link in the future chain . . . and that that link might be you."

"Because of my son—?"

"Precisely. That's another thing I've always admired about you, your ability to cut through the skin and get to the marrow." He frowned and cleared his throat. "Chester, there's a very legitimate concern about your files."

"Why?"

"Because certain members of your immediate—"

"Family?"

"Yes, and others, might have had access to them and could potentially compromise our position."

"My son, sir, is dead."

"Was he the one who gained access to them?"

"To what?"

"Your MKULTRA files."

"There weren't any."

"That's not what I've been told."

"Who told you otherwise?"

"A reliable source."

"*I'm* a reliable source."

"Of course you are, Chester. When I heard about your son I was shocked. I'd met him once and was very impressed with his intelligence. He was a son any father could be proud of, I would have been pleased to have called him my own . . ."

Sutherland resisted the temptation to respond sharply. Instead he said, "Clarence's death was a tragic loss to all of us close to him, and we're trying to cope with the horror

99

of it as best we can. If there isn't anything else, Bill, I'd just as soon get back to my family."

Stalk came around the desk and draped his arm around Sutherland's shoulders. "Chester, I'm sorry if I've intruded on sensitive ground. There's no need for that, national security or no national security. But I have an obligation to explore any possible area of weakness. You understand, I'm sure."

"Yes, of course. I enjoyed lunch, Bill, it was good seeing you again."

Stalk pushed a buzzer on his desk, then walked Sutherland to the door, his arm still over his shoulder. "You know, Chester," he said, "I realize we've discussed this before, and I promise you this will be the last time. Are you certain you didn't keep files of your own on MKULTRA?"

Sutherland placed his hand on the doorknob and turned it. He looked into Stalk's eyes and said flatly, quietly, "Yes, I'm certain. Enjoy the skeet shooting."

CHAPTER
17

EIGHT OF THE NINE SUPREME COURT JUSTICES SAT IN THE main conference room. Missing was Temple Conover. He had called to say he was ill but promised to come in later in the day.

Jonathan Poulson had presented his argument in favor of the state of Illinois in the *Nidel* v. *Illinois* case. Much of what he said had been contained in a long memorandum from him earlier in the week. It was a typical Poulson memo, long and rambling, filled with redundancies and lacking in clarity of writing and thought. At least that was the way most of the clerks viewed his written work, and their justices tended to agree.

What some of the justices found particularly upsetting about the memorandum was its stress on achieving a unanimous decision within the Court so that a clear and strong message on abortion would be available to lower courts across the nation. Poulson seemed to be saying that in this particular case it mattered less what each individual justice believed represented the facts of law in *Nidel* v. *Illinois* than a need to reflect the administration's antiabortion posture, which in turn reflected the nation's morality. "It's ridiculous," was the way one justice put it to his clerks. "If there's ever been a case that didn't lend itself to unanimity, this is it."

When Poulson had completed his arguments in the conference, the senior justice was next to speak. Since Conover wasn't present, his turn was passed on. One after another the justices presented their views of the case based on their reading of the briefs and the oral arguments heard in open court.

"I don't understand why we continue to deal with this matter beyond the scope of the legal issue," Justice Tilling-Masters said. "If it's the intention of members of this Court to render a sweeping opinion on abortion from legal, philosophical and moral perspectives, *Nidel* v. *Illinois* is not the case to base it on. I said that from the beginning. That's why I voted against accepting it for review."

"I agree," Morgan Childs said from his chair near the door. "This case is too narrow for that. In accepting it for review we're being asked to determine whether the federal government has a right to tell a state what it must do with its funding for health care. It isn't federal money we're discussing, it's state money." He picked up law books that had been opened to specific pages and quoted from previous cases he felt had bearing on *Nidel* v. *Illinois*. "It's my view that the state of Illinois has a right to determine its policies on state-funded medical care. Naturally, if an individual's rights are in question another element would be introduced, but I find that situation lacking in this instance."

Poulson nodded enthusiastically. "Can we take a preliminary vote?"

They went around the table, beginning with the Chief. It ended up four to four.

"I'm afraid I can't accept this," Poulson said. "Perhaps there are overlooked factors that we might reconsider." He started to present his views again when another of the justices, a thin, scholarly man named Ronald Fine, who was second in seniority to Temple Conover, and who often voted with the senior justice on social issues, interrupted. "Chief Justice," he said in a quiet, level voice tinged with a southern accent, "I believe we have a preliminary vote on this case. Naturally, Justice Conover's vote will be the deciding one, and I'm sure we are all . . . well, shall we say, relatively certain how the senior justice will vote."

Poulson knew Fine was right on both counts. Still, he did not want to leave the conference in the minority.

"Let me call Justice Conover," Fine said, "and inform him of the vote."

"Yes," Poulson said. A wave of anxiety had swept over him; he was anxious to return to the quiet of his chambers.

There was silence in the room as Fine placed the call to Conover's house. "Yes, Justice Conover, that's the way the vote went . . . Pardon? . . . Of course, I'll pass that information on to the others . . . Oh, just a second, Justice Poulson wants to speak with you."

He handed the phone to Poulson. "Temple, how are you feeling? . . . Good, glad to hear it. You're voting for Nidel I take it . . . Yes, I understand. I would like to speak with you when you come in this afternoon . . . Yes, thank you, you too."

"That makes it five to four," Childs muttered, "for the

plaintiff. Somehow, I can't help but feel that this won't represent a final vote."

"It usually doesn't," said Justice Augustus Smith, the Court's only black member. Known as "Gus" to his friends, he was the most easygoing of the nine; quick-witted and filled with gentle humor. "With Temple writing the majority opinion," he said, "there's no way somebody won't see some light on the other side. Did he say he'd write it himself?" he asked Fine.

"No, but it's a fair assumption."

Under the rules of the Court, the senior justice in the majority was empowered either to write the initial opinion or assign it to another member of the majority. Had Chief Justice Poulson been in the majority, that authority would have gone to him. As it now stood he would assign the minority opinion, and each justice was free to write a personal, dissenting judgment.

Poulson hid his anger until reaching his chambers. He realized that his failure to gain unanimity was not particularly relevant in light of the way the initial vote had gone. Not only would the Poulson Court fail to utter a call to the nation that would reflect President Jorgens's campaign promise to return decency to American life, but a distinct blow would be delivered to that pledge, resulting in an important victory for the social libertarians he and Jorgens abhorred.

But as he sat back in his high-backed leather chair and soaked in the calm of his office, his initial anger and anxiety faded. This was only the beginning. If there were ever a time for a chief justice to effectively lobby his colleagues on the Court, this was it. He thought about Augustus Smith's comment and realized how accurate it had been. Temple Conover would write a majority opinion that would go too far. Conover couldn't help it. His zeal for social reform, combined with the influence of age and his natural irascible personality, would see to it, and more moderate justices who'd voted in the majority just might shift their final votes.

Poulson lunched with an old friend from law school and his friend's son, also an attorney, at the National Lawyer's Club. The young man asked questions, which pleased Poulson. Poulson told him that of all the institutions in America, it was the Court that stood apart from political wheeling and dealing. It was, he said, a body of nine individuals who, by virtue of their backgrounds, education and experience could interpret the Constitution without being mortgaged to any person or group. He ended up by giving the young man what had become a canned speech, but as he continued, checking now and then to measure the son's interest, he felt genuine pride. He'd always revered the sanctity of the law, which was why he'd worked as hard as he had to gain his first appointment to a bench to escape practicing law with all its deals and bargaining, its infighting and corruption.

The young man asked about Poulson's views of secrecy in the Court. He phrased the question carefully so as not to hint at recent media criticism of the Poulson Court as being the most secretive in history.

Poulson smiled. "I'll answer that by quoting my predecessor, Chief Justice Warren Burger. I always remember a speech he gave to the Ohio Judicial Conference about ten months before being sworn in as chief. I may not have it 100 percent correct, but it will be close enough. Justice Burger said, 'A court which is final and unreviewable needs more careful scrutiny than any other. Unreviewable power is the most likely to engage in self-indulgence and the least likely to engage in dispassionate self-analysis.' But these words really sum up Justice Burger's feelings, and mine. 'In a country like ours no public institution, or the people who operate it, can be above public debate.'"

The young attorney's father kept his smile to himself. His friend, now Chief Justice, had, in fact, clamped a heavy lid on the Court far beyond anything experienced in the past. He couldn't help thinking back to his younger days when he and Poulson were struggling to get started. A mutual friend had termed Poulson "the most paranoid guy I've ever met." When told of the comment, Poulson had laughed and said, "Just because you're paranoid doesn't mean they aren't following you."

"Well, I really must be getting back," Poulson said. "Good luck to you, young man, in your career. If there's anything I can do for you, please feel free to ask. Your dad and I go back a long way together."

As they prepared to leave the dining room Poulson's friend asked about major cases pending at the Court. Poulson hurriedly listed a few, including *Nidel* v. *Illinois*.

"How does that one look?" his friend asked.

A laugh from Poulson. "You know better than that, Harold. If there's one thing in the Court that demands secrecy it's the voting on cases. You'll have to read the papers like everybody else."

Poulson had his driver stop at a drugstore on the way back to the Court to buy Preparation H and a bottle of aspirin. They were for different problems. Once back in his chambers he took two aspirins for a headache that had begun during lunch, instructed his secretary that he did not want to be disturbed, settled in his chair and picked up a private phone. He dialed. It was answered on the first ring. "The office of the attorney general," a woman said.

"Hello, this is Chief Justice Poulson. Is Mr. Fletcher available?"

"Just a moment, Mr. Chief Justice."

A few moments later Attorney General Walter Fletcher came on the line. "Good afternoon, Mr. Chief Justice," he said. "What can I do for you?"

106

"Nothing at the moment, Walter. I just thought I'd better call and tell you that preliminary voting on the abortion case did not go well."

There was a pointed silence on Fletcher's end.

"I'm not discouraged," Poulson said. "These things shift, especially something as sensitive as this. I wouldn't be surprised if we ended up with an almost unanimous decision in favor of Illinois once the dust settles."

"But as of now, it doesn't look good. Is that what you're saying?"

Poulson tried to act nonchalant. "No need to worry, Walter. You might tell the President that we've got things under control."

"Can I tell him that with conviction, Mr. Chief Justice?"

"Absolutely." (Well, you can tell him, but it's not in the bag.)

"Fine. Thank you for calling. By the way, if the President wants to discuss this with you, will you be available later today or tomorrow?"

"I'll make myself available any time that's convenient for him, Walter."

It was appropriate, but these were difficult times, he told himself, rationalizing. If the nation under President Jorgens's leadership were to regain its former balance and prestige—and the need for that he *was* unequivocal about— it would take definite, even bold steps by every governmental institution to bring about that change.

"'The law, wherein, as in a magic mirror, we see reflected not only our own lives but the lives of all men that have been,'" Poulson said aloud, quoting Oliver Wendell Holmes, Jr., and felt a sense of relief displace his doubting mood. He poured himself a glass of vodka and sternly addressed himself. "You've been appointed Chief Justice of the Supreme Court by the President of the United States," he said, "and you'll do what's *right*, damn it, for the President, for the Court, and for the American people. *No matter what* . . ."

CHAPTER
18

"WHO?" TELLER ASKED THE DESK SERGEANT WHO'D CALLED from downstairs the following morning.

"Mrs. Temple Conover. She wants to see you, says it's urgent."

"Send her up."

He couldn't imagine the senior justice's young wife visiting MPD headquarters unless she had something that related to the Sutherland murder. Well and good. He'd just come from his nine o'clock meeting with Dorian Mars and it hadn't been pleasant.

Cecily Conover was ushered into Teller's office.

"I'm sorry to barge in on you this way," she said, "but it couldn't wait."

"Please sit down, Mrs. Conover. Now, what couldn't wait?"

She crossed her legs, fussed at her blonde bangs. Teller couldn't help but react to her sexiness. She was a naturally attractive woman who seemed to feel a need to reinforce what came naturally. She also acted nervous; acting or for real, he wondered?

"I'm not sure I should be here," she said, "but I didn't know what else to do."

He leaned forward on his desk and smiled. "Whatever brings you here, Mrs. Conover, I'm sure we can talk about it."

"I've never been so confused in my life," she said as she shifted her weight in the chair, her skirt riding up on her thighs.

"How is your husband?" Teller asked.

"Fine, just fine. He's an amazing man, Lieutenant Teller, but I'm sure you know that. Every American knows of my husband's contributions to the law . . . and justice."

"True. I don't know how he does it. Somebody told me the other day he's written more than twenty books. I see things by him in magazines too. I hope I'm half that active when I get—"

It was a smile intended to put him at ease. "Yes, my husband is old, detective, and has his physical problems, but he doesn't stop for a moment. He's a very virile man."

He wished she hadn't used the word *virile*. Why mention something so intimate to a stranger? He shifted gears and asked her whether she enjoyed being in the public eye.

"No, I hate it. I'm a very simple person, a very private one."

"I'm sure you are."

He was getting fed up with her posturing. He wished she'd get to the point. When she didn't, and after a few more meaningless exchanges, he put it to her. "Why did you come here this morning, Mrs. Conover? Does it by any chance have to do with the Sutherland case?"

She pursed her lips and looked away.

"If you have something to contribute, anything, you might as well do it now. Frankly, I can use all the help I can get, even if it's painful for you. We can talk frankly and privately."

She looked at him. "Can we? I mean, can I discuss things with you and be *sure* it will stay in this room?"

Teller sat back and lit a clove. "That depends," he said as a blue cloud of smoke headed for the ceiling. "If you want to share a confidence with me, I'm sure there'll be no problem in keeping it confidential, but if it has a bearing on the investigation, I can't promise. I guess you'll just have to trust me."

"Funny, but I do trust you, detective. You have that kind of face."

"Thank you." (What the hell kind of face was *that*?)

"I'm concerned about how I'll be seen by you...and others. After all, a wife is supposed to stand by her husband for better or for worse. A wife can't testify in court against her husband, can she?"

"She can't be forced to. Can if she wants to."

"Then you understand my dilemma."

"No, I don't. You haven't told me anything yet."

"I'm sorry." He couldn't see any tears but she dabbed a corner of her eye with a tiny embroidered handkerchief. "All right, Detective Teller. Here." She reached into a floppy oversized purse, pulled out a brown paper bag and handed it to him. "Go ahead, look at it," she said.

He pulled a handkerchief from his pocket, reached inside the bag and pulled out a Charter Arms Pathfinder .22-caliber pistol with a seventy-six millimeter barrel.

"Yours?" he asked.

"My husband's."

"And?"

She looked down at her lap. "It might be the gun used to kill Clarence. It's the same kind of pistol described in the newspapers."

Teller weighed the pistol, examined it. "It's easy to ascertain whether it was the murder weapon."

"Yes, you can do that sort of thing, can't you?"

"That's right. But before we get to the technology, Mrs. Conover, I'd like to know more about why you think this weapon might be the one used in Clarence Sutherland's murder?"

"I told you, it fits the description in the papers."

"So do thousands of other .22-caliber handguns. If everybody who owned one turned it in after reading about Sutherland, we wouldn't have room to store them."

"But those other people don't work in the Supreme Court, nor did they know about Clarence or have a reason to—" She stopped abruptly.

"Are you actually telling me you think that your husband might have used this weapon to kill Clarence Sutherland?"

She gasped, opened her eyes, then shook her head. "*No*, I'm not suggesting anything like that. He kept the gun in his chambers. I guess someone who knew that took it to kill Clarence."

"If it's the murder weapon."

"Well . . . but you can find that out, can't you?"

Teller shrugged. "How did *you* know your husband had this weapon, Mrs. Conover?"

"I . . . Justice Conover and I once had an argument, a silly spat. He waved the gun at me. It was over as fast as it started."

"You argued in his chambers?"

"Yes."

"And he waved a gun at you?"

112

"It was all so silly, just—"

"Maybe life has passed me by, Mrs. Conover, but from where I sit a man waving a gun at his wife sounds like more than just a silly spat."

She stamped her foot. "I'm sorry I ever *mentioned* it. God... I thought it was right to bring the gun to you. I was just trying to help..."

"Did that *spat* with your husband involve Clarence Sutherland, by any chance?"

"Of course not. I don't remember what it was about."

Teller looked at her hard. "All right, I'll have ballistics check this out."

"There's something else... I'm afraid..."

"You think your husband is capable of killing you?"

"He's... he can be volatile at times. He's very jealous and imagines things—"

"Was he jealous of Clarence Sutherland?"

She opened her eyes and dabbed at them with her handkerchief. "He's jealous of *everyone*."

"I'm going to take the pistol to ballistics now, Mrs. Conover. You're free to stay if you'd like, but you don't have to."

"I think I'd like to leave," she said. "I do ask that if it is the murder weapon you let me know before anyone else."

"We'll see."

He helped her on with her coat and held the door open. "It was gutsy of you to come forward like this," he said, not meaning it but feeling he had to say it.

"I had to," she said. "Thank you for being so decent about everything..."

He watched her move off to the elevators, then went to the ballistics lab, found its director and handed him the pistol. "The Sutherland case," he said. "It's hot."...

The chief of ballistics came to Teller's office immediately

113

after the tests. "It's the weapon," he said. "Perfect match. Bullet and muzzle. No question."

"Prints?"

"Partials, maybe enough for a positive ID, maybe not. But there's no doubt about the weapon itself, Marty. Sutherland was shot with it."

Teller spun around in his chair and looked out his window over a gray, wet Washington.

"Who's it belong to?" the lab chief asked.

"Somebody I wish it didn't. Keep this cool until I have a chance to talk to Mars. Not a damn word to anybody."

"Okay, Marty, but move fast. These things are hard to sit on for very long."

Ten minutes later Teller was meeting with Dorian Mars. He told him about Cecily Conover's visit, her handing over the murder weapon. Mars listened, no change of expression. After Teller had finished, Mars lit his pipe, clicked the stem against his teeth and said, "Silence is golden, Marty."

"So I've heard. The lid stays on?"

"Tight."

"How long?"

"I'll get to the commissioner right away. Hey, this guy is the senior justice of the United States Supreme Court—"

"Owning the gun doesn't mean he used it, Dorian. His wife says someone must have taken it from his chambers. Maybe she did. Implying her husband just might have done it...a jealous man, and really diverting suspicion from herself...after all, she's a few light-years younger than he is. Maybe he was getting in her way. The bloom was off the rose of playing a justice's wife?..."

Mars dropped the pipe on his desk and picked up his phone. "I'll call you later, Marty. Stay available."

As Teller was leaving he heard Mars say into the phone, "... I don't care what he's doing or where he's doing it, this can't wait, and if you make *me* wait you'll be a new statistic on the unemployment rolls."

CHAPTER
19

SUSANNA PINSCHER CALLED MARTIN TELLER AT THREE that afternoon.

"You promised to keep me informed about any developments on your end. You didn't."

"Don't know what you're talking about—"

"Yes, you do. I'm talking about the gun you got into your hot hands this morning."

It took him a moment, finally, "I don't believe it."

"Come on, do you think something that important can be kept a secret?"

"Who told you?"

"It doesn't matter, somebody here at Justice."

"It does matter, damn it. If there's a leak from here I want to plug it."

"Later. The important thing is that you have the murder weapon. What now?"

"It's being discussed. It's not like your run-of-the-mill murder weapon, Susanna. The damn thing belongs to Justice Temple Conover. Not only that, his wife brings it to MPD, which is not what a run-of-the-mill wife does."

"Can we get together?"

"Sure. When?"

"A drink, dinner."

He was about to leave his office at six to meet her when Dorian Mars came through the door.

"I was just leaving," Teller said.

"It'll take a minute. Look, Marty, first of all the commissioner, along with other heavy rollers, wants the Conover thing hushed up for a few days."

"It's probably all over town already," Teller said. He didn't mention his conversation with Susanna.

"Maybe so," Mars said, "but I want it kept tight to our vest."

"Tight to? . . . Right. I really have to run."

"One more minute, Marty. You told me that you were working close with Justice."

"I have a contact."

"Maybe you should find another one."

"Why?"

"The scuttlebutt is that Justice has developed an important lead in the case."

"What is it?"

"I don't know, but I sure as hell want to. It's still MPD's responsibility to resolve this case and I'll be damned if I'll stand still for those people over at Justice doing our job and rubbing our noses in it."

"I'll see what I can find out."

"Fill me in at the nine o'clock meeting."

"I'll do my best."

* * *

HE MET Susanna at Coolbreeze's, a neighborhood bar on Eleventh Street, where they ordered Italian specials of the day from a blackboard and a bottle of Corvo red. Teller told her about Cecily Conover's visit. When he was finished, she asked what the MPD intended to do with the evidence.

"Nothing for the moment. Conover will have to be questioned again, but right now everybody's bracing for a confrontation with the Court's senior justice over the fact the murder weapon belongs to him."

"I think everybody at MPD is very naive," she said.

"Why?"

"I guarantee you that by noon tomorrow the gun will be front-page material. It's already all over Justice, and I'm sure it's the same at MPD."

Teller nodded. "You're right, but it sure isn't going to come from me. Now, let's talk about you and Justice. You sounded annoyed on the phone that I hadn't called you with the gun story. You do understand why, don't you?"

She shook her head and sipped her wine. "No, I don't. We agreed to share information. Telling me isn't like telling a reporter from the *Post*."

"I know that, but I was in a spot. While we're on the subject of sharing information, what's the so-called big breakthrough at Justice?"

She shrugged. "What big breakthrough?"

Teller held up his index finger. "No games, Susanna. I leveled with you—"

"Only after I called you on it."

"Doesn't matter. I've filled you in about Conover's gun. Your turn."

"What I came up with is minor league compared to the gun. I've been assigned a couple of nice bright young interns to help with the investigation. I had them go back over

118

everything ever written about public figures in the case, Conover, Childs, Poulson, Dr. Sutherland, anybody who piqued a journalist's interest."

"Why?"

"Because I didn't know what else to have them do. Frankly, Marty, it's all been a dead end for me. I envy you having the murder weapon plopped in your lap."

Teller bit his lip and poured the last of the wine into their glasses. He hated to admit she was right. He hadn't done a thing to bring about possession of the pistol, couldn't point to painstaking digging or innovative thought.

She continued. "At any rate, one of my interns came up with an intriguing bit."

"Go ahead."

"Chief Justice Poulson has been a patient of Dr. Chester Sutherland. What do you think?" she asked.

"A man is entitled to see a doctor, including a shrink."

She looked annoyed. "But if that shrink's son was his murdered clerk, and the patient happens to be Chief Justice of the Supreme Court?"

"Sure, it's an interesting linkup—"

"What if Clarence Sutherland knew about Poulson's psychiatric problems through his father and held it over his head? Remember I told you about my lunch with Laurie Rawls, how she said no one could understand why Clarence wasn't fired? Even granted his ability. Maybe that's how he kept his job."

Teller said, "And maybe Poulson killed his law clerk to keep his mouth shut?"

"Maybe."

"If so, the kid must have come up with some pretty damaging information. Do you think Poulson's gay?"

She shook her head, then changed tack. "Who knows? Stranger things have come out. A homosexual Chief Justice would blow the lid off the whole nation, not to mention the career of the President who appointed him, a President awash in moral rectitude and a Chief Justice who publicly is known to share his sentiments . . ."

Teller nodded. Farfetched, but so was Watergate and the idiotic Bay of Pigs . . . "By the way," Teller said, "when you mentioned Laurie Rawls it reminded me of something. I talked to a close friend of Clarence Sutherland, a guy named Plum. Plum says Laurie was crazy in love with Clarence, called him at all odd hours, made huge scenes when he was with somebody else."

"It seems to fit his pattern. I want to see her again. I think I could keep our relationship going. I must say I like her—I'd hate to see her come up guilty."

"Come on, lady, you're investigating a murder. I'll take whatever, whoever I can get. You get that way after a few years in this business."

He paid the check and they went outside. "How are your kids?" he asked.

"Fine. How are yours?"

"Good, last I heard. Nightcap?"

"Okay."

"I'd suggest my place but the cleaning woman hasn't been in for six months."

She took his arm. "Mine was in this morning."

They sat in her living room for several hours, talking about their lives, families, exchanging gossip about people in Washington, and some of the cases they'd been involved with.

She yawned. "I guess I'd better call it a night—"

He slid close to her, took her in his arms and kissed her, gently at first, then more urgently. She fell back into soft corduroy cushions, her arms around his neck, their bodies pressed tight together . . .

Afterward he said, "If I wanted to be flip, I'd say something brilliant like, 'Thanks I needed that.' What I'd like to say, if you can stand it, counselor, is 'Thanks, and you're quite a woman.'"

She smiled. "And thank you, Teller. And, not being flip, I'll say I really did need that . . . and enjoyed it . . ."

As he was leaving her apartment at two in the morning he said, "Something bothers me about this info on Poulson being a patient of Dr. Sutherland."

"What?" She was now wearing a purple velour robe and slippers.

"How your interns came up with it by reading old newspaper clippings. It's not the sort of thing that makes the papers."

She kissed him on the cheek. "Elementary, my dear Teller. One of the interns has a father who owns a pharmacy frequented by the high and the mighty, including Chief Justice Poulson. He's had prescriptions filled there that were prescribed by Sutherland. And I'll let you in on another shocking revelation."

"Yeah?"

"Somebody in the Chief Justice's family has hemorrhoids."

"I see. Good night, Susanna."

"Good night, Teller. Sleep tight."

CHAPTER
20

MORGAN CHILDS RECEIVED CLEARANCE TO LAND AT NEW
York's Kennedy Airport. He banked his Piper Colt into a
tight left turn, slipped into the prescribed landing pattern
and set down smoothly on Runway 21 Right. He braked
the small aircraft to a quick stop, turned off the runway and
taxied to a designated small-plane area.

After arranging for tie-down facilities he asked a dispatcher to call him a cab. "I'm catching American's nine
o'clock flight to San Francisco," he told him.

"Are you Judge Childs?" the dispatcher asked.

"Yes."

"Happy to drive you over myself, sir."

The dispatcher, a gregarious fellow, did not stop talking
all the way to the American Airlines terminal. Childs half

listened; his thoughts were on recent events in the Court and on the purpose of his weekend trip to California. He was scheduled that night to address a western regional meeting of Sigma Delta Chi, the journalism fraternity, on the subject of freedom of the press. He'd originally turned down the invitation, but called the program chairman a week before the meeting. The chairman was delighted. "It'll be quite an honor, Mr. Justice, and a pleasant surprise for our members," he'd said.

Childs boarded a 747 through Gate Three and glanced inside the flight deck as he passed it on the way to his seat in First Class. The three-man crew was busy preparing for departure, and Childs wished he could be up there with them rather than strapped in as a passenger. Nothing relaxed him more than being at the controls of an airplane in the vast ocean of air above the earth, the problems of everyday life far below and losing importance with every foot of altitude. He could have made a connection later in the day to San Francisco from Washington, but opted for the New York flight because it gave him a little solo time aloft.

"Good morning, Justice Childs," a flight attendant said. "We've been expecting you aboard."

"Good morning. Nice day for flying."

"Yes, beautiful. Can I get you anything?"

"No, I'm fine, thank you."

He settled back in his seat, opened a briefcase and took out a handwritten draft of the speech he would give. The doors to the aircraft were closed and, engines whining, the huge aircraft rolled away from the gate. Fifteen minutes later it lifted off the ground and began its long, carefully prescribed journey west.

Childs had a Bloody Mary before breakfast and worked on the speech, deleting paragraphs, inserting new ones. Satisfied that the notes did not contain inappropriate references to pending cases, he returned them to his briefcase.

He peered out the window at the panorama thirty thousand feet below, then looked across the aisle where another passenger was reading a paperback book. A copy of that morning's New York *Times* was next to him. He noticed Childs and said, "Help yourself."

Childs took up the paper and scanned the front page. He'd left his house that morning before his Washington *Post* had been delivered, and had deliberately avoided turning on his car radio on the way to the airport. With so little time for silence and reflection, he husbanded every moment he could find.

He started to turn the page when an item at the bottom from United Press International caught his eye. The headline read: SUTHERLAND MURDER WEAPON FOUND.

He read the lead:

The .22-caliber pistol used in the killing of Supreme Court clerk Clarence Sutherland has been uncovered by the Washington Metropolitan Police Department, it was learned last night. The report, unconfirmed by MPD spokespeople but attributed to a reliable source within the department, claims that the pistol has been subjected to ballistics testing and that it is, in fact, the murder weapon.

The story, which was continued inside the paper, went on to recount the details of Sutherland's death. It ended: *Dorian Mars, chief of detectives for the MPD, refused to comment when reached at his home, but promised a statement later today.*

The flight arrived in San Francisco at 12:15 California time. Childs went to a phone booth and placed a credit-card call to his home in Virginia. His wife answered.

"What have you heard about the weapon being found?" he asked.

"It was on the news this morning. Some reporters have called."

"Why would they call me?"

"They're trying to find out more about it, I suppose. Morg, I'm very concerned."

His laugh was forced. "Why?"

"Why did you call about it?"

"Curious, that's all. I read about it on the plane and thought you'd have picked up more than the initial dispatch I read." There was silence on the other end. He asked, "Has there been any word on how the MPD got hold of the weapon, or who it belonged to?"

"Not that I know of. Are you all right?"

"I'm fine. I just arrived and am heading for the hotel. I'll call you from there."

"All right."

"Peg."

"What?"

"I wish you were with me."

"I should have come."

"Yes, you should have. If another reporter or someone from the police call, tell them nothing. Understand? Just say, 'No comment.'"

"All right. Call me later."

"I will."

The SDX dinner committee had booked Childs into a suite on the fifteenth floor of the Mark Hopkins Hotel. A bouquet of flowers, a basket of cheese and two bottles of wine had been sent up by the hotel's assistant manager, who had escorted Childs to the suite.

"Is there anything you need, Mr. Justice?" he asked before leaving.

"No, thank you, everything looks fine."

"Have a pleasant stay with us. We're honored to have you."

125

Childs stepped onto a glassed-in terrace that overlooked the city. Bright sunlight streamed through the windows and created a small rainbow in one corner. It was silent in the suite, and very calm. Yet, in the midst of beauty and peace, he was apprehensive. It was a feeling he hated, one that said weakness, loss of control.

He did what he usually did when anxious. He exercised. He stripped off his clothes and in his boxer shorts went through a half-hour of knee-bends and push-ups, stretching and pulling. He observed himself in a full-length mirror. He was in excellent shape for his age, which made him feel better. He tended to be scornful of people who didn't take care of themselves. He'd survived his Korean captivity because he'd been mentally and physically strong, and if the need ever arose again to survive, he intended to still be ready.

The banquet chairman called to inquire whether everything was satisfactory, and to go over the schedule for that night's dinner, which would be held downstairs in the Peacock Court. He invited Childs to have drinks with the officers of the organization but Childs declined, claiming he had reading to do on matters before the Court.

He showered, napped for an hour, then called home. Sue, the youngest of his four children, answered. They chatted for a minute before Childs asked to speak with her mother.

"Mom's not here, dad. She had a fashion show to go to, at Garfinckel's, I think."

"Yes, I forgot. By the way, honey, anything new about the report I heard that they found the gun that killed Clarence Sutherland?"

"Gee, I don't know. Somebody from NBC called and asked to talk to you, but I told them you were gone until Sunday. I guess it was about the gun. Mom told me not to say anything to anybody."

126

"That's right, honey. Well, take care. I'll see you to-morrow night."

"Okay, dad. Give a good speech."

"I'll try."

He turned on television and searched for a newscast. It was too early in the day; he'd have to wait until that night to pick up new information about the gun.

He looked at the phone, then at the TV screen. A college football game was in progress. He turned down the sound, picked up the phone and dialed a number. A woman answered.

"Hello," Childs said, "may I speak to Dan Brazier?"

"He's not here. Who's calling?"

"A friend. Who is this?"

"Sheryl. I expect Dan back in an hour or two. Give me your name and—"

He dropped the phone in its cradle, got up, dressed in tan corduroy slacks, a white shirt and a dark brown crew-neck sweater and rode the elevator to the lobby. He entered a waiting cab and gave the driver an address in North Beach.

He walked along Broadway, stopping to peer in shop windows and to read large, garish signs extolling sexual favors available inside. His reaction to them was visceral. He hated pornography, and had voted in a number of cases to curtail its proliferation. The First Amendment, he felt, did not grant the right to create and prosper from materials that were blatantly offensive, that degraded women, victimized those who were exposed to it and generated revenue for mob-controlled interests to feed a mushrooming drug traffic. His eldest daughter had recently joined a women's march against porn in New York's Time Square, and he'd been very proud of her.

Still, he deeply believed in the First Amendment and, in most court cases, had focused on the distribution of por-nography rather than the curtailing of its production. If there

127

were those in society who needed pornography to compensate for inadequate personal lives, all right, so be it, but no one should be exposed to it who did not want to be...

He glanced up at a number above a doorway, crossed the street and looked at it from that perspective. He tried to see through the windows of an apartment on the second floor but a reflection made it impossible.

He stayed for a half-hour, watching, checking his watch, leaning against a building. He might have stayed longer if a teenage girl dressed in a pea coat, jeans and wearing a purple feather in her hair had not approached him and asked, "Want to party?" Childs walked away from her, found a cab and returned to the hotel, where he read briefs until it was time to dress for dinner.

There were two hundred people gathered in the Peacock Court. Childs was warmly welcomed by the officers of the group, who led him to the dais, where he was seated in the center of a dozen people.

"I hope you don't mind the publicity, Mr. Justice," a woman to his immediate right said. "We were so excited when we heard you'd decided to accept the invitation that we crowed about it."

"I haven't seen any," he said.

"It was in the papers today," she said, "and on radio and television. We have working press here tonight to cover your speech."

"Well, I hope I say something worth their trouble."

She laughed and touched his forearm.

The banquet chairman asked whether he'd consider holding a brief press conference with reporters, informal, of course, and guaranteed not to take more than fifteen minutes. He agreed and followed the chairman to a tight knot of men and women at the end of the dais. One of the group, a bearded young man with an intense expression on his face, said, "Justice Childs, we'd like to ask you a few questions."

"Go ahead," Childs said, "but first let me ask you one." They laughed. "What's this rumor I've heard about the gun used to kill Clarence Sutherland being found?"

"We wanted to talk to you about that," a young woman said. "I was told as I was leaving the office that the gun belongs to Justice Conover, and that his wife was the one who delivered it to the police."

"I didn't . . ." Childs held back words that would betray his shock at what she'd just said. He smiled. "I hadn't heard that, and naturally would not want to comment on it until I had a chance to confirm the facts."

"But what if it's true, Justice Childs? You've sat on the bench with Justice Conover for quite a long time now. Do you think he's the sort of man who would be capable of—?"

"I think that's an inappropriate question, young man. I don't want to discuss the Sutherland matter any further. If you have questions about my appearance here tonight, please ask them."

"Do you have an advance copy of your talk?" another journalist asked.

"No. I work from notes."

"Please, Mr. Justice, just one more question about the gun that was found. Were you aware that Justice Conover kept a weapon in his chambers, and if so, do you—?"

"I'd better get back to my seat," Childs said. "Thank you for coming."

He returned to the center of the dais. His speech went well. He was confident he'd struck the right note, combining a stated reverence for the First Amendment with a call for responsibility among the media.

Afterward he took advantage of the first lull to excuse himself, said good-night to his hosts and made his way toward the door. Eventually, after being stopped numerous times enroute, he reached the lobby. Piano music drifted from the lower bar, and Childs recognized the familiar strains of "Tomorrow." He paused in the center of the lobby, unsure whether to return to his suite or to go outside for a walk. He decided to go upstairs and call Peg. As he walked toward a bank of manually operated elevators, an anachronistic nicety he always enjoyed about the Mark Hopkins, a voice from behind said, "Play ball."

Childs stopped in his tracks, the words ringing in his ears.

"Home run," the voice said.

Childs slowly turned his head. Ten feet away in a wheelchair was Dan Brazier, dressed in a brown suede jacket, flowered open shirt and khaki pants pinned over the stumps of his legs.

"Dan?"

"In the flesh, Morgan." He closed the gap between them and extended his right hand. Childs took it, held it for a moment, then vigorously shook it.

"What are you doing here?" Childs asked.

"Waiting for you. Hell, when my old buddy hits town to give a speech I figure I have to catch him. Your picture was in the paper today. Thanks for looking me up."

"I called."

"She told me, but you didn't leave a name."

"I was . . . Well, it doesn't matter. How've you been, Dan? You look good."

"I feel great, ready to run the mile."

Childs winced, then stepped back a few paces and said, "When I heard you say, 'Play ball,' I couldn't believe it."

"I figured it would grab your attention."

They had used the phrase "play ball" to signal their escape from the North Korean prisoner-of-war camp. Baseball terms had been used as a code throughout their days of internment, and the system had worked, their captors having little idea of what they were saying to each other.

"How'd your talk go?" Dan asked.

"Fine."

"I used to belong to SDX but dropped out years ago. If I was still a member I would have been there."

The initial shock at seeing Brazier was now replaced by awkwardness, a need to escape to the solitude of his suite. But he knew he couldn't simply shake hands and walk away, not after so many years, and memories.

"Buy me a drink," Brazier said.

"Sure," Childs said. "In there?" He pointed to the lower bar, which was just off the lobby.

"Why not?"

They found a table and ordered. Childs was quickly aware that Dan was a little drunk. He slurred some of his words, his eyes had a hard, glassy cast to them. After they'd been served, Childs asked, "What's new, Dan?"

"What can be new for a former hack without legs? I keep going."

"Who's Sheryl?"

"The woman I live with."

"You look good, Dan. You live around here?"

"You know where I live, Morgan, the place you stood across from and watched this afternoon."

Childs started to protest but Brazier added, "Sheryl told me about this guy standing across the street and looking at the place for an hour."

"What makes you so sure it was me?"

"Old newshawk's intuition. It's like a woman's. It was heartwarming to know that you cared enough to check out where you've been sending the checks. The neighborhood ain't great but it has its advantages. By the way, Mr. Justice, you should have taken the kid up on her offer."

"What kid?"

"Bobbi, the hooker who sent you hightailing it from the street. Word is she's good, gives—"

Childs cut him off. "Are you doing any writing?" he asked.

"No. I decided sitting at a typewriter and putting little marks on paper is a dumb way for a grown man to spend his day. No, I just sit and watch the flow go by my window and live the retired life, thanks to a little help from the United States Government and my friends."

The bitterness was not lost on Childs. He held up his glass of bourbon. "Here's to baseball, Korean style."

Brazier looked at him without picking up his own glass. His stare was hard, unremitting. A thin smile formed on his lips.

"Please, join me," Childs said.

"Why not?" Brazier lifted his glass and clicked it against Childs's. "Here's to life, Mr. Justice, or to what passes for a reasonable facsimile."

Childs looked over his glass. "I'm sorry you're so bitter, Dan."

"Bitterness is in the mouth of the taster. I've tasted. It's bitter. Period."

The pianist returned and launched into a medley of Broadway show tunes.

"What can I do for you, Dan?" Childs asked. "I often wish we'd stayed close, but it was your decision to put space between us. I've continued to do what I think is right—"

"And necessary? You always were the ultimate pragmatist, Morgan, a survivor above all else—"

"Is that so wrong? We all survived, didn't we—?"

Brazier looked down to where his legs should have been.

"Forgive me, Dan, and I know it's easy for me to say, but it beats being dead." Childs slowly turned the glass in his hands and gazed into its amber contents. "I remember a story about Louis Armstrong. He had an old black fellow who traveled with him. They called him Doc because his

132

only job was to see that Armstrong took his medication while on tour. Artie Shaw came backstage during an intermission, noticed that Doc wasn't around and asked where he was. Armstrong said, 'Doc's dead.' Shaw asked what was wrong, and Armstrong said, 'When you're dead, *everything's* wrong.'"

"Jesus, Morgan, you're a little too old to play Pollyanna. I don't need parables, especially from you."

"What do you need from me, Dan? More money?"

Brazier shook his head. "No, I don't need more money. It may not look it to you but I live pretty good. Sheryl's a good woman, takes good care of me. I eat good, drink good, even make love good, and..." He held his index finger in the air. "And, Morgan, I sleep good. How are you sleeping these days?"

Childs glanced around the lounge, which had filled up. He said firmly, "I sleep fine."

"The survivor at the height of his powers. I need another drink."

"I have to go. I'm catching an early flight."

Brazier gripped his arm. "Another drink, Morgan, for old times. Who knows, we may never see each other again."

Childs checked his watch. A woman at a nearby table recognized him, came to their table and asked for his autograph.

"I really don't give autographs," he said. "I think—"

"Don't disappoint your public, Mr. Justice," Brazier said, tightening his grip on his arm.

Childs scrawled his name on a slip of paper the woman handed him. "Thank you, sir," she said. Childs forced a smile as Brazier caught a waitress's attention and ordered another round.

Brazier talked about the Jorgens presidency. He didn't like Jorgens. Childs said little, neither agreeing nor disagreeing.

133

Eventually, the conversation shifted to Clarence Sutherland's murder.

"I heard on the news they found the weapon. Know anything about it, Morgan?"

"Just what I read."

"Sounds like a break in the case." Before Childs could respond, Brazier added, "When I heard it, I immediately thought of you."

"Oh? Why?"

"You've been a big gun collector since the service. I saw your collection when I was in Washington. Very impressive."

"If you're wondering whether the gun belonged to me, it didn't. Apparently it belonged to Justice Conover."

"I know. Who do you figure killed Sutherland?"

"I have no idea."

"He called me, you know."

"I heard."

"From him?"

"Who else? You didn't bother telling me."

"He was a nasty little bastard," Brazier said.

"He wasn't exactly liked."

"What did he tell you about the call to me?"

"It doesn't matter."

"Of course it doesn't. He's dead, which is good for you."

"I resent that."

"Resent it, but it's true, isn't it?"

Childs downed the remaining bourbon and ran his fingers over his mouth. "It was good seeing you again, Dan. Best of everything."

"Don't dismiss me, Mr. Justice."

"Call me Morgan. We're friends."

"That's right, Morgan, maybe even more so these days. Sutherland saw to that."

"I don't see how."

"Yes, you do. Do you have a nice room here? They give you the bridal suite? By the way, how's Peg and the kids?"

"They're fine."

"Are you staying in a big suite?"

"Dan . . ."

"I'd like to see it."

"Another time, Dan."

"How about now, buddy?"

"Don't push me, *buddy*."

"I'm not pushing. Dr. Sutherland would term it being assertive, stating my needs and wishes, being up-front. He taught me to take stock of my assets and to ignore my failings—"

"Damn it," Childs muttered as he searched the crowded room for a waitress.

"Calm down, Morgan. You were always so calm in Korea."

Childs ignored him and continued looking for the waitress. He found her, literally yanked the check from her hands and put down cash on the table. "I have to be leaving."

"There's more to talk about," said Brazier. He tipped over his empty glass.

"Another time."

"Now, damn it."

The people who'd recognized Childs were aware of the rising voices at his table, which embarrassed him. He turned his back to them and looked at Brazier, who smiled and said, "Invite me up, Morgan. Like I said, we have more to talk about."

They rode up in the elevator, Brazier in his wheelchair, Childs standing rigidly in a corner. The operator called their floor and wished them a good night. Childs opened the door to the suite and held it as Brazier wheeled himself inside.

"Very nice," Brazier said as he pivoted in the center of the living room.

Childs took off his suit jacket and tossed it on a chair. "There's only wine," he said.

"We can order up."

"I'd rather not." He turned around and leaned over Brazier, his hands on the wheelchair's arms. "Get it out, over with, Dan. The only reason I accepted this speaking engagement at the last minute was because I intended to look you up. I tried, said the hell with it. Fine, *you* looked me up and here we are. I'm tired. I have an early flight in the morning and there are things I need to do tonight before turning in. Get to the point you want to make and then get out."

"Wine always gives me heartburn. If you have Tums around I don't mind. If you don't, I'd just as soon have a bottle of gin, on me, of course."

"I don't need Tums."

"Looks like gin it is." He went to the phone and called room service. "A bottle of Beefeater, two glasses and some cold shrimp." He turned in his chair, raised his eyebrows at Childs, then said into the phone, "And a bottle of Old Grand Dad, lots of ice."

"I have to call Peg," Childs said after Brazier had hung up.

"Let me say hello when you do. I always liked Peg. She's real people."

Childs dialed the number and, after preliminaries, said, "There's an old friend here with me, Peg. Dan Brazier. He wants to say hello."

It was obvious to Brazier that Peg said something that would have been awkward for Childs to respond to. He took the phone and said, "Hello, Peg, a voice from the past."

"Hello, Dan, what a surprise."

"Well, when I heard Morgan was going to be out here I couldn't resist seeing him again. We're having a hell of a time, living it up, telling war stories, recapturing our youth."

"That sounds nice, Dan. I'd love to see you again the next time you're in Washington."

He almost commented on the icy tone of the invitation but didn't. Instead, he said, "I'll take you up on that offer, Peg. In this whole world my two favorite people are Justice Morgan Childs and his lovely wife Peg. Good talking to you. Here's the judge."

Childs ended the conversation quickly. Room service arrived with an elaborately adorned cart, ice in a silver bucket, a mound of shrimp on a bed of lettuce and iced bottles of gin and bourbon. Brazier fished two dollars from his pocket and handed it to the young man who'd delivered it. "Looks great," he said as he wheeled himself to the cart and poured gin for himself, bourbon for Childs. "This is the way to live, ol' buddy." He handed Childs his glass. "To us, Morgan, to being friends and respecting the dark side of our lives." He downed his gin and poured another. "You know, Morgan, there's something nice about friends sharing a secret. It's like kids pricking fingers and becoming blood brothers, if you know what I mean."

"I know what you mean."

"It's good, positive, binds people together, especially when one of the friends has so much to lose."

"Are you talking about you, Dan?"

"Hell, no, Morgan, we know who I'm talking about."

Childs removed his tie, unlaced his shoes and put them under a desk, then unbuttoned the cuffs of his shirt and rolled the sleeves up to his biceps.

"You look like you're getting ready for a fight," Brazier said.

"Maybe I am."

"Really? Who are you going to fight with, the guy who

137

delivered the booze or your old friend? If it's me, I'm ashamed of you. I'm sort of at a disadvantage."

"All that means is that you can't run."

"But I wheel a mean hundred-yard dash. Look, Morgan, there's no need for you to get antsy with me. I've proved ever since Korea that I'm a true friend, discreet and trustworthy. If I hadn't been, things might have been a lot different in the life of Morgan Childs, justice of the Supreme Court, American hero, inspiration to youth—"

"Shut up!"

"It's *okay*, buddy, I understand. You're under the gun with this Sutherland thing, pardon the pun ... You know something, Morgan, the way I see it, mankind was done a service by whoever knocked off Clarence Sutherland."

"I'm not sure I look at it that way, Dan, and I am sorry for blowing up—"

"Hey, we all have our moments, even a Supreme Court justice ... Sutherland was a *big* moment for you, wasn't he?"

"I don't know what you mean."

"Well, you knew he called me and asked me all those questions about Korea. He didn't need answers—he already had 'em. What did he say to you, that he had the goods on you and would spill unless you did him a favor—"

"Of course not. Don't be melodramatic—"

"Never kid a kidder, Morgan. Frankly, if I'd been in your shoes I would have killed him myself."

"Enough, Dan. You've had too much to drink."

"I'm just getting started."

"Not here, you haven't. It's time to leave."

"Some way to treat a friend. He knew everything, Morgan, all the nitty-gritty—"

"He knew what you'd told his father during your therapy."

"Who would have figured that being open with a shrink

would cause trouble? When I told his father things about Korea, I assumed it stayed with him. I only went to him because the orthopedic doctors thought I could benefit from psychiatric counseling to . . . how did they put it? . . . 'to help resolve my inner feelings about loss of limbs.' Ain't that a hot one?"

"You didn't *have* to get into Korea with him, did you? There was no need to talk about it—"

"Come on, Morg, free association is the ticket in therapy. You sit there and everything is so calm and relaxed, so nonjudgmental. It's pretty easy. I knew the minute I started talking about us and Korea that I was getting into deep water, but what the hell, he's a doctor and I'm a patient. It's all confidential, unless . . . unless your shrink happens to have a son who manages to snoop through his father's records."

"He knew a good deal about a good many, it seems."

"I know. You walk around with that kind of information and somebody's liable to take a shot at you."

"I didn't."

"Duly noted, your honor . . . Anyway, somebody did. Who else did his father treat and keep records on?"

"I wouldn't know."

"Good stuff. Even though I don't write anymore, the old instincts keep coming through. It's a hell of a story, a Supreme Court clerk whose father is a psychiatrist treating big shots reads his father's files and holds trump cards over the big shots. That's power, Morgan, like J. Edgar Hoover had."

"Not worth murder."

"Depends. Have you ever told Peg about Korea?"

"It doesn't matter."

"Of course it does."

"Not to you."

139

"I'm your closest friend, Mr. Justice, except for your wife, but that's a different friendship—"

"Very different."

"All I'm saying is that we're in this together. No matter what you had to do to handle the Sutherland thing, I want you to know that you can trust me to the grave."

"I never doubted that, Dan. If I did—"

"That's what I like to hear, still the hard-nosed survivor to the core."

Childs poured himself another drink. He was beginning to feel the effects of the alcohol. His thoughts at that moment were ambivalent—he wanted Brazier to leave, yet was enjoying a certain pleasure at having him there. Acute, painful images of Korea flashed through his mind . . . the rotting flesh of prison camp, the sounds of North Korean guards laughing as they beat a prisoner . . .

"You're an important man, Morgan," Brazier said. "Think about it. There's only nine of you in the world."

"I'm aware of that."

"But what is true importance, Morgan? I mean, take away the black robes and you're like everybody else, getting old, losing touch, dying."

"I don't see it exactly that way."

"Nobody likes to, but it's reality. Remember how we used to talk about staying ready every minute until the break came? You were obsessed with that, which is probably what saved us. You'd hop off that straw cot every morning, yell for us to wake up and start your damn calisthenics, and I'd curse at you through every push-up and every step of running in place. But you were right, Morgan, you got us up and kept us ready. And here we are. Well, more or less. Are you still ready?"

Childs smiled at the challenge. "As ready as ever, Dan. Remember, I'm a survivor."

Brazier slipped out of his jacket, unbuttoned his shirt,

yanked off his tie and tossed them to the floor. His naked torso was thick and heavily muscled.

"What are you doing?"

"Getting ready, Morgan. Come on." He slid from the chair and assumed a position on the carpet from which to do push-ups. "Thirty minutes worth, Morgan. We'll count. The winner gets ... well, how about a hundred?"

"Don't be silly."

"Lost it, Morgan? Sorry to hear that. I read once that some guy did almost two thousand push-ups in a half hour, world record. Count 'em off for me."

Brazier began, massive arms lifting his body easily from the carpet and lowering it again, up and down, the tempo increasing. At first Childs didn't count, and Brazier picked it up at ten. When he got to fifty Childs took over.

"Check your watch," Brazier said.

"A hundred and twenty. Don't worry, I'll keep time." He refilled his glass and continued to count as Brazier raised and lowered himself in a steady cadence. A half hour later he'd done nine hundred push-ups. His body glistened with sweat, and strands of black hair hung down over his face. He lay on his back, arms spread to the sides, and started to laugh. After a while, there was no way for Childs not to join him.

"What'd I do, nine hundred?" Brazier asked. "Want to take a shot at breaking the Dan Brazier middle-aged, legless record?"

"No, I think it's time we called it a night."

"I guess you're right." Childs held the wheelchair as Brazier lifted himself into it. "You know, Morgan, this has been a sort of historic night. Here I am, former newspaperman and starmaker doing push-ups in a fancy suite while a Supreme Court justice counts 'em off. Who'd believe it?"

"It was good to see you again, Dan. I'd just as soon keep this evening between us."

"Hey, you know me, Mr. Closed Mouth. I've been proving that for years, right, ever since Korea."

"What happened wasn't so terrible—"

"Of course not. They used us both for a so-called greater good, the war effort, patriotism, victory over the gooks. You came out of it a hero, Morg, and I'm proud as hell to have helped create you." He put on his clothes. "I'm also glad Sutherland got it," he said when he was dressed.

"Are you?"

"Yup. It brings it back to the way it always was, just you and me against the world."

Childs started to say something, held the words that had formed on his lips and said only, "You know, Dan, that if you ever need anything you just have to give a yell."

"Oh, yeah, Morgan, I've always known that. Don't worry, you'll hear me all the way across the country." He wheeled himself to the door, opened it, looked back and said, "It was good seeing you again, Mr. Justice. Best to the wife and kids."

CHAPTER
21

Two press conferences were held on Monday.

In the morning Senior Supreme Court Justice Temple Conover, his wife at his side, sat before a bank of microphones and television cameras in a room in the Department of Justice. He wore a dark gray vested suit, white shirt and muted green tie. He'd removed his topcoat but kept his red wool scarf around his neck throughout the session.

He began by reading a short statement he'd written that morning:

> *I understand that the Metropolitan Police Department has in its possession the weapon used to kill court clerk Clarence Sutherland. That weapon, a .22-caliber pistol, belonged to me. Until now I was not aware*

that it had been used in the commission of a crime, nor do I know who took it and under what circumstances. This represents the sum and substance of my knowledge of the matter.

One of fifty reporters in the room outshouted the others and asked, "Is it true that your wife, Mr. Justice, was the one who gave the gun to the MPD?"

"I have no comment other than the one I have given you."

Another reporter called out to Cecily Conover, "Did you bring the gun to the MPD, Mrs. Conover?"

Cecily, who wore a tight straw-toned cashmere-and-silk dress, responded, "The circumstances under which my husband's pistol was uncovered are not a matter of public record. It was a pistol he's owned for some time and—"

Conover glared at her, then said to the questioners, "You were told that I would not answer questions, that my appearance here this morning was solely for the purpose of making the statement I have just read. Thank you for coming. Good day." He stood, turned so that an aide could help him on with his coat and limped toward the door, his right arm securely in his crutch, his face tight and pained.

Cecily smiled at reporters who pressed close and fired questions at her. She held up her hand and said, "Not now, please, not now." She joined her husband at the door, took his arm and they disappeared into the hallway.

Susanna Pinscher had been standing at the rear of the room. She felt a kind of sadness about what she'd witnessed. There sat an old, brilliant and distinguished jurist dishonored by his young and beautiful wife. Bringing his pistol to the MPD had been, to put it mildly, an unfaithful act, more than her rumored infidelities. Susanna found herself actively disliking Cecily Conover. A real little bitch...

An old friend from CBS-TV spotted her and asked if she

144

knew whether Cecily Conover had turned in the gun. "I can't get a confirmation from MPD," he said.

"I have no idea," Susanna said, wondering who at MPD had leaked the story. It couldn't be Teller...

The second press conference took place at three in the afternoon. It was held in the White House. President Jorgens announced he had named a well-known Texas trial attorney, Donald Wishengrad, as special prosecutor in the Sutherland case.

Jorgens delivered a long statement, ending with, "... *this unfortunate murder and resulting developments have threatened to shake public faith in our highest institutions and officials. By naming a special prosecutor, I hope to bring this matter to a swift and just conclusion and to restore that shaken faith.*"

He took a limited number of questions, one of which was whether he was referring to justice Conover when he spoke of shaken public faith in high officials. He quickly replied, "I referred to *no* specific individual. The Supreme Court is our highest tribunal, and anything, or anyone, who puts a cloud over it does a profound disservice to the nation."

After Jorgens left the room reporters buzzed about whether Temple Conover was, in fact, being singled out. Jorgens's feelings about the senior justice were a matter of public record. He'd attacked Conover's liberal stance on many occasions, and once had commented during a televised fireside chat, "Some of our more dedicated liberal thinkers, such as the distinguished Justice Conover, see nothing wrong about turning the country over to pornographers, dope addicts and criminals in the name of freedom. I don't call that freedom for anyone, except for a small, zealous number of social misfits. Indeed, I call that license." He'd then added, "I forget the sage who said it, but I think he was onto something when he said, 'there's nothing older than an old Liberal.'"

Conover had sent Jorgens a letter following the telecast, chiding him for his lack of good taste. He did not receive a reply.

"The real question," said one of the reporters to her colleagues, "is whether Conover might have killed Sutherland."

"It depends on whether his wife is the piece of business they say she is, and whether she and Sutherland ever got it on together," said another.

"And," put in a third, "whether the old man had the goods on them and cared enough to do something drastic."

AT SIX o'clock that evening Susanna Pinscher circled a block in Washington's northwest district. A car vacated a parking spot and she quickly took it. She looked around to get her bearings, then walked in the direction of an address written on a small slip of paper, stopped in front of an older building that had recently been converted into apartments, confirmed the number over the door and stepped inside a small lobby. Mailboxes and buzzers were to the left. She leaned close to them and squinted in the dim light. L. RAWLS—2C. She pressed the buzzer. The answering signal tripped a lock on the lobby door.

"Hi," Laurie Rawls said when she answered Susanna's knock.

"Hi. Sorry I'm late, but I had trouble parking."

"Everybody does. Come in."

The apartment was small but airy. She'd entered directly into the living room. A kitchen was immediately to the right and there was a pass-through to the living room. A dozen hanging plants covered a picture window. The room was painted a pale yellow and trimmed with white. The furniture was green, which, with the plants, gave the space a pleasant outdoorsy feeling.

"Sit down," Laurie said. "I don't have much in the way

of booze but I do have wine. I think there's some Scotch, too, maybe a little vodka."

"Wine would be fine, Laurie, red or white."

Susanna sat on the couch. A glass-topped coffee table was piled high with books, including *The Brethren*, a former best-seller that provided unflattering insight into the Supreme Court.

"Must have been required reading," Susanna said of the book when Laurie returned with the wine.

"I guess so. Bacon and eggs all right for dinner?"

"Sounds fine." She raised her glass. "Here's to better days."

"I'll drink to that."

"I love your plants. Your thumb is decidedly green."

"They grow in spite of me." She sipped her wine. "I appreciate your coming here, Susanna."

"When you called this afternoon I was a little confused, not about the call but about how you sounded, and that you wanted to avoid public places. Why do you feel that's necessary?"

Laurie shrugged. "Maybe I'm getting paranoid. They say that if you hang around Washington enough you get that way."

"Especially when you're involved in a murder investigation."

"Yes, that helps. Did you see the press conference today?"

"I was at Justice Conover's. I heard about the President's."

"I saw them on the early news. I'm back clerking for Justice Conover."

"Really? How did that happen?"

"He complained about the Chief taking me away from him, and I guess he won."

"How do you feel about it?"

"Ambivalent, especially now that the gun has been found."

It was obvious that Laurie wanted to talk about the gun but had some reservations. Susanna decided not to push, and switched to chitchat about the Washington Redskins.

"I don't follow football," Laurie said, "although it's hard not to in this town. Everything is so hard in *this town*. Excuse me." She went to the bathroom, returning with a smile on her face, her voice reflecting a new, although determined, lightness. "I think I'll get dinner going."

"Can I help?"

How about doing the eggs? I usually manage to mix in the shells. I hope you're better at it."

They went into a small white kitchen where Laurie handed Susanna an apron. "One of these days I'm going to get my kitchen act down and become Earth Mother. I always wanted to be a good cook but was told it was old-fashioned and that the way to a man's heart these days definitely isn't through his stomach." She said it with a lilt, but there was a touch of bitterness mixed in.

"Have the rules changed that much?" Susanna said as she gathered things to set the table. "I'm just enough older than you to have experienced something different." She turned, shoved her hands in her apron's large front pocket. "I happen to think it's okay if a woman wants to cook and bake and make a man happy. I guess I'm not much of a feminist. At least not orthodox."

"But you don't live your life that way."

"A matter of choice, and circumstances. Laurie, I do think, though, that a woman who makes the other choice ought to be respected, not be accused of having sold out."

"What about abortion? It's the hot topic even in this town, as you know. I mean the case before the Court..."

"Well, I don't see how anyone can be *for* abortion, but I also believe in a woman's right to make a choice..."

"I think the Court will rule in favor of a liberal position. I mean in *Nidel v. Illinois*."

"Why do you think it will go that way?"

Laurie whipped eggs in an aluminum bowl with a whisk. "Being a clerk in the Supreme Court puts you on the inside of a lot of things, Susanna . . . sometimes I wish I didn't know—"

"Puts a burden on you, doesn't it?"

"You might say that . . . They've taken a preliminary vote on *Nidel v. Illinois*." When Susanna said nothing, Laurie added, "It was five to four in favor of Nidel."

"Why are you telling me this? Should you be?"

Laurie dropped the whisk in the bowl, turned and rubbed her hands on her apron. "Probably not, but it's all *relevant*, Susanna. So many things happening in the Court are related to what happened to Clarence."

"Do you want to talk more about it?"

"Yes and no."

Susanna let it go at that during dinner. There were times when she wanted to reach out and tell Laurie how much she liked her, that she could consider her a friend, but knew she shouldn't. She was there because Laurie had called and asked her to be there, had gotten her to the apartment with the promise of revealing further information about the Sutherland case. Stick to the ground rules, she told herself.

"More wine?" Laurie asked when they were finished.

"Coffee, I think."

They had coffee in the living room. Laurie put on a recording of *Die Zauberflöte*, Mozart's *Magic Flute*. "He was commissioned to write it," she said, "by a theater owner in Vienna who wanted a magic opera. Mozart approached it as light clowning but the more he worked on it the more it became a kind of serious celebration of man."

Susanna laughed. "If anything positive comes out of the

149

Sutherland case it will be an education for me in opera."
Teller first and now Laurie.

They listened to one side of the record in silence. Laurie
turned over the disc and returned to the couch, where Susanna had leaned her head back and closed her eyes. Susanna
asked without moving, "What did you want to tell me,
Laurie?" She almost added, You can trust me, but didn't,
knowing that would be unprofessional.

"The gun..."

"What about it?" She opened her eyes and turned so that
they faced each other.

"Justice Conover threatened his wife with it."

"I'd heard that."

"From whom?"

"That's not important. Nothing stays secret very long in
this town."

"Justice Conover threatened his wife with it because she'd
been having an affair with Clarence. Did you know that
too?"

"There's been a lot of speculation—"

"It's true. When Justice Conover found out about it he
went sort of berserk, broke things in his chambers and..."

"And what?"

"And said...said he'd kill both of them."

"How do you know this? Were you actually there?"

"I was close enough to hear. It was an awful scene, the
judge pulled out the gun...God...for a moment I really
thought he was going to shoot her."

"But of course he didn't."

"No."

"What about Clarence? Did Justice Conover confront him
about it?"

"Yes."

"Did you hear that conversation too, Laurie?"

She shook her head. "Clarence told me."

150

Susanna sat up straight. "He did? Why would he do that?"

"I never knew . . . unless it was another way to hurt me . . ."

Susanna reached out and touched her shoulder. Damn it, she could be *human*, couldn't she? "I'm sorry, Laurie, it must be very painful to drag this up."

"It's all *right*." Except obviously it wasn't. In spite of herself tears formed in her eyes. "Clarence liked to make sure I knew about his other women. I wouldn't have minded so much, I think, if he'd actually fallen in love with someone else, but that was never the case. It was always the sex he'd brag about, somebody he'd picked up in a bar or at a party, or someone . . ."

"Someone like Cecily Conover."

No answer. But the silence spoke volumes. "How long did their affair last?"

"I don't know if it ever ended. He'd tell me . . . they'd meet at his apartment or a hotel or even in the Court—"

"In the *courtroom*?"

"No . . . in Clarence's office. The only time I think he ever did anything like that in the actual courtroom was . . . I'm embarrassed to tell you . . . was with me. Pretty sick, right? Was this what my parents put their darling daughter through law school for . . ."

Susanna's natural reaction was sympathy, but she also wanted Laurie to go on. She didn't have to prompt her.

"It only happened once," Laurie said, "and it really isn't quite as terrible as I've made it sound. We didn't go all the way in the courtroom, but we came damn close. Clarence had a pixyish—some might say quirky—side to him. He often worked late and liked to go into the courtroom and pretend to be chief justice. He'd sit in the middle chair and issue proclamations to the room, which, obviously, was empty and dark, except when I was with him."

"Was that often?"

"No, just once in a while—"

151

"And one night you made love there?"

"He did become affectionate, and we, to use an old-fashioned term, necked, petted. I was worried that one of the building's security people would come in but Clarence didn't seem at all worried. If it had been up to him we probably would have—"

Susanna smiled. "Another old-fashioned term . . . gone all the way?"

"Right."

The second side of the record ended. Laurie stood up and asked, "More of the same, or something lighter?"

"Something lighter."

She put on George Shearing with strings and went to her plants, touched them with exaggerated tenderness, turned and said, "I'm pretty damned frightened, Susanna."

"Of what?"

"Of being there."

"In the Court?"

"Yes. Oh, God, I don't want to come off strange or nutsy, paranoid, but, after all, somewhere in the United States Supreme Court it seems there's a murderer . . ."

Susanna went to her. "Is there something you aren't telling me? Did Clarence confide something to you—?"

She started to deny it, then nodded. "Yes, he did . . ."

"And?"

"I think one of the justices must have done it . . ."

Susanna pointed to the couch. "Let's sit down. Now, go ahead."

"Clarence used to say how he had a key to every lock, to every person on the Court. He knew compromising things about the justices."

"How, specifically?"

"I don't really know, although I suppose just being close to them, listening, would account for it. He'd worked closely with Justice Poulson, and claimed Poulson was nothing but a puppet of President Jorgens and that he could prove it."

"Lots of people have said or implied that about Poulson, Laurie. In fact, that sort of charge has been made about chief justices for years."

"I think there was more to it than that," Laurie said. "It's one thing for a justice to be influenced by the political philosophy of a president who's appointed him to the bench, but it's another to have the White House play a direct role in your decisions on specific issues."

"Has that happened with Poulson?"

"Clarence claimed it had, and he told me he had documents to prove it. He said that if they were released they'd blow the lid off the Court, and maybe the Presidency too."

Susanna whistled. "I'd like more coffee," she said. "And some brandy if you've got any."

"I do."

They continued to talk about Justice Poulson and his links to the White House. Laurie didn't have much more to offer because she hadn't actually seen the proof Clarence had referred to, but she seemed convinced that it represented a real threat to the Chief Justice, and even to the President. Enough to provide a motive for murder.

"What about the other justices?" Susanna asked. "You've told me about Justice Conover and his wife's affair with Clarence. Are there others whose private lives might have been compromised by Clarence?"

"He seemed to have something on *all* of them, Susanna. I remember him once talking about Justice Childs. He laughed and said, 'Some hero. He's a phony.'"

"Justice Childs? His heroism in Korea is well documented—"

"I don't have any answer for that. All I know is that I wake up in the middle of the night and see the justices' faces. I dream that all nine of them stand in front of the

153

bench. Clarence sits in the Chief's chair . . . just like he did when he was killed. He laughs at them, calls them fools and fakes. Each justice has a pistol, and one fires and hits Clarence in the head—"

"Which one?"

"I don't *know*. It's a dream, I wake up, thank God."

"If you had to go with your gut instinct, Laurie, which would it be?"

A nervous laugh. "I wouldn't know, Susanna, but if I had to narrow it down, I'd say Conover, Poulson or Childs. From what I know, they had real motives. I know how much has been made of Clarence's relationships with women, but I don't think a woman killed him. I'd turn the old saying around, look for the man, Susanna . . ."

Twenty minutes later Susanna sat in her car. She started the engine, gripped the wheel and said to herself, "Look for the man. Look for the woman. Look somewhere else but, of course, don't look at me . . ."

IN CHEVY Chase, a two-man team finished searching Dr. Chester Sutherland's offices.

"That's it," one of them said.

"Right," said the other. "We've got the MKULTRA files. Whatever the hell they are. That's what they wanted. Let's go."

CHAPTER
22

"I'M CERTAIN OF IT," VERA JONES TOLD DR. CHESTER Sutherland the following morning. "Look..."

He looked over her shoulder at an unlocked file drawer with the label MNOP. "Are you sure you locked it last night before you left?" he asked.

She looked at him. "I have locked and checked these files for twenty-two years, doctor, and last night was not an exception."

"Yes, of course, I'm sorry. Have you found out whether anything is missing?"

"Not yet. I thought you should know before I did anything."

"Have you checked my office?"

"No."

Sutherland, who'd been eating breakfast when she called from the office, and who still wore a robe over silk pajamas, entered his private office, Vera at his heels.

"Everything looks in order," he said. "Have you gone through the unlocked file?"

"I told you—"

"Yes, yes, I know. Why don't you do that now. I want to check in here."

She started to leave, then turned, hands on hips. "Should I call the police?" she asked.

"No. First let's see what's missing, if anything."

She closed the door behind her. Sutherland went to the paneled wall behind the curved couch, touched a spot and a section opened. Built into the wall behind the concealed door was a safe and two locked, wood-grained file cabinets. He turned the dial on the safe; it was secure. So were the cabinets. He fished a key from a pocket in his robe and inserted it into the top cabinet. The drawer slid out easily on nylon casters, and a row of red plastic file folders with typed labels stared at him. He did not have to touch them to know some were missing. The supporting bracket behind them had always been in the right position to hold them erect and neat. Now they slumped against one another.

"Damn it, god*damn* it."

Vera knocked.

"Just a minute," he said, locking the file and closing the wall's hinged panel. "Come in."

"I've checked," she said. "Nothing seems to be missing. Perhaps I did forget to lock it after all."

"That would be uncharacteristic of you."

"I'm human."

He took a step toward her, then stiffened and went to the glass coffee table that was his desk.

"Was anything disturbed in here?" she asked.

"No . . . no, nothing at all. Are you sure everything outside is secure?"

"Yes."

"That file that was unlocked . . . it contained the Ps. Was Justice Poulson's file there?"

"Yes, of course."

"Good. Vera, perhaps we should talk."

"About what?"

"About Clarence's murder."

"Why? What is there to discuss?"

"I'd call that denial and resistance."

"Please doctor . . . Clarence's death was a tragic blow to us all. We grieve, we try to recover, retrench and get on with our lives."

"Come, sit down." He patted a spot on the couch next to him. "Please, sit a minute."

She uneasily joined him on the couch, long, slender fingers smoothing her skirt over her knees. He put a hand over one of hers and smiled. "We've been together a long time, Vera, been through a good deal . . ."

She said nothing.

"People who share as we have tend, inevitably, to become close, sometimes closer than even blood relations." She continued to look straight ahead, her breasts rising and falling beneath her blouse that was buttoned to her neck, her hand, though, rested perfectly still on her knee beneath his hand.

"Life is an accumulation of episodes, Vera. We all tend to function day by day, and what we do is shared by a limited number of people that we let into our lives. These are the people we most trust with our secrets."

She turned now so that she faced him. "If this is your way of finding out whether my loyalty to you and to *your* secrets is intact, I must say I resent it—"

He started to say something but she went on quickly.

157

"No, Chester, you don't have to worry about me, and I think you know that. We've been sucked into something that ended up destroying Clarence. It's over now. His death, as tragic as it was, has at least seen to that."

Sutherland sat back, straightened out his fingers and examined his nails, positioning them on the palm of his other hand like a jeweler creating a scrim for his gems. Apparently satisfied with their condition, he looked at her and said, "It will all work out, won't it, Vera?"

"Of course it will, doctor."

"Thank you, Vera."

"There's nothing to thank me for," she said, going to the door. "We do what we have to do . . . I mean, we go on . . ."

Sutherland sat on his couch after she was gone and stared at that portion of the wall where the file cabinets and safe were hidden behind. He went to the phone in his smaller office, consulted a small black book he'd taken from his desk, dialed a number. William Stalk, director of the Central Intelligence Agency's science and technology division, who at the moment happened to be playing a video space-invader game with his son, answered. "Good morning, Chester. To what do I owe the pleasure of this *early* morning call to my home?"

"I'm sure you know why I'm calling, Bill."

Silence.

"There's been a break-in at my office. It happened last night."

"I'm sorry to hear it. Any damage?"

"No, but my files were invaded."

He laughed. "I hope they didn't snitch anything juicy about your patients. That could be embarrassing for a lot of people."

Sutherland started to mention the missing MKULTRA

files but held back his words, saying instead, "I'd like to see you, Bill."

"I'll be at home all morning. My wife reminded me a few weeks ago that I'd been spending too little time with my boy, so I blocked out part of today. We've been playing one of those games on TV where electronic enemy blobs keep coming at you fast and furious. He's a lot better at it than I am, but then again he gets more practice. The damn things are addictive."

"When can I see you?"

"How about this afternoon, at my office? Three o'clock."

"I'll be there, count on it."

VERA JONES sat behind her desk. A lighted button on the telephone went out. She picked up a pencil and began writing on a pad. Moments later Sutherland came into her office. "Cancel any patients I have today," he said.

"All right. There were only four. I'll call them."

"And you might as well go home after you've made the calls. I'll be gone all day."

"Perhaps I will. Thank you."

She stayed at the office the rest of the day, rearranging files, typing dictated notes of patient sessions left for her by Sutherland and doing what was an obsession with her—retyping pages in a master telephone book that contained not a single handwritten entry or cross-out.

At six-thirty, after washing her coffee cup, she took from a concealed compartment in her desk a file folder with a typed label at the top that read, POULSON, J., opened the cover and read the first page, then went through a dozen additional pages, each filled with lines of pristine typing. Had someone taken the time and interest to compare the pages in Poulson's file with materials in other files, they might have wondered why his pages, presuming to cover months of sessions and resulting notes, were all freshly typed, as though they'd been done in a single sitting, which was the case. Vera was aware of the inconsistency and wished it weren't so, but there had been no other way to duplicate the missing file. She'd typed the new pages from what she'd remembered of the originals, the doctor's comments and analytic perceptions. It was the best she could do and, she reminded herself, the chances of it being discovered were remote. The Poulson file was a dead one. He hadn't been a patient in a long time. There was no reason for Dr. Sutherland to review his case, which was why his asking about it concerned her. She'd kept the reconstructed file in her special hiding place ever since making it, reluctant to put it to the test in the MNOP drawer. Now, she knew she would have to. She double-checked every lock in the office, turned out the lights and went to her car, where she sat for some ten minutes, the motor running, her body trembling against the cold and inner anxiety. Once the heater had come to life she drove off to her apartment. She sat for a moment in front of it, trying to decide whether to go inside or to go on. The thought of spending a long night alone was nearly unbearable. She shifted into DRIVE and headed down the Rockville Turnpike, south on Wisconsin to Connecticut Avenue and down Connecticut to Lafayette Park, where she sat at a red light and stared at the White House. Most of its windows were alive with pale yellow light, and the porte-cochere designed for Thomas Jefferson that covered the north entrance, and that was favored by visiting heads of state, was illuminated by spotlights. The traffic light turned green; she continued to stare. A motorist behind her blew his horn. She came erect, glanced in her rearview mirror and proceeded through the intersection.

She felt the onset of panic. She drove by rote, passing corner after corner, wanting to turn at each of them. Eventually she crossed the Kutz Memorial Bridge and parked along the Tidal Basin under Japanese cherry trees that were waiting for spring.

"My God, what's happening to me," she said as she gripped the wheel and tried to squeeze control into her body. She hated herself when she allowed this to happen. It was weak, pathetic, dangerous. It always frightened her to become confused. She was usually the one who could see things clearly in the midst of chaos, focus on the real issues, make crucial decisions to restore order and resolve conflicts.

But now she sat alone and afraid, and desperately wished there was someone to comfort her, to grab hold of, to touch and be touched by. The sense of weakness was overwhelming. She started the car and drove to M Street, Northwest, in Georgetown, where after considerable searching she found a parking spot. As she walked up the street the sound of loud community singing and a piano came through the partially open front door of Club Julie. She almost turned and retraced her steps to her car but the pull of the music, the human voices, laughter, drew her inside.

The club was unusually crowded for a weeknight. The smoke was thick, which was why the front door had been propped open.

She'd decided that if she couldn't find a secluded place at the bar she wouldn't stay. She wasn't one for joining in community sing-alongs, although she rather enjoyed listening and watching others indulge. She'd felt uncomfortable the last time she'd been here, which was the only other time. Her escort had insisted on sitting close to the piano. She thought about that night and winced.

She glanced nervously about. A stool at the corner of the bar nearest the front door appeared to be vacant, so she went to it. A reasonably well-dressed man on the next stool smiled and said, "Hello there."

"Is this seat taken?" she asked. She noticed an empty beer glass in front of it.

"I think he left," the man said. "It's all yours."

She sat and waited to be served.

"Let me buy the lady a drink," the man told the bartender.

"Thank you, no," Vera said. To the bartender: "A vodka and tonic, please."

When the bartender returned with her drink he said, "Haven't seen you in a long time."

She was startled by the comment. "I've been very busy," she said, wishing he hadn't spoken to her.

"Yeah, right," said the bartender. "Anyway, good to see you again. Enjoy."

Julie played a song familiar to the man next to her, who began to sing, turned to her and said between the lines, "Know this one?"

She shook her head.

He stopped singing. "I've never seen you here before."

"I was only here once, a long time ago."

"Nice place. I don't get here much myself but I was coming home from a meeting and thought I'd stop in for a pop and a little music."

She sipped her drink.

"You live around here?"

"No."

"Work in the neighborhood?"

"No."

"I'm vice-president of a computer company. We're not very big but . . ." He pulled out a business card and shoved it at her. She tried to read it in the dim light.

"Name's George Jansson," he said, extending his hand.

She took it. "My name is Vera."

"Vera? Nice name, very old-fashioned." He scratched his head. "I don't think I've ever met a Vera before." He laughed. "Lots of Georges around, though. Can I buy you a refill?" He held up both hands to offset a negative reply. "No strings, no ulterior motives. I just enjoy talking to you."

He looked down the length of the bar and called out, "Robbie, another round here."

He shouldn't have had any additional drinks, Vera decided twenty minutes later. He'd become tipsy, not less of a gentleman, just sillier. She didn't dislike him. His hair was close cropped and gray at the temples, he had kind eyes.

"Another?" he asked.

"No, thank you, I really must go."

"It's too early. Come on, hang in, or at least keep me company."

"I'm sorry but it's been a rather difficult day and tomorrow will be the same..."

Julie announced that he was about to play a request and that a favorite regular patron would sing it. A portly man wearing a shirt collar too tight for him, and carrying a drink, stepped to the microphone and waited for Julie to play the introduction to "Chicago." He sang with gusto, pronouncing the title, "Chick-cargo, Chick-cargo."

Vera's bar companion called for another round of drinks.

"No, please, I can't stay—"

"How about a nightcap someplace else?"

"I'm sorry..."

He put his hand on her arm and looked at her. "Look, you don't have to worry. I'm a pretty nice guy, if I do say so. I just... well, I like being able to talk to a woman. I'm not hustling you, please believe me. We could just go and have coffee, just sit a little longer, that's all."

It was, of course, just what she wanted, in fact badly needed... "Well, all right, but just for a bit..."

"Do you have a car?"

"Yes."

"Tell you what. There's an all-night place six blocks straight up M Street. I'll meet you there. They have great cheesecake. You like cheesecake?"

163

"Yes, matter of fact I do." She found herself able to smile. He *was* nice.

"Good." He paid the checks, helped her on with her coat, said good night to the bartender and held the door open for her. The cold night air felt very good on her face.

"Where's your car?" he asked.

She pointed. "Two blocks up."

"I'll walk you."

"That's not necessary."

"My pleasure. Never mind what they say, chivalry isn't dead, and it doesn't cost a dime." He took her arm and they started up the street.

Their progress did not go unnoticed. Detective Martin Teller had pulled up at the curb across from Club Julie as they were leaving. He recognized Vera immediately. "What the hell is she doing here?" he asked himself. He considered following them but saw that they'd stopped at a car. The man opened the door and Vera got in.

"And who is that?" Teller asked himself as he got out of his car and went into his favorite club. The seats previously occupied by Vera and the computer executive were still vacant, and he took one. "Robbie," he called to the bartender.

"Hiya, Marty," Robbie said, "good to see you."

"Same here. Robbie, that woman who just left with the guy in the suit. Do you know her?"

Robbie shrugged, shook his head.

"Did she come in with the guy?"

"No. He bought her a couple of drinks and they took off. He comes in regularly, though."

"You never saw her before?"

Robbie leaned on the bar. "Yeah, I've seen her before, once, I think."

"In here?"

"Yeah, months ago."

164

"Tell me about it."

Robbie made another customer's drink, filled a waitress's order at the service end of the bar, then returned to Teller. "What can I tell you, Marty? I can't remember every woman who comes in here."

"Try."

"Important?"

"Maybe. Give me a gin while you go down memory lane."

He came back with the drink. "Okay, I do remember more about her than I might some others. She's a type, you know, very uptight, sort of prissy, pinched face like she kind of disapproves of everything. For some reason she didn't strike me as the sort who'd enjoy our place. Most everybody's pretty loose here, right?...Let me see. Oh yeah, there's another reason for remembering her. The real reason, I guess...She had a tiff with a guy at the bar and left."

"The same guy as tonight?"

"No, no, a lot younger."

"She pick him up here?"

"Nope. They came in together, and that was another reason I remember them. He didn't look like he belonged here either. He was young, a sort of snotty character if I remember right. Good-looking guy, though, dressed nice. They didn't fit in here, and they didn't seem to fit together either. Still, who knows who fits with who anymore? Anyway, they sat down there." He pointed to the end of the bar nearest the piano. "I served them and everything was okay for a while, but then they started arguing. I think I tried to finesse them out of it, offered a drink on the house, something like that."

"How'd it end up?"

"*That* I remember. She left and he stayed. I think he ended up leaving with another girl."

Teller drank half his drink. Robbie started to walk away but Teller said, "Wait, Robbie. Tell me what the guy looked like."

"I don't really remember. Like I said, he was young, blond, snotty, looked down his nose all night."

"Remember the picture of the Supreme Court clerk who was murdered?"

The bartender rubbed his chin. "Sure, what was his name?"

"Sutherland."

"Right . . . Jesus . . ."

"What?"

"That's right, that could have been the guy she was with that night. It looked like him . . ."

Teller sat back and threw up his hands. "Here I am investigating the most important murder case in Washington history, aside from Lincoln, and you, a trained observer of mankind, miss something like this. Was it the same guy or not, damn it."

"Could be. I'd have to see a picture."

Teller went to his car, took an eight-by-ten glossy photo of Clarence Sutherland from his briefcase in his trunk and returned to the bar. He led Robbie into the kitchen, where there was more light. Robbie examined the photograph.

"Well?"

"Yeah, I think it's the same one."

"You think?"

Robbie looked at Teller. "Come on, Marty, this place isn't a lineup. Lots of guys come through. I can't be *sure*, but if I had to lay a bet on it I'd say it's the same guy."

Teller leaned against a sink, drew a deep breath. "Don't tell anybody about this, Robbie."

"Why should I?"

"Just don't."

The chef, an illegal alien named Juan, grinned at Teller. "Hey, detective, you want something to eat?"

"Yeah, fries and a Julieburger, medium, and easy on the anchovies. But not too easy."

VERA PASSED the all-night diner and saw George, the computer executive, get out of his car. She didn't want to disappoint him, go back on her word, but any guilt about that took second place to a compelling need to be home. She accelerated, and the diner became a red neon dot in her rearview mirror.

CHAPTER
23

CHESTER SUTHERLAND DECIDED AS HE APPROACHED HIS house in Chevy Chase to drive around the back and then enter through his office. He noticed as he came up the long driveway that all lights in the house were off with the exception of his bedroom.

He did not immediately get out of his car. The last seven hours were a blur to him. After leaving the two-hour meeting with Bill Stalk at CIA Headquarters he'd gone to his club, where he had dinner alone. He then did something he had not done in years, went to the movies. He hadn't liked the film, an attempt at comedy by names he was only vaguely familiar with from having once watched "Saturday Night Live." The young people in the audience loved it though. It didn't matter, though, whether he liked the film or not.

It was something to do, a way to blot out what had happened during the two hours with Stalk.

The meeting had started pleasantly enough, Stalk again telling of his fascination with video electronic games and how he'd decided to take a few days off in the future and spend them practicing so that he could better compete with his son. Sutherland had listened politely, even offered comments of his own on the subject, but he knew the badinage would soon be over and the serious subject that had brought him there would take its place.

"So," Stalk said as he sat behind his desk and propped his feet on it, "you wanted to talk to me, Chester. You sounded upset on the phone, although I suppose if someone had broken into my office I'd be upset too." He laughed. "It's a good thing for us that you never did keep files on the MKULTRA Project. If you had I'd be concerned that whoever broke into your office might have taken a peek."

Sutherland knew Stalk was playing with him. If he'd had any doubts earlier about who had broken into his files, they no longer existed.

"Did the Company do it, Bill?"

Stalk assumed an expression of surprise, shock. "The Company? Why would we do such a thing to someone who's been an important, trusted part of our operation?"

Sutherland, who hadn't eaten since breakfast and then had only partially finished because of Vera's call, suddenly was hungry and would have liked a drink. He was, he knew, in a touchy position. If the CIA hadn't taken the files, his admitting that he had in fact kept them, despite his constant denials, would brand him a liar and, worse, a fool. Still, if it hadn't been someone from the Company, he felt obliged to report it to the man and the agency most jeopardized by the theft.

He decided to admit he'd kept files and that they were now missing, hoping that his candor would bring a parallel

169

honesty from Stalk. It did not work that way . . . After Sutherland finished telling Stalk the truth, the director stood, brought his fist down sharply on the desk. "Damn it, I knew it." He quickly went to the expanse of windows overlooking the woods, and for a moment Sutherland thought that he was going to put his fist through the glass. Instead he rolled the fingertips of both hands over the pane.

"I'm sorry, Bill," Sutherland said, standing and coming halfway across the room. "You must understand that I had several motives for involvement in the project. I do care about serving the country when and as I can, but I'm also an individual. I'm a scientist, or at least I'm involved with science, and for someone like me the payoff is in the excitement of discovery, of breaking new ground, creating understanding where it hasn't existed before. I couldn't devote all that time and knowledge without having something to show for it personally. I've never talked about it to anyone, and the files have been secured in my private office for as long as they've existed. But it was important to me that I at least had them."

"Like Nixon keeping the tapes," Stalk said. He was not amused. In fact, his face looked like granite. He went back to his desk, opened a drawer and pulled out a sheaf of file folders. Sutherland recognized them immediately as the ones taken from his office.

"It *was* you," Sutherland said.

"Of course it was us, Chester, and a damn lucky thing it was. A few years ago if we'd known these files existed we'd have done the same thing, only we would have been rather less discreet about it. The American public has seemed to demand more discretion these days with their break-ins."

Sutherland leaned forward. "But why take them now? I told you that no one has ever seen them except me. Every entry was made personally by me."

170

Stalk slapped the files back in the drawer and closed it hard.

Sutherland sat in a chair and drew a deep breath. He was afraid he knew what was coming.

"You weren't the only one to have access to those files, Chester, and you know it. Your son did too."

Sutherland looked at the floor. "Whatever my son might have been, or might have done, he's paid for it, Bill. Do we need to attack him now? Whatever he knew . . . about people, other things, whatever he might have done to hurt . . . God knows, he's been punished, and with no chance for appeal, no chance of parole. My son, sir, is dead. Isn't that *enough*?"

Stalk nodded. "I do sympathize with you, Chester. I was thinking about your son this morning while I was playing that video game with my boy. I suppose there's no greater loss than the death of a child, no matter the age."

Sutherland felt his stomach clutch.

"Are you all right, Chester?"

"Yes . . . I'm not happy with what your people did, but I suppose I can understand it—"

"Chester, it's been a very difficult period for us. We've been hit on from all sides, which does not exactly make our mission any easier. There have been so many leaks that damaged us, and we were forced to release some of MKUL-TRA under the Freedom of Information Act. Sure, we sanitized everything we could and held back more than some think we should have, but you know as well as anyone how compromised this nation would be if the entire project had been laid open. When we realized that material we hadn't released was beginning to surface, we became, to put it mildly, concerned. Our first assumption was that the leak was within the division, and we went to a good deal of trouble to find it and shut it off. But then we looked outside and uncovered that *your son* was making it known in certain

171

places he had access to his father's files. Naturally, I can't reveal the source of that information. What a shame, was what I said, and felt, when the picture became clearer. What a damn bloody shame."

Along with everything else, Sutherland found himself annoyed at Stalk's use of the British usage. That was something he'd always noticed about CIA brass, the tendency to affect the language and manner of their British counterparts.

Stalk locked Sutherland's files in the drawer, dropped the key into his jacket pocket, stood, came around the desk and slapped the psychiatrist on the back. "You know, Chester, this is a strange world we live in, and it sometimes takes extraordinary people, and acts, to inject some sanity into it. There is no clear-cut good or bad, Chester. Mostly it's a matter of survival. Some understand that, some don't." He removed his hand from Sutherland's back and went to his door. The point was made, the meeting was over.

At the door Stalk shook Sutherland's hand. "I'd be happy to have you back in the program, Chester, but I would understand if that should prove rather too difficult for you. If that is the case, I think it best that you never come here again."

The notion of ever returning to the CIA's top secret research program almost made Sutherland laugh. Still, he needed to ask, "Why would you invite me back into the program in the light of what's happened with the files?"

"Well, Chester, no offense, but once a man has made the mistake you have, he does tend to become rather more easy to control. I've enjoyed knowing you, Chester. Good luck in all your future endeavors. By the way, I'd heartily recommend getting one of those video games. A wonderful way to get your mind off real problems . . ."

Sutherland now got out of his car and went through the back door to his office. As usual, Vera had left a night-light on, a large translucent plastic goose he'd given her as a gift five years ago. A small bulb in the base illuminated the entire figure and cast a warm glow over the room.

He flipped on the overhead lights, took a key from his pocket and opened the file drawer marked MNOP. He touched the top of a folder marked *Poulson, J.*, almost removed it to read its contents, then closed the drawer and locked it. He made his way to the house, glanced at mail that had been left on a table near the staircase, then slowly climbed the stairs to the second floor, where he opened the door to his bedroom.

His wife Eleanor was on the chaise, reading.

"You're home," Chester said. "I thought the fundraiser would go later."

"I didn't go," she said, removing her glasses and looking up at him through narrowed eyes.

"Why not?"

"I couldn't get up the interest or strength." She didn't sound weary, her voice was strong.

He took off his jacket and hung it in the closet, took off his shoes and sat on the edge of their king-sized bed.

"Where were you?"

"I had a meeting, grabbed some dinner at the club and then went to the movies."

"The movies? You went to the movies? You haven't been to the movies for as long as I can remember."

"I needed a little diversion," he said as he unbuttoned his shirt.

"I'm impressed."

"Impressed with what? What's so unusual about going to a movie?"

"I don't mean the movies, Chester, I mean the need for diversion. I've never known you to express such a human need."

He understood too well that she was looking for an argument. He went to a bathroom off the bedroom, closed the door, took a fast hot shower, put on a terry-cloth robe and returned to where Eleanor stood in front of an eighteenth-century French escritoire. She held in her hands what she'd been reading on the chaise, a thick batch of letters. She was especially beautiful at the moment, her face etched with a sadness that had been perpetual since Clarence's murder. Champagne blonde hair was pulled up into a loose chignon on the top of her head, stray tendrils framed a full, lovely face.

"What are you reading?"

She answered so quietly that he didn't catch it. He asked again.

She turned. "Letters from Clarence, Chester, letters he wrote while in college and that you never had the time to read."

He abruptly crossed the room to his bureau. "Nonsense," he said over his shoulder, "I read everything he ever wrote us—"

"Only because I insisted on it. You'd sit and pretend to take in his words, pretend to respond to what he'd said, but the fact is none of it really mattered to you. You were never interested in your own son...Too bad he wasn't one of your patients—"

"That's enough, Eleanor. We've gone over this too many times before."

He watched as she lowered the letters to the desk, as though putting them in a fire. There was a discernible trembling to her hands as she gripped the edge of the writing desk for support. When she turned and faced him her blue eyes shone with anger. "He's dead, Chester, and I think you killed him—oh, you didn't have to pull the trigger, Chester. There are other ways to assassinate a human being without being the one at the other end of the gun—"

"I've heard *enough*, Eleanor. Have you been drinking?"

"Isn't that typical of you, Chester, and how *unanalytic*, to look for an external reason for something that displeases you. Have I been drinking? Should I be literary and say that I've been drinking the words of the son that I no longer have, that I'm drunk with the loss of him?"

"I'm tired, Eleanor, we can discuss this in the morning—"

Her action took him by surprise. She swept the letters from the desk, ran across the room and pushed them in his face. "Read them, Chester," she shouted. "Read them now that it no longer matters. Listen for the first time to what was in your son's heart."

The corner of one of the letters nicked his eye. He put his hand to it, turned and crouched in pain. "What *heart*?" he said.

She came up behind him, placed her hands on his shoulders and spun him around. "Why did you hate him so?" she asked. Tears now flowed down her cheeks.

He straightened, his hand still over his eyes. "I didn't hate him, Eleanor, I loved him, damn it . . . no, damn *him*. He was no good . . ."

"Is that an appropriate way for a psychiatrist to talk?"

"Maybe it is. Sometimes I think we do a disservice using so much jargon to describe behavior. There are people in this world, Eleanor, who are no damn good, and as much as it breaks my heart to say it, our son was one of them—"

He knew it was coming, didn't avoid it. Almost welcomed it. She brought her right hand across his face. When he didn't react she did it again, then grabbed his neck with both hands and dug her nails into his flesh. He took hold of her wrists and pulled himself free. Tiny rivulets of blood sprung from where her nails had broken the skin and ran down to the collar of his robe.

"Oh God . . . I'm sorry, Chester . . ." Her body was heaving.

"We're all sorry, Eleanor. Sorry . . . I'll sleep downstairs . . ."

CHAPTER
24

MARTIN TELLER GLANCED AT A WALL CLOCK AS HE MOVED through the bull pen at MPD headquarters. It was a quarter to nine, fifteen minutes until his morning ritual with Dorian Mars.

A detective assigned to the Sutherland case stopped him and said, "Got a new Polish joke, Marty."

"Not interested. Besides, Polish jokes are in bad taste these days."

The detective looked at a colleague and shrugged. "*Sorry,*" he said. Teller continued toward his office, entered it and slammed the door behind him.

It had been a bad morning. His cats had gotten into a fight during breakfast and spilled his coffee all over the rug. A few minutes later his ex-wife called from Paris, Kentucky, to inform him that their younger daughter was dropping out of college because she was pregnant. "Who did it?" Teller asked, now knowing what else to say. "I don't know, Marty, she's coming home in a few days and I'll let you know." Then, as he was leaving his apartment building, he read a notice posted on the wall that there would be no hot water for three days while the boiler was being serviced.

The detective who'd offered the Polish joke opened the door and asked, "You playing tonight, Marty?" He was referring to an intrasquad poker game.

"No, and instead of playing poker I suggest you and the rest of the brilliant young sleuths assigned to me spend the night hitting every bar in town, especially the singles' joints, with Clarence Sutherland's photo in hand."

"*Every* bar?"

"Start in Georgetown. Ask the bartenders, the broads hanging out, guys on the make. I want a list tomorrow morning of every joint you hit, and I want it before nine o'clock.

"That's a lot of overtime, Marty."

"You complaining?"

"No. What's with you? How come you're so uptight this morning?"

"The position of the moon relative to my sun."

"No kidding."

"No kidding. You got any kids?"

"None that I know of."

"They break your heart. Get moving."

"Yeah, have a good day."

Teller picked up a coffee cup stained from the day before, went into the bull pen and poured from a communal pot, leaving a quarter in a dish. He returned to the office, hung up his jacket and sat behind his desk. It was now 9:10. He punched in Dorian Mars's extension on his phone. "Marty?" Mars said. "Where are you? I'm waiting."

178

"Let's skip the meeting this morning, Dorian. I've got nothing to report. It would be a waste of time."

"Doesn't matter. We should meet anyway, every day. Brainstorming can open things up. You run a case like this through a grinder enough times and out comes the perfect hamburger."

"What?"

"Come up, Marty."

"No. I've got a lot of sorting out to do. Let's catch up later."

Mars sighed loudly. "All right, Marty. By the way, are you okay? You sound strange."

"I'm terrific, Dorian, tip-top, at peace with my fellow man. Life is truly a bowl of cherries, a virtual perpetual cabaret."

"Take it easy, Marty."

Teller called the desk and instructed the sergeant on duty to hold all calls until further notice.

"One just came in for you, detective. I was about to put it through."

"Who is it?"

"Your Miss Pinscher, from Justice."

"My? Oh, all right, I'll take it, but that's it for a while."

"Good morning," Susanna said.

"Good morning. How've you been?"

"All right. I thought you might have called me."

"I've been busy as hell. Sorry."

"That's not what I called about, though. I wanted to fill you in on a conversation I had with Laurie Rawls."

Teller found a pad of paper and uncapped a pen. "Go ahead," he said.

"Remember when I said I thought I might be able to establish a sort of big-sister relationship with her? Well, it happened . . . I had dinner at her apartment and she opened up."

"What did she say?"

She read from notes she'd made right after leaving Laurie's apartment—Laurie back clerking for Conover, the preliminary vote in *Nidel v. Illinois* in Nidel's favor, confirmation that Cecily Conover and Clarence had had an affair and that Justice Conover had confronted both of them about it. Teller listened, made his own notes until she got to the part about Clarence sitting in the Court at night and playacting, and that he and Laurie had almost made love there.

"In the Supreme Court? That is mighty high-level making out."

"Well, his liking for the Chief's chair could explain why Clarence was there the night he was killed. No one had to entice him into the room. He went there on his own almost as a matter of routine..."

"Go on."

"Laurie says that Clarence once bragged to her that he had... How did she put it?... He had the key to every lock and person in the Court. Evidently Clarence knew something damaging or embarrassing about everyone. At least that's what he told her."

"Where'd he get the information?"

"I asked her that too. She says he picked it up while working as closely as he did with the justices."

"What about his father? Did he come up?"

"In what context?"

"The fact that he treated the high and mighty, and that Clarence might have learned things through that connection."

"We didn't discuss it."

"Okay, anything else?"

"Laurie says that Justice Poulson is sort of a puppet of President Jorgens and that the White House plays a direct role in most everything Poulson does on the Court. She also claims that Clarence had documents to prove it that would...here's exactly what she said...'had documents to prove it that would blow the lid off the Court.'"

"Is the phone you're using secure?"

"I think so—"

"Don't think. Be sure."

"I'm in my office at *Justice*."

He wanted to tell her that a telephone in the Justice Department was probably as unsecured as any phone in Washington, but didn't. He wanted her to go on.

"There's not much more," she said. "She told me that Clarence knew that Justice Childs was a phony hero and that he could prove it."

"How?"

"I don't know and I don't think she does either. Anyway, her advice was to look for a man—"

"Seems I've heard that before."

"Childs said look for a woman. Remember?"

"Yeah...Do you think she did it?"

"Laurie? No, but my opinion doesn't mean anything. What do you think?"

"Who knows? You can't tell the players in this thing without a scorecard." He glanced up at his empty flow chart on the wall.

"Well, Detective Teller, I've shown you mine. Now, it's your turn."

"I'd love to, but I've never found that the phone was a substitute—"

"*Teller*...cut it out...have *you* learned anything new?"

"Not a thing."

"Sure? I'd hate to think this was a one-way street, my telling and your holding back."

"Free for dinner this week?"

"No. I'm taking a few days off and going with one of my kids to California to visit my father. By the way, did you know that Mozart wrote *The Magic Flute* because a theater owner in Vienna commissioned it?"

"Yeah."

"You did?"

"Sure. He started off writing a light piece but it turned out to be a serious work—"

"Damn."

"Call when you get back."

From the carton that had contained the wall chart he took an assortment of colored, magnetic plastic symbols and labels, spread them on his desk, then used an erasable marking pen to write the names of each suspect. He considered categories to group the names under—*personal* and *Professional, male* and *female, Court* and *family*. He decided on the last, wrote the words on the largest of the magnetic labels and put them on the board. He added a third heading, *personal*, to include those not in the Court or family.

He ran into a snag grouping names beneath headings. Those from the Court, people like Poulson, Conover and Childs, might well have had personal rather than professional reasons for killing Clarence. Or both? He'd let it go, at least where the chart was concerned.

When he was finished, the chart was resplendent in red, green, yellow and blue:

COURT	FAMILY	PERSONAL
Justices Poulson	Dr. C. Sutherland	Friends
Childs	Mrs. Sutherland	(Male)
Conover	Sister	(Female) C. Conover
Clerk L. Rawls		

He considered where to place Vera Jones. Seeing her at Club Julie and convinced that she'd had a personal relationship with Clarence certainly made her a good suspect. He started to put her name under *Personal*, then changed it to *Family*. A close call.

He narrowed his eyes and took in the chart as a blur of color. He slapped colored magnetic arrows on the board to link the names, realized it accomplished little. Besides, he wanted more room next to each name to write comments. He rearranged the board into a vertical configuration.

COURT

Justices Poulson

Childs

Conover

Clerk L. Rawls

FAMILY

Dr. C. Sutherland

Mrs. Sutherland

Sister

Vera Jones

PERSONAL

Friends

(Male)

(Female) C. Conover

He wrote Clarence's name in large letters and put it at the top of the chart, then took it down, changed it to DE-CEASED and returned it to the board. Next he sat at his desk and wrote out motives to be put next to each suspect.

Poulson—father's patient, White House sellout.

Childs—phony hero???? (He found orange magnetic

question marks and strung four of them next to his comment.)

Conover—jealousy, wife and deceased.

Dr. C. Sutherland—violation of his files???? (Again, a string of question marks.)

*Mrs. Sutherland??—*He didn't know, and had used up the supply of question marks. He took two from the other lines and placed them after her name.

Sister—nothing.

Vera Jones—woman scorned, possible affair.

Friends—He'd taken Laurie Rawls's name from the Court list and put it here. Next to her name he put *Jealousy.*

He created another heading, MISC. No suspects yet here; he left it blank, a category-in-waiting. ——

He decided he didn't want the others to see the chart so he called around the department until he found a large roll of brown paper that he taped over the chart. Finally he went downstairs to a public phone booth and called Paris, Kentucky. His ex-wife answered.

"Anything new?" he asked.

"She called. She'll be home tomorrow."

"What'd she say?"

"She was crying."

"Look, be sure she tells whoever this guy is that her father's a cop."

"Why?"

"What do you mean, why? Maybe he won't run so fast if he knows I'm a cop."

"Or maybe he'll run faster . . . except I don't think he's trying to run anywhere, Marty. She says they're in love."

"Wonderful. Call me the minute she gets home."

"I will. Please don't get all riled up about this. I'm sure it will all work out."

"Sure it will . . . just like everything else."

184

CHAPTER
25

SUSANNA, FEELING BETTER THAN SHE HAD IN WEEKS, RE-
veled in her first day at her father's modest, yellow stucco
home in St. Helena. She sat on the patio, a tart, icy banana
daiquiri from the blender on a wrought-iron table next to
her, her feet in sandals, sunglasses shielding her eyes from
a blinding afternoon sun as she watched her father and her
son toss a baseball about in the backyard.

Later, after a barbequed chicken and corn-on-the-cob
feast, she sat with her father on the patio, illuminated by a
single flattering gas lamp. They sipped coffee and caught
up on their lives.

"I wish you could stay longer," he said. "It's good having
you here."

"Me, too . . ." And she told him about the Sutherland investigation and the strain she was under.

"Do you think you'll ever find out who did it?"

"We'd better . . . I thought I'd spend part of tomorrow looking up Dan Brazier." She'd told him about Brazier's link with Morgan Childs and her hunch that the former journalist just might be able to shed a little light on the case.

"Is a Supreme Court judge really a suspect?"

"Could be." She cut it short, not saying that not one but at least three, Childs, Conover and Poulson, were legitimate suspects.

"By the way, who's *we*?"

"People working on the case, including a detective from the Metropolitan Police Department named Martin Teller." She told him a little about Teller. When she was through, he smiled. "What's funny?"

"It sounds like you're falling a little for a cop."

She laughed. "Who knows? He's not your everyday cop . . . loves opera, calls his female cat Beast and male cat Beauty."

Her father shrugged, changed the subject, as he most always did when she began to talk too much about men in her life. "This Dan Brazier," he said. "Do you have an appointment with him?"

"No. I was going to call but decided I'd just drop in. I have his address."

"I don't like it."

"Don't like what?"

"Any of it, you involved in investigating a murder. Why don't you get out of it, get out of Washington for that matter, come back here."

"I couldn't be that far from the kids, dad."

"Bring 'em with you. They belong with their mother anyway."

"Please, let's not get into that again."

He touched her hand. "Okay, but I'll tell you this, Susanna. No one will ever convince me that a judge of the United States Supreme Court could kill someone, let alone in cold blood in the courtroom and, as I understand it from the papers, in the Chief Justice's chair."

"Truth's stranger than fiction, dad. Which I guess is why fiction is rarely the truth. I mean, who would believe it . . . Anyway I don't *know* whether one of the justices did it. It could have been an old lover, a coworker, even someone from the family."

As he stood and stretched, she noted the beginning of a potbelly. "*If* it's any one of 'em, Susanna, I'd put my money on the old one, Conover. Jealousy . . . it's one damn powerful emotion, and destructive as hell. Some states automatically acquit a man for killing his wife's lover, did you know that?"

"I do now." They watched television with her son until ten, when she announced she was turning in. "Don't worry about tomorrow," her father said. "Rich and I will make out just fine." He cuffed his grandson on the head.

"Thanks," Susanna said. "I know you will."

SHE LEFT the house at ten the following morning, driving her father's 1976 Mercury station wagon. She passed through towns that made up California's wine country—Rutherford and Napa, Pleasanton and Mission San Jose, down through flat and dusty plains on either side of Route 680, past the vineyards of Charles Krug and Beringer, Beaulieu and Christian Brothers until traffic thickened as she neared the Bay Bridge linking San Francisco to Oakland. It was a short drive up the Embarcadero to Broadway in North Beach. She found Brazier's apartment and rang the downstairs bell. No response. She decided to walk, and to call Brazier's number from time to time.

She strolled the length of Fisherman's Wharf, stopping

in shops along the way, buying a leather address book from a sidewalk artisan, a nubby cotton pullover from another. She tried Brazier's number a few times, always without success. She lunched at the Buena Vista, where Irish coffee had been introduced into the United States, and had espresso late in the afternoon in one of Ghirardelli Square's cafes.

She took a cab back to her car. Since it was parked only two blocks from Brazier's apartment, she decided to try again. This time the bell ring resulted in Sheryl Figgs opening the upstairs door.

"Hello," said Susanna. "I'm looking for Dan Brazier." She wasn't sure whether Sheryl's face reflected disappointment or confusion or both.

"He's not here."

"Will he be back? I'm sorry, I'm Susanna Pinscher. I work for the Justice Department in Washington and—"

"Yes, I know you, I know your name. I read about you."

"Oh? Well, I'm here visiting my father in St. Helena and . . ." She realized she was shouting up the flight of stairs, and so did Sheryl.

"I'm sorry," Sheryl said. "I don't mean to be rude. Would you like to come up?"

"Yes, thank you."

Susanna stepped into the small, cluttered apartment.

"You'll have to excuse the mess," Sheryl said. "I got home from work an hour ago and decided to do some cleaning. Once I get in that mood I lose my head. Dan's not here, but I expect him home pretty soon."

Sheryl, wearing a soiled red apron decorated with sewn felt knives and forks, wiped her hands on the apron. "I read the article about you and the Supreme Court murder not too long ago. You interviewed one of the judges up in his plane."

"Yes . . . Look, I'm sorry to barge in on you this way but I did try to call."

188

"I was at work. I work with computers. Dan must have . . . well, he likes to get out in the fresh air."

"It's beautiful weather."

"I know, I hate to be cooped up too." She raised her eyes. "What a mess. I wanted to have it all put back together before Dan came home. He's a neatnik, a regular Felix. I'm an Oscar, I'm afraid."

Susanna glanced into the bedroom. On a double bed that took up most of the room were dresser drawers. Sheryl quickly said, "I wanted to straighten them out before Dan got home. I get in this mood sometimes and—"

"Me, too," Susanna said, "but not often enough."

Sheryl, whose responses always seemed to be a delayed reaction, said, "I shouldn't have started it so late in the day. I have to start supper."

Susanna looked at photographs of Brazier and Morgan Childs. "These are interesting pictures," she said.

"They were such good friends . . . Dan went to see him when he was out here a few weeks ago."

Susanna turned. "He did?"

"Yes. Justice Childs gave a speech and Dan had a drink with him after. More than one, actually." She smiled. "They got sort of drunk together, Dan said, and he ended up doing push-ups while Judge Childs counted . . . Dan should be home soon. I'm sure he'll be happy to meet you. I . . ."

Susanna looked at her. If she read Sheryl's expression accurately, maybe Dan Brazier would not be too happy to meet her. She considered leaving, decided not to. She wasn't in a popularity contest. She was on a murder investigation. "Could I use your phone? I'd like to call my father and tell him I'm running late. My son is with him and they're probably wondering where I am."

"Oh, sure, it's in the kitchen." She butted her forehead against her hand. "Sorry . . . it's not working and I promised Dan I'd call the phone company and report it. You can use the one in the bedroom, if you can find it under all that mess."

Susanna started for the bedroom.

"Miss Pinscher."

She stopped. "Yes?"

"Would you like to stay for supper? I don't know where Dan is but sometimes he gets talking and doesn't quite make it home for dinner. It's always a waste. I cook for two and it ends up just me. Anyway, if he does come home . . . well, I don't think he'd mind some company." (Again, she didn't sound very convincing on that score.) "Please stay, I'll make meat loaf."

"One of my favorites."

"I'll get it going right away." She snapped her fingers. "I knew I forgot something. I *always* forget things. I need some ingredients . . . I'll run out and get them. Only be a minute."

Susanna waved and said, "Please, don't go to any trouble. I really should be heading back and have dinner with my family—"

"No, I insist. You just stay and make yourself comfortable until I get back. Only take a few minutes. Would you like a drink? There might be some gin left. I drink wine and don't even like that much, but I like to keep Dan company. I'll pick up some wine." She put on a tan raincoat, slung her purse over her shoulder and opened the door. "I'll be back before you know it."

The slam of the door reverberated throughout the apartment. Susanna looked into the bedroom, where a princess phone could be detected beneath a pile of sweaters. She picked it up and dialed her father's area code and number. "My long-lost daughter," he said. "Where are you?"

"At Dan Brazier's apartment. Dad, I've been invited to stay for dinner. Do you mind?"

"Sure you want to?"

"Yes. He isn't here but his girl friend...I guess that's what she is...his girl friend has invited me and I'd like to take her up on it."

A long pause. "Why don't you come home, Susanna? It's a long drive, I worry about you."

"I won't stay long, I promise." She looked at the pile of things on the bed. One drawer that had been emptied of clothing contained a pile of small, leather-bound books. She picked one up and opened it...

"Well, Susanna, if you insist, Rich and I will fend for ourselves," her father was saying. "He'll have to suffer through my cooking but I suppose it won't kill him."

"What?"

"I said my cooking won't kill him."

But she heard nothing he said. Staring up at her from one of the pages she'd been almost idly flipping through was: *Dr. Chester Sutherland, Psychiatrist*, followed by his Chevy Chase address.

"He doesn't want chicken again, I don't know what else I have here, I don't cook much for myself and—"

"Dad, I'll see you later."

She snapped the book closed and was about to drop it back into the drawer when a presence in the bedroom doorway made her spin around.

She dropped the book.

"Who the hell are you?" he asked.

"I'm..."

He turned his head, said to an unseen man, "Yeah, thanks for the help upstairs, Harry. See you tomorrow." The door slammed shut. Brazier returned his attention to Susanna. "Like I said, who are you? And what the *hell* are you doing in my bedroom?"

Susanna forced a smile. "Both very good questions ...I'm Susanna Pinscher, Mr. Brazier. Your...Miss Figgs invited me to stay for dinner. She went out to—"

"What do you think you were looking at?"

"What? Oh . . . I wasn't really looking at anything. I called my father to tell him I'd be late, he lives in St. Helena—"

"Come off it. You had something in your hand when I came in. One of those books from the drawer—"

She looked down into the drawer. "Books? No, I wasn't looking at anything." She took a few steps toward the door, which was blocked by Brazier and his wide, metal chair. She extended her hand. "I'm visiting from Washington," she said. "I'm working on the Clarence Sutherland murder case for the Justice Department and thought that while I was out here I'd look you up."

"Why?"

"Because you were close to Justice Morgan Childs . . . and he's, well, after all, he's a member of the Court—"

"Get out." His voice was ragged, he even raised a fist. She knew he was drunk. "Get out *now*."

"All right, but I can't go anywhere unless you move."

He glared at her with watery eyes, his fist still in the air. He seemed unsure whether to vacate the doorway or stay there, blocking her. Susanna took a deep breath, took a step closer to him. "I'm leaving," she said. "Excuse me."

He hesitated, then rolled his chair backward, providing just enough room for her to pass. She went quickly to the front door, opened it. Sheryl was on her way up the stairs, her arms full of brown bags.

"I'm sorry," Susanna said, "but I have to go. My son isn't feeling too well and my father thinks I ought to head back right away—"

"I bought steaks and wine—"

"I am sorry. Another time." She waited for Sheryl to reach the landing, then quickly descended the stairs and burst through the outside door to the street. Had she lingered for another minute or two she would have heard the sound of Dan Brazier's hand hitting Sheryl across the face, and the thud of her body slamming against a wall.

She ran to her car and drove as fast as she could back to St. Helena. Her father and son were deep in a game of checkers.

"Quick dinner," her father said.

"Yes. And I'd love a drink."

"Daiquiri?"

"Bourbon. Straight."

CHAPTER
26

"WHY CAN'T YOU TRUST ME?"

Temple Conover, who'd just come downstairs for breakfast, brought his cane across the back of a chair. "Trust you, Cecily? *Fide, sed cui vide.*"

"You and your damn foreign words. What does that mean?"

"Trust, but take care *whom* you trust."

The argument, which had erupted upstairs in the bedroom, was precipitated by a phone call from Martin Teller asking for another interview with Cecily.

She came around behind her husband and touched his neck. He twisted in his chair, grimaced at her. "How could you have done that?" His voice was raspy.

"I told you, Temp, I was frightened, scared to death,

matter of fact. You *threatened* me with that gun, I didn't know what to do . . ."

He sipped his orange juice while she came around the other side of the table and plopped down in a chair.

"Get that pout off your face," he said.

"Don't tell me what to do with my face."

He grabbed the cane that was resting against his chair and extended it toward her. She got to her feet and screamed at the top of her lungs, "Don't ever raise that thing at me again. Don't ever threaten me again, Temple, ever, ever again." Tears. "God, I hate you."

His voice was calm. "Yes, I know that. You took the gun to the police, you've been unfaithful and let me know it. This house is my Gethsemane. You serve me hemlock with my juice."

"I don't understand your damn fancy talk and you know it—"

"You understand betrayal, though, that comes easy as pie, not to mention lying and cheating." The palms of his hands slapped against the tabletop. Juice slopped over the rim of Cecily's glass, staining the pale blue linen tablecloth.

She had been standing with her back to the table as he spoke, her arms around herself. Now that she had stopped crying, her face, which he could not see, was relaxed. She heard him take another drink of his juice, then the sound of his fork against his plate as it scooped up scrambled eggs. Without turning she said, "I turned in the gun, Temple, because you killed him."

His second forkful was halfway to his mouth. It remained poised there as he looked up over his glasses.

"Did you hear me, Temp? I said—"

"I heard you. Along with all your other sterling qualities, you're pretty stupid."

She turned slowly. "Am I? Temple, you're so full of hate. You couldn't stand having Clarence walk the same

195

earth with you. What had he done to you, Temple, provided a little warmth and fun for a woman you claim to love, or at least used to..." She stopped and waited for the invariable outburst, the cane, thrown dishes. It did not come. He sat back and actually smiled.

"Maybe it was his ambition you couldn't stand, a young man on the way up, making you feel so old?..."

"Go on."

She wasn't sure how to react, what to say next. She sat down and drank cold black coffee. "Was it his White House job, Temple, that broke the camel's back?"

"Having someone like Clarence Sutherland considered for an important job in the administration of our government would be more than most decent people could bear."

She shook her head. "You love to rub it in that I'm not as smart or *decent* as you, don't you, Mr. Justice. Well, maybe I'm not so dumb after all."

He reached for a buzzer that would sound throughout the house, part of a system installed after his first stroke so that he could summon aid from any room. Moments later Karl appeared in the doorway.

"Call the Court motor pool and tell them not to send a car this morning. You drive me, Karl."

Karl glanced at Cecily, nodded and disappeared.

Conover pushed against the arms of his chair and stood. His ability to walk had improved over the past few months, and he'd been able to shuck the elaborate Canadian crutch for a more conventional cane, which he took in his right hand. "My best to the detective," he said. He paused, then added, "You may be interested in my plans..."

"What plans?"

"First, we're conferencing this morning about the abortion matter. I intend to see that a free choice means something in this country, even for poor women. Afterward I shall resign from the Court and spend whatever time I have

196

left *alone*, what's left of my peace of mind intact. My resignation from the Court will coincide with my action for divorce from you."

"Well, Temple dear, I surely wouldn't fight either decision. I would only expect my fair share as a dutiful and loving wife for more than five years."

He managed to hold his anger in check as he slowly crossed the room.

"I'll *fight* for what's mine," she said.

He paused, turned, leaned on his cane. "Cecily, for the past six months your every move has been noted by a firm of private investigators—"

"You had me *followed*? How *tacky*, Temple."

"Yes, I agree, but sweets to the sweet. Well, like they say, have a good day."

He took his coat from a hall closet, put it on and stepped out to the front of the house, where Karl waited behind the wheel of a shiny red cadillac. Conover said nothing as he settled into the back seat and looked at the house. Cecily stood at the window. "So damned beautiful," he murmured. "Damned is the word..."

As Karl drove off, Martin Teller pulled up in his car. Conover looked at him, turned away and closed his eyes. Karl glanced in the rearview mirror. Conover often fell asleep on the way to the Court, which was fine with Karl. He didn't like talking to the old man.

Teller rang the bell. A housekeeper answered it, took his card and returned a few moments later. "Mrs. Conover will see you," she said in an Irish brogue.

Cecily was seated at the breakfast table in the sunroom. "Good morning," she said. "Coffee?"

"No, thanks. I appreciate you seeing me like this, Mrs. Conover. Usually I try to schedule things further in advance but I needed to talk to you today."

"My pleasure, sit down."

197

Teller, who'd given his coat and hat to the housekeeper, took the chair that had been occupied by Justice Conover.

"Any progress on the case?" Cecily asked.

"It never works fast, Mrs. Conover. You go day by day, put a piece together now and then, here and there. If you're lucky you end up with enough of the puzzle to recognize the face."

"I see. Well, what can I do for you?"

The folds of her robe had fallen open and the upper part of her breasts was looking at him. He looked away as he asked, "Why did you bring me your husband's gun, Mrs. Conover?"

"I told you why. I was afraid. Temple had threatened me with it—"

"Because of Clarence Sutherland?"

She began an answer but he cut her off. "Look, Mrs. Conover, I'm a cop but I don't enjoy poking into people's personal lives. What people do is their own business, unless it affects me, my job... Your relationship with Clarence Sutherland had nothing to do with me personally, but it might with my murder investigation. Did you have an affair with Sutherland?"

"Yes."

"That simple."

"What else do you want me to say?"

"I guess I'm used to people beating around the bush over questions like that. Okay, let's get back to you turning in your husband's weapon. You say you were afraid of him using it on you. Is that the only reason?"

She opened her eyes wide, started to say something, then cried softly, a perfect teardrop running down each rouged cheek. "Excuse me," she said, standing and getting a tissue from a table. She dabbed at her eyes, wiped her nose and sat down again. "I suppose you deal with weepy women all the time in your profession."

198

"Sometimes," Teller said, waiting for the act to finish.

She looked down at her lap. "I haven't been completely honest with you, Detective Teller."

"Well, you're only human."

"Yes. I'm sure you'll understand why when I tell you what I've held back."

"I'll try my best, Mrs. Conover."

"I delivered the gun to you because... because my husband murdered Clarence Sutherland." (No change in her tone of voice.)

Teller looked around the room, ran his finger under his shirt collar. A very cool little lady. "You're sure?"

"Yes, I'm sorry to say, but I am."

"Proof?"

"If you mean did I see him do it, no. Did he tell me he did it? Well, not exactly, but he surely hinted at it enough times."

"Why do you think he did do it, because of your affair with Sutherland?"

"Of course, that, but Clarence's rise to power inside the Court, his success, the offer to him of a job on President Jorgens's staff... they all contributed—"

"Sutherland was offered a job in the White House?"

"Yes, in so many words. It wasn't definite, but he was very excited about it."

"What sort of job?"

"Something to do with legal affairs, I guess. Imagine, someone that young going up so fast. My husband couldn't *bear* it. It ate away at him like a cancer—"

"Because a young man was getting ahead?"

"That young man had slept with his wife, Detective Teller."

"Are you willing to testify that your husband killed Clarence Sutherland?"

"How testify?"

199

"Make a formal statement. If you do, it at least will be enough to ruin him, even if it doesn't stick in court. It'll be front page in every newspaper in the country, the world. Sure you want to do that to him, Mrs. Conover?"

She drew a deep breath, rubbed her forehead. "This may be hard to swallow, I know... after what I've said and done, but I care about Temple... I really do... but if you lived with a person you knew in your heart had killed another person, well... what would you do?..."

"We're talking about you, Mrs. Conover. Is there anything else you can give me by way of proof?"

"I'm afraid not, but I'm sure if you question him it will come out... I wish I could be more helpful. I'm trying... this is very difficult, as I'm sure you understand..."

"Oh, I think maybe I do, Mrs. Conover. And thank you." He stood up and extended his hand.

A thin smile crossed her lips. Her robe had fallen even further open, one bare leg now dangled over the other. "Please keep in touch," she said. "This is the most difficult thing I've ever faced in my life, and I'm not an especially strong person..."

"I'm sure... well, thanks for your time. And have a good day..."

No sooner was he gone than she picked up the phone and dialed her husband's office. Laurie Rawls answered. "Miss Rawls, this is Mrs. Conover."

"Good morning," Laurie said. "How are you?"

"Not too well, I'm afraid."

"I'm sorry, anything I can do?"

"Yes... Justice Conover is on his way to the office. I would appreciate your not telling him that I called."

Silence.

"Miss Rawls, of all the clerks my husband has had work for him, you've always been my favorite. I don't wish to

200

sound as though I'm, so to speak, currying favor, but it happens to be true."

"Thank you."

"Are you alone?"

"Yes, I am. Why do you ask, Mrs. Conover?"

"Miss Rawls, let's talk woman to woman. I'm sure you're aware that certain . . . tensions between Justice Conover and myself have existed during our relationship—"

"Mrs. Conover, I'm not sure whether this sort of conversation is appropriate. I—"

"Please, hear me out. Things have reached a very bad point . . . I'm even afraid for my safety—"

"Again, I think that—"

"Miss Rawls, there's a file in my husband's office that relates to me and our marriage. I'm at my *wits'* end. *That* file contains, well, what could be damaging personal information about me. I suppose there have been times during my marriage when I might not have been quite as careful as I should have been . . . Miss Rawls, I *need* that file."

"Mrs. Conover, Mrs. Conover I couldn't—"

"*Please*, I'm begging you. I understand your position, but you must understand mine too. I'm talking to you not as an employee of the Court. I'm talking to you as one woman to another . . ."

"Mrs. Conover, I sympathize with you, but it's still out of the question. I have no idea what file you're talking about, and I don't want to. I'm a clerk on this Court. That's a position of unique trust, as you know. I can't compromise it for *any* consideration, regardless of personal feelings," (which include not liking you, lady).

The importuning abruptly stopped. "All right. You will forget that I called?"

"I can assure you of that. It never happened."

"Thank you."

Laurie heard the phone click on the other end, slowly

hung up, leaned over and looked down at a red file folder on her desk. She opened it and, once again, looked at the many pages lying within. On top, the very top, was a picture of Cecily Conover entering a motel with Clarence Sutherland.

KARL PULLED the Cadillac up in front of the justices' entrance to the Supreme Court building. His passenger, Senior Justice Temple Conover, appeared to have slept throughout the trip.

Karl got up and opened the back door. Conover did not move. "Justice Conover," he said. Still no reply. He reached inside, gently shook Conover's shoulder. It was only then that he noticed that the justice's tongue protruded at a peculiar angle from a mouth twisted grotesquely. He stepped back as the judge slumped toward the door, his head coming to rest over the curb, his red woolen scarf dipping into stagnant water in the gutter.

Sic transit gloria mundi, Judge Conover might have said, if he were talking.

CHAPTER
27

SOME TWENTY MINUTES LATER A DETECTIVE ASSIGNED TO
the Sutherland case walked into Martin Teller's office. "Did
you hear, Marty?"

"Hear what?"

"Justice Temple Conover had a stroke right in front of
the Supreme Court."

"I just left his house . . . Dead?"

"No, but close. In a coma."

"Where'd they take him?"

"Capitol Hill, on Mass."

"Have somebody monitor his progress," Teller said. "And
round up everybody for the meeting."

Teller and four detectives sat in his office, three coffees,
one tea and one chicken soup. They reviewed the Sutherland

case from the beginning, each man contributing what information his area of investigation had uncovered. There wasn't all that much, and Teller knew it. He sat with his feet up on his desk and twisted his toes in his right shoe. The inner leather lining had split and curled up in the front of the shoe. "Excuse me," he said, removing the shoe, pressing the lining flat, then quickly slipping his foot inside. "That's better," he sighed. "Okay, let's go over the logs from the surveillance."

A detective picked up a thick sheaf of papers, handed portions of it to the others, "I've got the log on Justice Poulson."

"Go ahead, read," Teller said. "And everybody listen up. If something rings a bell, yell."

The detective recited the entries on the first page of the log on Poulson, stopped and laughed.

"What's funny?"

"Putting a tail on the Chief Justice of the Supreme Court. You could get arrested for that."

"Just read," Teller said. He hadn't lightly made the decision to put a twenty-four hour surveillance on three Supreme Court justices. But what else could he do? And Dorian Mars had added to the squeeze when he said during one of their 9:00 A.M. meetings, "Marty, all the line is out. Unless we get a fish on the hook damn soon we're all going back on foot patrol." To which Teller had replied, "What if it's a big fish, Dorian?" And Mars had said, "Just as long as the net we use is strong enough." And Teller had said, "There's plenty of fish in the sea, Dorian. Too damn many." And the conversation had ended with Mars, lover of the extended metaphor and cliché, saying, "Then stop trolling and get out the harpoon."

Justice Poulson's movements under surveillance didn't provide much. He divided his time between home and the

Court, with time out for two speaking engagements in Washington, one in Virginia and three visits to the White House.

"Is that a lot of visits for a Supreme Court Justice to the White House?" Teller asked.

The detective shrugged. "Why should it be? They're top guys in the same business. Telling the rest of us what's up."

"What about Childs?"

The log on Morgan Childs's movements were also not especially revealing.

Pretty much the same for Temple Conover, except that the officer assigned to cover Conover had made a note that it was his opinion that Mrs. Conover was also being followed. He'd asked whether someone from MPD was on her case and was told no.

"You didn't have a tail on her, did you, Marty?" one of the men in his office asked.

He shook his head. "Maybe her husband had her followed."

"From what I hear about her, it probably wouldn't be a bad idea," someone said, which started a series of lewd comments about Cecily Conover.

"Knock it off," Teller said. "Let's get on with the rest of them. What about Dr. Sutherland?"

Sutherland's surveillance log was read. The detective reading the log said, "The doc makes house calls at the CIA. Makes sense, a shrink making house calls to the crazies at Central Intelligence."

Teller scratched under his arm and lit an odious clove.

"Come on, Marty, please."

"Hold your breath if you don't like it ... Let's look at this a minute. Why *would* he be going to the CIA?"

"Maybe *he's* a spook. Remember those stories a couple of years back about all the strange drug experiments the CIA was into? Lots of doctors involved, if I remember right, civilian doctors ... maybe he was one of them."

"Go back over those stories," Teller said. "See if he's mentioned anywhere."

When they'd finished with the logs, Teller asked for a review of background checks on the suspects.

The voices droned on, and Teller found himself at one point on the edge of nodding off. He struggled against it, even resorted to digging a fingernail into the palm of his hand. His mind wandered—the last opera he'd seen, Puccini's *La Fanciulla del West*, "The Girl of the Golden West," which he hadn't liked . . . a former girl friend calling and suggesting they get together for "old times' sake," which he'd declined to do . . . the lyrics to "You're the Top," which he'd forgotten while trying to sing it at Club Julie . . . bills that were overdue . . . his younger daughter, she'd come home and told her mother everything. She was planning to marry the father of the child as soon as he finished college, which was two years down the road. She planned to have the baby, live with her mother and find a job until the wedding. Teller had asked his former wife for the young man's name. She reluctantly gave it to him on his promise that he wouldn't call and make trouble. "I saw his picture," she said. "He's blond, adorable . . ." "Wonderful," Teller had said.

He came out of his reverie as the detective reading from the report said, "There's this one year while Poulson was sitting on the Court of Claims that's hard to nail down."

Teller sat up. "Why?"

"Well, he took a year's leave of absence and according to what I can piece together, used it to write a book."

"What kind of a book?"

"About suing the United States government. It's a textbook."

"Was it published?"

"Sure. I got a copy. You approved it on my expense sheet."

"What's this court about?"

"It only hears cases against the United States, I'm told."

"So what's so strange about that year? He takes a leave of absence and writes a book."

"Right, but he didn't stay at home to write it. The first four months of the year he sort of disappeared."

"Sort of?..."

"Yeah, his family was home, but he holed up in a place called Sunken Springs, Delaware."

"Why? Do they own a summer place there?"

"No."

"Where did he live in Sunken Springs?"

"Nobody seems to know. Four months later he comes home and goes on with his work on the book. Then he's back on the bench, the book's published and everything else is laid out clean for the record."

"Check it out."

"How?"

"Troll the waters. Let out all the line. Use a strong net..."

"Huh?"

"Just do it, Maurice."

He spent the rest of the day rearranging his flow chart, taking phone calls and thinking about his daughter, and about Susanna Pinscher...

He stopped in a music store on the way home and bought the sheet music to "You're the Top," committed the lyrics to memory over a dinner of frozen Welsh rarebit, toast and bacon, talked on the phone with someone from MPD who reported that Justice Conover was still in a coma and might not survive, took a nap, then went to Club Julie, where he sang loud and bad until the wee hours.

CHAPTER
28

NEWS OF TEMPLE CONOVER'S STROKE PERMEATED EVERY corridor and filtered through every door, open and closed, in the Court. His secretaries, Joan and Helen, cried, as did a black cleaning woman who said, "Lord have mercy on him." Conover had been the Court's leading champion of minority rights ever since coming to the bench.

A conference that had been called for that morning by Chief Justice Poulson to discuss *Nidel v. Illinois* was delayed an hour. When it was finally convened in the main conference room, Morgan Childs was absent. Justice Tilling-Masters asked where he was.

"He's running late," Augustus Smith said. "He'll be here shortly."

Poulson couldn't hide his annoyance at Childs's absence. He slapped a pencil on the table and looked at his watch.

"How's Justice Conover?" Justice Fine asked.

"The same, I suppose," Poulson said. "One of his clerks is at the hospital and is keeping in touch. I'm afraid it doesn't look too good."

"He's survived them before," Smith said. "He comes from hardy stock. And we certainly can't afford to lose him." Smith meant lose a liberal's vote on the Court, and Poulson knew what he meant.

Poulson looked sharply at him, then at Tilling-Masters. "Have you had a chance to go over my memo?" he asked.

"I'll need another day."

The door opened and Morgan Childs entered the room. "Sorry," he said as he took his seat and opened a folder.

"Well, we can begin," Poulson said. "Naturally, we all share grief over what has happened to Justice Conover, and we pray that his recovery will be swift and complete."

No one in the room said what he, or she, was thinking. It wasn't a matter of doubting the Chief Justice's sincerity about Temple Conover. Despite what some considered his inadequacies on the bench, he was not without compassion . . . There were no formal rules to deal with the sudden and complete incapacitation of a justice. It was up to the remaining eight justices to decide the disposition of cases that were pending before the condition. Were Conover to recover sufficiently to be able to communicate his thoughts, his final vote on the abortion issue could be cast from the hospital by phone, through a clerk or another justice. But he was in a coma, and the prognosis was not good.

"We might as well address the immediate issue," Poulson said. "Justice Conover is not in a position to vote on pending cases. I think we agree that of all the cases before this court, *Nidel v. Illinois* is the most pressing. I wonder whether—"

"I'm not certain that's true," Justice Fine said. "Sorry to

interrupt, Mr. Chief Justice, but because *Nidel v. Illinois* does have importance as a precedent-setting decision that will influence social programs in this nation for generations to come, it might be prudent to hold it over until Justice Conover has recovered."

"If he recovers," Justice Tilling-Masters said. "And what if he doesn't?"

"We could hold over the case for next term," Augustus Smith said. An action he personally did not favor. Smith's problem as a liberal was that if Conover was unable to return to the bench, President Jorgens would appoint a more conservative replacement. *Any* stalemated vote held over for the arrival of the new justice would, in all likelihood, mirror the administration's views. As for the abortion issue, well, he wasn't sure . . .

"I'm against that," said Poulson. "The nation is waiting for this Court's decision on abortion. To delay will only indicate indecision on our part." He didn't state the real reason for wanting to push forward on a vote. His personal lobbying efforts had resulted in what he perceived as a wavering on Augustus Smith's part. Smith had voted in favor of Nidel during the initial vote. Now, with the vote four to four, if he had a change of heart it would make it five to three in favor of Illinois and against abortion.

There was more discussion about what to do in Conover's absence. Finally Poulson suggested another preliminary vote.

"Are we really ready for that?" Smith asked.

"I think so," said Poulson. "Let's see where we stand."

Tilling-Masters said, "It seems to me that we know where we stand. It obviously still falls four-to-four, now that Justice Conover can't vote. Perhaps we should hold the case over until the next term."

Poulson knew that holding it over until the President could appoint a conservative to the bench was, on the face of it, safer. But one could never be sure. Judges sometimes changed stripes once they got to the Supreme Court . . . look at Black, a Klu Kluxer turned liberal, and Eisenhower surely never expected Earl Warren to lead the fight to strike down the "separate but equal" doctrine . . . *And* if his instincts about Smith were right, *Nidel v. Illinois* could be settled quickly, and the way he wanted. The Poulson Court would have acted, the nation would have clear guidelines on a nasty, divisive issue, the administration's pledge would be fulfilled and he, Poulson, would have delivered what he'd promised.

"Let's vote," Justice Fine said, removing wire spectacles and rubbing his eyes. "If there's been a change, we might as well find out."

Morgan Childs cleared his throat, held up a finger. "I think another vote is premature," he said.

"Why?" Poulson asked.

"I'm not ready, Mr. Chief Justice."

"Not ready?" Poulson couldn't help but smile. Childs's conservative views were well known, solid. Certainly, Poulson reasoned, Childs couldn't be considering changing his vote in favor of the plaintiff Nidel.

Childs went on, "I've read every position paper that's been generated since the last vote, along with a stack of related materials. This is the sort of issue that naturally stirs up very personal feelings that tend to influence sound legal reasoning. I'd be less than honest if I didn't admit that this has happened to me, but when I strip away my private views, I keep coming back to a very narrow and clearly defined legal issue. I haven't reached a firm decision as yet, but my reaction to the legal aspects of this case is different from what it was earlier."

"I'm surprised," said Poulson. It was the mildest reaction he could manage.

"Well," Childs said, "surprised or not, that's where I stand at this moment."

Justice Smith, a wry smile on his face, asked, "What if you had to vote right now, Justice Childs? What would it be?"

"Hypothetical votes don't interest me," Childs said.

"They don't count, but they're interesting," Smith said, still smiling.

They spent another half-hour discussing other pending cases and deciding what to do in light of Conover's situation. Eventually it was decided to table voting on all cases until a clearer picture of the senior justice's physical condition could be determined.

Poulson went to his chambers and slumped in his chair, his stomach a knot, his nerve ends alive. He tried to calm down, took deep breaths, considered having a drink.

It was inconceivable to him that Childs might vote for Nidel. How many times had they sat together over lunch or dinner and discussed their views on life, not as Supreme Court justices but as men, husbands and fathers, observers of society and of the moral deterioration it had suffered at the hands of liberal gurus? A man doesn't change that much, he told himself, and if he did, it would surely be to become even more concerned about the shredding of the American fabric, to become even more conservative. He refused to acknowledge, even to himself, that Childs's narrow legal focus on the case might be sound. It didn't matter what the legal technicalities were. There was a greater issue at stake, one beyond strict legal considerations. There was decency to be upheld, moral leadership to be exercised . . . and a President in the White House who had appointed him and expected him to live up to his commitments.

Anger displaced anxiety. He picked up the phone and dialed a number in the White House. It rang in the office of Craig Lauderman, special assistant to the President. A secretary answered, told Poulson to hold and entered Lauderman's private office. "Sir, the Chief Justice wishes to speak with you."

Lauderman, thirty-five years old, thick brown hair neatly combed over a thin, patrician face and wearing tortoiseshell glasses, raised his eyebrows, and then his patrician face. "Thank you, I'll take it."

"Mr. Lauderman," Poulson said when he came on the line, "I hope I'm not interrupting some important affair of state." He laughed a tentative laugh.

Lauderman did not laugh, or smile. "Is there something I can do for you, Mr. Chief Justice?"

His coldness was not lost on Poulson, who hesitated before saying, "I'd like to speak to the President."

"He won't be available to anyone until tomorrow afternoon."

"That's a shame."

"Is it urgent?"

"Yes."

"Perhaps I can help."

"I don't think so, Mr. Lauderman."

"Try me, Mr. Chief Justice."

Poulson resented the tone used by the younger man. Who the hell was he, just another middling bright and over-weeningly ambitious young man with a position of influence in Jorgens's administration, lording it over everyone in Washington—senators and congressmen, cabinet officials and even Supreme Court justices. He wanted to tell him what he thought of him and his kind. Instead he said, "It has to do with *Nidel v. Illinois*."

"I suspected that was the purpose of your call, Mr. Chief Justice. The President is on top of it and is taking steps he considers appropriate—"

"I don't think you understand, Mr. Lauderman. There have been developments that—"

"How is Justice Conover?"

213

"The last we heard, he was still in a coma and the prognosis is guarded."

"It was a shock . . . Well, perhaps the President could get back to you, Mr. Chief Justice. As I said, he's quite up to date on the case, and so am I."

Poulson's voice now filled up with anger. "Perhaps you'd better tell the President, Mr. Lauderman, that it seems Justice Childs is considering changing his vote. Perhaps you could suggest that thought be given to Justice Childs and his vote—"

"I will, Mr. Chief Justice. Thank you for calling."

The line went dead. Poulson took his coat from a closet and headed into the hallway. He needed time to think. Maybe a walk would help. As he proceeded down the corridor Laurie Rawls came around a corner. "Good morning, Mr. Chief Justice," she said.

"Good morning, Miss Rawls."

"Any word on Justice Conover?" she asked.

"Nothing new," Poulson said. "We're all hoping. Good day," and he walked past her.

LAURIE RAWLS left the building and drove home, where, after rummaging through closets, she chose a tailored brown tweed suit, taupe blouse with a button-down collar, stockings and plain brown pumps. She checked herself in a mirror, playing with her hair and makeup. Finally, apparently satisfied, she returned to her car and drove slowly toward the center of Washington, checking her watch every few minutes and varying her speed accordingly. She parked in a garage on Eighteenth Street near the General Services Building and walked toward the White House. She'd been told to enter through the south portico, which she did. A guard took her name and checked a list, then called Craig Lauderman's office. "Yes, Miss Rawls, you're expected," the guard said. "Someone will be here to escort you in a minute."

Lauderman's office was large, free of clutter. He was in shirt sleeves. He stood up and offered his hand. "Nice of you to stop by, Miss Rawls."

"I appreciate your finding the time for me—"

"Don't be modest. The President is impressed with you and what you've offered us."

She seemed almost embarrassed. "Thank you, that's very flattering."

"Yes, well, I know what you mean. I sit close to the most powerful leader in the Free World. Few people have that opportunity. Right here is where the buck stops."

Well, almost, she thought. Like more than one top presidential aide, Lauderman tended to so identify himself with the top man that he began to think he *was* the man. No question, though, that he had the President's confidence, and that no one had access to Jorgens unless cleared by the Jorgens Militia, a cadre of arrogant, aloof young men with ambition in their veins and steel in their hearts. This one tended to frighten her, as he did so many others . . . but he also attracted her. Montesquieu said power corrupts . . . well, it also seduces, she thought . . .

"I want you to know, Miss Rawls, that I speak for the President when I say to you we appreciate the information you have offered us about Dr. Chester Sutherland's research files. I don't think I overstate it when I say that those files, were they to end up in the wrong hands, would have posed a grave threat to national security."

"Well, Mr. Lauderman, when I learned . . . through his son . . . that such files existed, I knew something needed to be done. It wasn't an easy decision. Clarence Sutherland was a friend and . . . and close colleague. Were he still alive, I would not, to be perfectly honest with you, have informed the White House of the existence of the files. But once he

215

was gone I did what I thought was right. I hope I made the right decision."

"You did, Miss Rawls. One must follow one's best instincts in these things... Tell me about yourself, Miss Rawls."

"What would you like to know?"

He smiled. It was not really much of a smile. Tight-lipped. She wondered whether he ever let go, laughed out loud.

"Tell me about the essential Laurie Rawls, the Laurie Rawls who might end up working with me every day and who, in that event, would work at the right hand of the President of the United States."

She shifted in her chair, organized her thoughts. Be precise, she told herself, and she was. He listened impassively, his eyes never leaving hers, his mind like a computer taking in her words and committing them to chips to be instantly replayed when and if needed.

"Very impressive," he said when she was through.

"Thank you." Good, he'd been impressed with her performance. She felt more in control now and actually felt his peer, every bit as bright, and calculating, as he was. An even match.

He offered her a glass of water. She declined. He poured himself a glass from a crystal pitcher wrapped in glove leather. "Do you drink?"

"Drink? Alcohol?"

"Yes."

"I like wine." And quickly added, "with meals."

"Drugs? Smoke pot?"

"No."

"Never?"

"Well, I did once or twice a long time ago but..."

"Any skeletons in the Rawls closet? Sordid romances, insanity in the family, cheating on college exams, unpaid

216

parking tickets or college loans, people holding something over your head..."

"No."

"Good." He leafed through a file folder, looked up and said, "You do know, Miss Rawls, that this job can be yours if things progress as we hope they will."

"I'm not sure I understand exactly what you mean, Mr. Lauderman. Clarence Sutherland and I were close. He told me about your interest in having him come to work here at the White House and—"

"How close were you?"

"Will honesty ruin my chances?"

"Honesty will help insure them."

"We were very close. Very..."

"And you're understandably upset by his death...but you still have your priorities in order. I like that, Miss Rawls. You're a pragmatist." He leaned on his elbows as he said, "Your late friend, Clarence Sutherland, was close to being named to our team here at the White House. At first I balked at the suggestion. After all, what could he offer us that any bright law graduate couldn't offer? Bright law school graduates are a dime a dozen, and being a clerk in the Supreme Court doesn't mean all that much. We know how he got the appointment, which, I might add, is no crime. His father, because of his *close* relationship with Justice Poulson, did what any caring father might have done, used a delicate relationship to benefit a son. I would do the same thing. Would you?"

"I think so."

"Well, the important thing is that Clarence Sutherland had certain information, because of his father's profession, that was valuable to this administration. Does that offend you?"

"Why should it?"

"It would some. I'm glad it doesn't you."

"As you said, I'm a pragmatist."

"And ambitious."

"Yes. I would imagine you would understand that."

He allowed a grin. "Yes, I do. When you first came here with the information about Dr. Sutherland's files, I was skeptical of you. I asked myself what you wanted, what your game was, what your price was. That's what I'm paid for."

"Was it because I'm a woman?"

"Why should it be? I'm no sexist. Just a realist. Miss Rawls, you want the job Clarence was being considered for and I admire you for that. You say you have the same information he had because of your—"

"Because I was very close to him. Yes. When you're that close to someone, you tend to share everything..."

"Yes...well, I'm aware of that. But can you stop the sharing if necessary. I'm speaking of what you would learn here at the White House?"

"Absolutely." She looked directly at him when she said it.

"Good. Now...we need a...continuing factor inside the Court. Mr. Sutherland held that out to us. Now, he's no longer in a position to provide it. Perhaps you are."

"I think I am."

"As I said, I'm a realist, Miss Rawls. Give me some results to convince me."

"Such as?" Actually she knew the answer.

"Help insure that the vote on *Nidel v. Illinois* goes the way it should. The way the administration, *and* the American people believe it should."

"That isn't easy—"

"Sutherland said it was."

"I'm not Clarence Sutherland."

"But you're peddling the same thing."

"I'm not *peddling* anything."

218

"Sorry, Miss Rawls. I'm afraid I'm not as good at the legal niceties as you are. Let me put it this way. Justice Childs may be a problem. I understand you might know something about him to help moderate his perhaps overly rigid *legal* principles."

"I might."

"If you want this job, Miss Rawls, you'd better."

"It comes down to that?"

He nodded.

"Well, there are certain inconsistencies in Justice Childs's background that might be helpful in persuading him to—"

"See the light?"

"Yes."

"You know what they are?"

"Yes."

"Can you prove them?"

"I think so."

"Childs is swaying in his position. His vote, I understand, is now crucial to the outcome of *Nidel v. Illinois*."

"I thought he was solidly for the state of Illinois."

"Not as of this morning. Can you do something about that?"

"Yes."

"Glad to hear it. As I told you at the beginning of this meeting, the job of judicial liaison can be yours, provided you can contribute to certain conditions within the Court—"

"Count on me, Mr. Lauderman. There is nothing Clarence Sutherland knew that I don't know. Nothing he could do that I can't do."

"I'm going to enjoy working with you, Miss Rawls. I have a good sense of people. You're good people, and I intend to tell President Jorgens exactly that."

"Thank you."

They stood and shook hands. "Maybe we could have

219

dinner some night," he said. "Since we're likely to be working together for what I hope is a long time, we really should get to know each other. Don't you agree?"

"I certainly do. Thank you. You'll hear from me shortly, Mr. Lauderman."

"I look forward to it."

CHAPTER
29

THE BRIEF, VOLATILE CONFRONTATION WITH DAN BRAZIER had left Susanna temporarily shaken, and by the following morning, highly annoyed with herself for having exited so hastily before asking the questions that had brought her to the apartment in the first place.

She'd told her father about the incident the night it happened. He was adamant about her getting off the Sutherland case. When confronted with her decision to return to see Brazier, he became angry.

"I have a job," she said.

"Your job is *also* to be a mother to your children." Which once again started all the business of her having given custody to her former husband. By the time she left the house for Brazier's apartment, a thick cloud of tension trailed behind.

She deeply regretted that but forced herself to forget about the argument and to concentrate on what she would say to Brazier. She knew that ordinarily she was not a particularly brave person, tended to avoid confrontation . . . Except, damn it, that wasn't completely true, she reminded herself as she passed over the Bay Bridge. It had taken real courage, no matter what anyone said, to end her bad marriage and especially to give up physical possession of her children. She'd stood up to it, had made a good career in a male-dominated world without sacrificing herself as a woman, without forgetting that she was a woman. Or a mother. She was still a good mother, even though she did not have everyday possession of her children. But their relationship was better than it had ever been. No, she had nothing to apologize for, feel guilty about, and was not about to create something now by avoiding Dan Brazier.

She planned her approach, went over it a dozen times. It didn't matter how he reacted, whether he hit out at her, just as long as she got to ask her questions.

She rang the downstairs buzzer. Sheryl Figgs opened the door at the top of the stairs and squinted against a shaft of bright sunlight that backlit Susanna. "Who is it?" she asked.

"Susanna Pinscher. I'd like to speak to Mr. Brazier."

"Oh, no, I don't think that's—"

Susanna quickly climbed the stairs. "Please, Miss Figgs, I won't stay long. I'm sorry about dinner the other night, but it was a difficult situation."

Sheryl glanced nervously into the apartment. She was wearing a faded pink robe and was barefoot, her hair was tousled. Obviously she'd just gotten out of bed.

"Is he here?" Susanna asked, looking past her.

"He's . . . we just . . ."

"I'll only stay a minute," Susanna said, stepping around her and into the living room.

"Who is it?" Brazier called from another room.

"It's me, Susanna Pinscher. I'd like to speak with you."

Sheryl came up behind her. "I really don't think it's a good idea. He was so angry after you left last time he——"

Brazier wheeled himself from the bedroom, chest bare, a dollop of shaving cream still beneath his right earlobe.

"Why did you come back?" he asked, wiping water from his neck with the towel.

"To ask you a few questions." Susanna looked into his gray eyes, at his powerful upper body that could have belonged to a weight lifter. "I won't stay long, no longer than the last time," she said, determined not to wilt under his intense gaze.

"I have nothing to say to you."

"I really think you do." She summoned up the line she'd rehearsed in the car. She had nothing to back it up, only Laurie Rawls's comment based on something Clarence had told her. She'd decided not to ask it as a question, she'd challenge and hope for the best. "Morgan Childs isn't what he's cracked up to be——"

"What the hell are you talking about?"

"About his so-called heroic deeds in Korea? I understand that was all made up, and you helped."

He started to respond, then wiped the back of his hand across his square, lined face as though to dismiss the subject, and her.

"Why?" Susanna pressed.

"What do you know?" he said, turning his chair and wheeling to the window. "What the hell does anybody know any more about heroes?"

"I know I like them better if they're legitimate."

Sheryl Figgs approached him. "Dan," she said, "if you'd rather have her leave——"

He waved her away, fixed Susanna with a look and pointed his index finger at her. "How do you know what you say you know?"

"It's my job, Mr. Brazier. I'm investigating a murder, and this could be relevant."

"How?"

She couldn't backtrack now. He'd all but acknowledged it, at least he hadn't denied it. "Clarence Sutherland knew about Justice Childs's so-called exploits in Korea. Sutherland was a man who used information for power. If he held damaging knowledge over Childs's head, it might have provided a real motive for your friend to have killed him—"

"Don't be ridiculous. Whatever Morgan Childs is or isn't, he's not a murderer."

"And Nixon wasn't a crook, and the boy next door who killed his family was always so polite and nice...It's an old story, Mr. Brazier. Appearances can deceive...anyway, the fact is that a substantial part of Justice Childs's public image revolves around his having performed all sorts of heroic deeds in Korea, which isn't exactly true."

"So?"

"So? Is that all you can say? A whole country was misled by a fantasy *you* wrote. Why did you do it?" She hoped she hadn't gone too far...after all, she wasn't really certain how much he was involved in Childs's Korean scenario.

He tugged on the arms of his wheelchair as though not sure which way to move, then looked up and asked, "What's your politics, Miss Pinscher? Liberal, conservative? Don't give a damn?"

"Moderate, I suppose."

"What does that mean?"

"I try to go by the issues. Sometimes I come down on what's considered to be the liberal side, other times the conservative."

Brazier looked at Sheryl, who leaned against a wall. "Get

me a shirt, will you?" She returned from the bedroom with a wrinkled red plaid shirt that he slipped over his massive shoulders, leaving it unbuttoned.

Susanna said, "My politics really haven't any bearing on this, Mr. Brazier. What I'm wondering about is why you and Justice Childs would get together on a sham—?"

"That's your word."

She pulled out a chair from the desk, sat down and said as calmly as she could, "Mr. Brazier, I'm not here to make trouble. What happened in Korea between you and Justice Childs is no one's business but your own, unless, of course, it bears on Clarence Sutherland's murder. I'm not your antagonist. I'm doing my job, or trying to . . ."

"Then you should understand."

"Understand what?"

"That we did what we had to do."

"I'm sorry, I don't follow you."

"Korea needed a hero. *Before* Vietnam. Maybe if we'd been more successful there'd have been no Nam. Anyway, nobody quite understood what was going on. It was a United Nations action, mostly manned by the U.S. MacArthur got everybody confused about not being allowed to win the war —Harry Truman had to fire him for insubordination . . . for forgetting who was Commander in Chief. Harry was right. But the country badly needed something to be proud of, we made the most of a brave man . . . Childs . . . who was a natural for the hero's role—a kind of rallying point for back home. Hell, the flag-raising photo on Iwo Jima that hit every front page in America during World War II was a phony too, a sham to use your word, staged by a military public relations guy to give the folks back home a sense of the glory and courage of their troops—which was no sham. So . . ."

"I think I understand," she said, "but when something

225

is that calculated, it seems to me it loses its value. I mean, I can't quite buy the end justifies the means—"

"*Okay*, Miss Pinscher, enough."

"Mr. Brazier, again, I tell you I'm not trying to stir up trouble, but I'm sure you can understand that—"

He lit a cigarette and wheeled himself into the kitchen, returning with a bottle of gin. "Drink?" he asked.

"No, thank you."

"We have wine," Sheryl called from the bedroom, where she'd gone to dress.

"You look like a wine drinker," Brazier said as he poured himself a tumbler full of gin.

"If that means what I think it means—"

"It means I'm tired of your judging me, or Childs, Miss Pinscher. All right, so you've discovered the deep dark secret of Korea and Morgan Childs. Where'd you get it, from that scum Sutherland?"

"Clarence, or his father?"

He cocked his head and closed one eye. "You're pretty good, lady."

"What do you mean?"

"You've got me talking too damn much." He shook his head and drank down more of the gin. "Where *did* you get the story about Childs and me?"

She was relieved *he'd* mentioned Sutherland and decided to go with it. "Clarence Sutherland found out about it from his father's files." She remembered having seen Sutherland's name in Brazier's old appointment book. "I take it you were a patient, and you told Dr. Sutherland about Childs and Korea. The son picked up the information somehow from his father's confidential files and used it to blackmail Childs..."

It was pretty much all supposition on her part, but Brazier's expression seemed to confirm it. He again filled his glass and looked toward the window. Sheryl came from the bedroom, dressed in slacks and sweater. "You've done a job, Susanna Pinscher. I toast you." He raised his glass. "Here's to Sherlock Holmes, Philip Marlowe, Travis McGee and Susanna Pinscher, sleuths of a feather, and so forth...so you know a deep, dark secret...what are you going to do with it?"

"Nothing, unless, as I said, it bears on the Sutherland case—"

"And if it does?"

"It it does, I'll have to—"

"Look, what if Morgan Childs did kill the Sutherland kid, which of course I'm not saying he did...I mean, what did we lose except a cheap, venomous, blackmailing snake ready and willing to sell a national hero down the tubes for his own private gain? Think about it, lady, put them on a balancing scale. Sutherland was filth. Morgan Childs represents to millions of Americans the sort of man we hardly ever see anymore. Name someone these days who's worth being called a hero, someone to look up to, to *stand* for something good in America. Athletes? That's a laugh. The only thing they've left kids to look up to are the size of their contracts. Movie stars? Forget it. Politicians? Those that aren't under indictment, or taping illegally, are busy getting rich in payoffs from the folks that financed their election campaigns..." He leaned forward in his chair. "Morgan and I have our problems, but they're ours, not yours or anybody else's. He means something to you, to me, to every person in America. He sits on the highest court in the land and votes his convictions about whether something is or isn't constitutional. He hasn't mortgaged himself to anybody. He stands for decency and honor, things we don't have much of anymore. There's a network of boys' groups in America that goes by Morgan Childs's name and that exists because he raises millions every year for them—"

"I understand all this, Mr. Brazier, and I happen to agree

227

with much of what you say. My father often talks the same way. I have three children of my own, and I worry about who they'll be able to look up to. I've met Justice Childs, went flying with him, matter of fact. I liked him, he reminds me of my father ... *but* if Clarence Sutherland threatened him enough to drive him to murder, that's obviously over-riding—"

"Leave it alone," Brazier said.

"I can't—"

"*Drop* it," he said, not turning. "There's a bigger picture to be considered—"

"Mr. Brazier, a person has been killed, and—"

He spun the chair around so fast that his glass flew from his hands and landed at Sheryl's feet. She picked it up, scooping ice cubes into it with her hand. Brazier shouted, "Morgan Childs counts for something, damn it. He means something to America, and to me. He saved my life in Korea and—"

"I understand what you're saying and I sympathize with it, but I've got to ask ... did your good friend Morgan Childs murder Clarence Sutherland?"

His words came slowly, measured by the anger he was suppressing. "Just ... get ... *out. Before I do something vi-olent.*"

She backed into the hall, followed by Sheryl, who closed the door behind her.

"I'm sorry, Miss Pinscher. Dan is ... well, he's very difficult at times, especially when it involves this country and Korea and Morgan Childs. He really cares so much, has such deep convictions that sometimes it gets the better of him."

"I understand," Susanna said. She touched her arm.

"I love him so much," she said. "He's been through a lot. He's a decent, fine man in pain. I've had pain in my life, but nothing like what he's suffered."

"I respect him," Susanna said. "Please believe that."

"I do." She wiped her eyes. "You know, he could have been an important man, Susanna."

"He was. His by-line was in every magazine in America."

"But he could have been even bigger."

"Why didn't it happen?"

"He became so bitter, so terribly negative. I tried to snap him out of it, tried to encourage him to write again but he refused."

"He hasn't written anything in how long?"

"Years. When we first met he was almost finished with a book, but he never finished it. It just sits under the bed collecting dust."

"What sort of book?"

"It's about how the CIA tested drugs on people years ago." She partially swallowed the final words.

"I'd read newspaper reports about it when the CIA was forced to release its files. How did Dan get interested in it?"

"Oh, it doesn't matter...he'll never finish it...He's so damned worried about protecting people and his country. Even the doctors that were involved in the experiments—"

"Doctors? Dr. Sutherland, for example?"

Sheryl quickly shook her head. "I don't know," she said. "Dan got involved in the project when he was at a clinic somewhere in Delaware, a place called Sunken Springs."

"Was Dr. Sutherland mentioned in Dan's manuscript, Sheryl? Is that why Dan had his name in his appointment book?"

"What book?"

"The one in your bedroom, the one he saw me looking at the last time I was at your apartment."

"He didn't tell me that."

"Oh. I thought—"

"He just said he didn't want anybody snooping around his life. He was so mad at me for letting you in . . ."

"I'm sorry I've caused you grief."

"You haven't. I accept what goes with being in love with someone like Dan. I know lots of men who wouldn't cause such problems, but they also wouldn't give me what Dan gives me."

"Yes . . . well, thanks again, Sheryl, for taking me into your confidence. It's been a real . . . experience meeting you, and Dan Brazier . . ."

CHAPTER
30

SUSANNA AND HER SON ARRIVED BACK HOME IN WASHington at eight in the evening. She delivered him to his father's house, drove to the Justice Department, went to her office and, by the light of a desk lamp, reviewed notes she'd made during the flight. She dialed Martin Teller's home number. No answer. She tried MPD headquarters. An officer at the desk said he thought Detective Teller was still in the building. After a few minutes Teller came on the line.

"Martin, I'm back. I need to see you. Are you free?"

"Come on over, I'll be in my office."

It was close to eleven when she arrived. Teller was in shirt sleeves, wearing a dark five-o'clock shadow. He closed the door, sat in his chair. She perched on the edge of the desk.

"Okay, let's have it."

She did, at first leaving out items that might link her two meetings with Brazier to the Sutherland murder.

"Brazier sounds a little *crazy*. How does it relate to the case?"

"Here's how. First, Morgan Childs isn't quite what he's cracked up to be, although I don't think any the less of him because of it, at least not from Brazier's version of the whys. What matters, though, is that Childs was vulnerable because of charming Clarence Sutherland's knowledge of his true Korean background. Dan Brazier laid it on a bit thick in his stories once they got back home and Childs went along. Was, I gather, persuaded to go along by Brazier, who felt the country deserved a hero out of that war and Childs was ideal material. He did apparently save Brazier's life, but I didn't get the details on that. Anyway, reluctant hero or not, Childs is open to a journalistic field day if what Brazier did and he went along with ever comes out. It could indeed be made to look like he's been a fraud, he might well face impeachment by the Congress . . . it's sure as hell a motive for murder and makes him a suspect. Even good guys panic when they see their life going up in smoke. Agreed?"

Teller nodded slowly. "How did Clarence get the information?"

"From his father's psychiatric files. Brazier had been his father's patient while he was in Washington."

"Go on."

"I found out from Brazier's girl friend, Sheryl Figgs, that he'd been working on a book exposing the CIA's mind-control experiments. Evidently he'd been institutionalized as Sutherland's patient in a place called Sunken Springs, in

232

Delaware. I can't prove this right now, Martin, but I know that—"

"That Dr. Sutherland was connected with the CIA experiments?"

"Yes . . . how did you know?"

"We've been working on Dr. Sutherland, some things broke while you were away."

"What? You've nailed down Sutherland's role with the CIA?"

"Yeah . . . I'll tell you something else. Chief Justice Poulson was probably in that same Sunken Springs funny farm. At first Sunken Springs meant nothing to me. We were supposed to believe that Poulson had spent some time there writing a book. We did a little checking. Besides a drugstore, meat market, shopping center and a movie theater open on the weekends, Sunken Springs has a very private and protected facility where the rich and famous can get their heads together when they start to come unglued. And rumor has it that the CIA uses the place as a halfway house, a retreat for spooks who've come in from the cold and need a rest, not to mention it's a research clinic for CIA experiments. I just got the report in late this afternoon. According to it there's a—"

"Are you *sure* Justice Poulson was there? Was he a patient?"

"It's a pretty reasonable assumption, wouldn't you say?"

"Then busy busy Clarence would have had *that* to hold over his head. If it had come out that Poulson had been institutionalized, he never would have been confirmed as Chief Justice. Or kept the job if it came out afterward. Did the White House know?"

Teller shrugged. "If I were writing this script, I'd have them knowing it . . . Clarence Sutherland was offered a job on President Jorgens's staff."

233

"He was? Wow..."

Teller got up and walked to the wall chart, untaped the brown paper and stepped back.

"What's that?" Susanna asked.

"My wall chart, obviously. Cost a hundred bucks. It's sort of comforting to me. Makes me feel less confused than I really am. Now... you may ask why would Clarence be offered a job in the White House..."

"Not to be a wise guy, Mr. Detective, but I think it's now fairly clear. Clarence used his knowledge of Poulson's institutionalization to pressure the President and his men to give him a job. Poulson was and is Jorgens's man."

"Right, but maybe there's more. If Clarence had the goods... you should forgive the expression... on Childs, he could have used that to swing weight inside the Court on the President's behalf. I mean with Childs."

She nodded.

"He was a nasty little bastard, wasn't he?" Teller said.

"Worse... what else have you learned since I was away?"

"That's about it."

"You're sure?"

"I'm sure. Now let's get organized."

She joined him in front of the chart. "There they are," he said, "the suspects all laid out. Time to refine it."

"Who are you ruling out?"

He folded his arms and squinted. "Let's see. Laurie Rawls. Aside from her anger at Clarence for his fooling around, is there any other reason to suspect her?"

"That might be good enough reason to keep her on the list."

"It might be, but I really think we should focus in. There's too many players with a maybe motive. I vote for taking her out of the game."

"All right."

234

He moved her magnetized nameplate from the board. "Who else?"

"Dr. Sutherland?"

"Why?"

"He was Clarence's father. Do fathers kill sons in cold blood? It happens in fits of anger or passion, but this killing was premeditated."

Teller nodded. "Except what if the son were blackmailing his own father over involvement in CIA drug experiments on people who didn't know how they were being used, some of whom died from the experiments? We went back through the files the CIA released, the MKULTRA files. The people in that business come up with some real screwy names for their little projects...*Artichoke, Bluebird*...grown men playing cloak-and-dagger games...Anyway, I don't figure papa shrink doing it, though with a son like Clarence he might have done himself in out of guilt for what he perpetrated on the world. I vote for taking him from the board."

"All right. It's your board."

"Don't be a wise guy." But he smiled when he said it, and removed Sutherland's name. "Next?"

"Justice Conover?"

"You heard?"

"About his stroke? Yes. How is he?"

"Last word he was still in a coma."

"Poor man."

"Yeah. I interviewed Cecily Conover again. 'Poor man' is right."

"If *Cecily* were the victim I'd have to vote him to the top of the list."

"Is he coming down from the board?"

"What do you think?"

"Yes..."

"Done." Conover's name joined Sutherland's and Laurie Rawls's on the desk.

235

"Cecily Conover?"

"As much as I'd like to see her *numero uno* I don't think so. That lady, and I use the term loosely in her case, really covers her tail. She'd get someone else to do it."

Susanna reached out and took Mrs. Sutherland's and Clarence's sister's names down. "Any argument?" she asked. "I'd say they're more to be pitied for having been related to Clarence. Especially Mrs. Sutherland."

"I agree."

"What about the 'friends' category?" Susanna said.

"Off with 'em."

Susanna started to remove Vera Jones's name from the board.

"Hold on."

"Why? From what we have on her she's not in the running." When he didn't respond she asked, "Are you holding out on me about her, Martin?"

"You know what I like about you, Susanna, along with a few other things?"

"What?"

"That you call me Martin. With most people it's plain Marty. Like the poor character in Paddy Chayefsky's play. You and my mother...Martin...except she did it when she was sore at me."

Susanna laughed and told him to stop being so adorable or she'd have to break off business and take him to her apartment.

"Sorry," he said. "And *adorable* nobody ever called me."

He told her about meeting up with Vera Jones at Club Julie, and about what the bartender said.

"But that would only put her in the same category as Laurie Rawls. Another woman spurned. Is that enough?"

He shook his head. "No, she has more going for her than that. She's been with Sutherland for years, must know all about a lot, including his CIA games. I'd like to leave her on the list... and I think we have to add a few."

"I thought we were trying to make the list smaller."

"We are, but that doesn't mean ignoring live ones."

"Who do you want to add?"

He muttered something under his breath.

"What?"

"How would you categorize the White House and the CIA on the board?"

"The White House?"

"If Jorgens appointed Poulson Chief Justice knowing he'd been in a mental institution, well... that speaks for itself. And if Jorgens has been exerting improper influence on Supreme Court business through what is in effect blackmail, courtesy of Clarence's access to his old man's files, that makes the President of the United States an accomplice to blackmail, to say nothing of violating the concept of separation of powers—"

"I'm not sure I can deal with it—"

"We have to... and the same with the CIA. If Clarence knew about the drug experiment programs and was holding that kind of information out for grabs, the friendly folks at our Central Intelligence Agency wouldn't mind seeing him... removed. Maybe they call it neutralized, or terminated, but it all spells death." He sat behind his desk, took out two strips of paper, uncapped his marking pen. "Do we lump them together under *Government* or do we make separate plates for *CIA* and *WH*. White House. I wouldn't want to spell it out on the board. Might get people shook up if they looked under the brown paper."

"Make them separate, *CIA* and *WH*."

He did and put them on the board. "There, how's it look?"

They stood back and took another look at the revised chart before he covered it.

DECEASED

POULSON—blackmail

CHILDS—blackmail

VERA JONES—personal, and access to same knowledge as deceased

CIA—secrets compromised

WH—blackmail

Teller walked her to her car.

"Want to come back to the apartment?" she asked.

"I'd like to, but I'm not going to."

"Why?" She touched his cheek.

"Tired, stuff on my mind. My youngest kid is pregnant. She dropped out of school."

"Oh, I'm sorry, Martin."

"Yeah, well, like they say, life is what happens while you're making other plans. Give me a rain check, okay?"

"You got it. Good night." She kissed him lightly on the lips. He pulled her close and pressed his mouth hard against hers. When they came apart, and she was about to open the door to her car, he said, "How about going out to see Dr. Sutherland and Vera Jones tomorrow?".

"Good idea. Confront them. It worked pretty good for me with Dan Brazier. What time?"

"I'll call them in the morning." He shrugged. "It is morning."

"Just let me know when, Martin. And get some sleep."

238

CHAPTER
31

IT WAS TWO DAYS BEFORE TELLER AND SUSANNA WERE able to see Dr. Chester Sutherland and Vera Jones. If Teller hadn't pressed hard during his third call to Vera it probably would have taken even longer.

Vera escorted them now into Sutherland's inner office and turned to leave.

"I'd like to have both of you here," Teller said.

"I have work to do—"

"So do we, Miss Jones."

Vera looked at Sutherland, who nodded, then sat down in a straight-backed cane chair, hands folded on her knees, eyes straight ahead, her pale, cameo face empty of expression. She wore a brown tweed skirt that flared wide below the knees. A beige cashmere sweater with a large, thick collar seemed to prop her head up above her shoulders. Her hair was drawn back into a severe chignon. She wore no makeup.

"Well, Mr. Teller, how are you progressing in the investigation?" Sutherland asked. He sounded pretty damn detached, Teller thought, considering that the investigation happened to involve his murdered son.

"Pretty good, doctor. Matter of fact, the last few days have given us some important new information." He glanced at Vera, whose face grew even stonier.

Even Sutherland reacted. He sat forward on his couch and asked, "What sort of information, Detective Teller?"

"We'd like to ask you and Miss Jones some questions."

Sutherland smiled. "Go ahead and ask. I've tried to be completely candid with you, as I'm sure Miss Jones has."

When Teller didn't immediately follow up with a question, Susanna, remembering her experience with Dan Brazier, said flatly, "We know, Dr. Sutherland, about your involvement with the CIA's experimentation programs, and that Clarence also knew about it and let you know that he knew..."

Sutherland, who'd relaxed into the couch's cushions, uncrossed his legs and said without looking up, "That's nonsense, Miss Pinscher, and you know it."

"It's fact," Teller said. "But there's more than that, Dr. Sutherland. We know that Chief Justice Poulson was a patient of yours, and that you institutionalized him in Sunken Springs, Delaware—"

"Now, look here... I resent this intrusion into a confidential area." Sutherland stood up abruptly.

Susanna put in quickly, "Dan Brazier was also a patient, Dr. Sutherland, and Clarence learned the truth about Justice Childs's Korean War record through *those* files—"

"*Damn it*," Sutherland said, crossing the room.

"Take it easy," Teller told him. "How these things relate

240

to your son's murder is speculative, but it's our job to follow through on them, see where, if anywhere, they lead to."

"This is horrible," Vera Jones said.

"It sure is," Teller said. "Look, neither Miss Pinscher nor I have any personal interest in either of you. All we're interested in is who killed your son, Dr. Sutherland. Now, if your son was blackmailing people on the Court, if he had information to make that blackmail a genuine threat, well, that makes for a motive for murder."

Sutherland, who'd had his back to Teller, turned now and said, "You pry into people's private lives. I am a physician. My relationship with patients is privileged under time-honored ethics and, I might add, under law. My patients—"

Vera broke in now, obviously capable of staying cooler when the heat was on than the good doctor. "None of this matters," she said. "If you've come here to ask Dr. Sutherland or me direct questions, please do, then leave. Anything else, any*one* else is none of your concern."

"That's your opinion," Teller said. "Everything seems to link back to this office, to the files you keep, and as long as that link exists, I intend to pursue it. I think I speak for Miss Pinscher too."

Vera glared at Susanna. "Do you need someone to speak for you, Miss Pinscher?"

"No, Miss Jones, not usually, but in this case it happens to be true."

"Let's get back to it," Teller said.

"Please, leave this office," Sutherland said.

"Not just yet," Susanna said more calmly than she felt.

"Didn't you hear me?" Sutherland said. "You're trespassing on private property. Do I have to call—"

"The police?" Teller said.

"I'll report you," Sutherland said, his hand poised above the phone, then slowly lowered it to his side. "Detective

241

Teller, are you seriously suggesting that my own son was blackmailing me?"

"We're not suggesting anything," Susanna said, "but we are *saying* that Clarence's murder is connected, in some way we don't fully understand yet, back to you, his father, and to this office. Surely in light of what we've found out about Justices Poulson and Childs, and your involvement with the CIA, the logic in what we're saying is evident."

"If you'll excuse me," said Vera Jones, standing and going to the door.

"Not yet," Teller said. "What about the psychiatric files on Poulson and Dan Brazier?"

Sutherland was now markedly calmer, more self-assured. Presumably he'd administered some tranquilizing therapy to himself, Susanna thought with amusement. "Did your son take them?" she asked.

"Of course not."

"How secure are your files?" Teller asked.

"Very," said Vera, and she said it with genuine conviction.

Sutherland nodded vigorously. "You're making assumptions about Justice Poulson and Mr. Brazier. You're wrong. I can sympathize with your frustration. This, after all, was my son who was killed—"

"Sure . . . well, look, doctor, we *know* Poulson was your patient, ditto Brazier. What goes on between you and a patient is private. We respect that, don't want to know what problems Poulson had that made you put him into an institution for treatment. Same for Brazier's therapy. All we're saying is that your son got those people pretty damn mad at him, very possibly the Central Intelligence Agency too, which is not exactly an outfit to have mad at you. Whoever killed your son may well have done it because of something he learned and took with him from this office . . ."

Silence.

242

"Would you excuse us, Miss Jones," Sutherland finally said. Teller and Susanna looked at each other, then at Vera, who stood ramrod straight, hands at her sides, then slowly reached for the door, opened it and was gone.

"Miss Jones has been with me a very long time," Sutherland said when she had gone. "She's loyal, efficient and . . ."

"And? . . ." Susanna nudged. She was getting a bellyful of Dr. Sutherland. The man's son was a creep, but he seemed singularly unaffected by his murder.

"People like Miss Jones are wonderful, loyal, but sometimes just a little too set in their ways—too rigid—for, I hasten to add, all the right reasons. In any case, I've decided to do something she would hardly approve of and I'm not sure I do either. Still, sometimes we need to bend. You've found out that Jonathan Poulson, Chief Justice of the United States Supreme Court, was once a patient of mine. You've also learned that Dan Brazier was treated by me, and that his relationship with another justice of the Court was discussed. There are things that, no matter how hard we try, become known to others—"

"Dan Brazier isn't really important," Susanna broke in, "but what he had to say about Justice Childs is."

"Yes, Miss Pinscher, I understand that . . . By the way, while your information about certain people having been patients of mine is correct, you're wrong about Clarence. I mean to say, even if he wanted to do what you've suggested, he could not possibly have gotten into my files. My files are secure. There are two sets of keys to them, and two sets alone. I have one, Miss Jones the other."

"What about Miss Jones?" Teller asked.

"Please, don't be ridiculous. You've seen how she is, how even more rigid about confidentiality than I am—"

"Did Clarence and Miss Jones have an affair?" Susanna asked abruptly.

"From the ridiculous to the absurd. But even if that were

243

true, she would never compromise those files...not for anyone. I would entrust my very life to Miss Jones. And I say that as a psychiatrist whose job it is to know a little something about people. She is just too conditioned to loyalty and honor to deviate. Sometimes this may not always be to her advantage, but there it is, and it is certainly to my advantage and that of my patients. Past and present...But as I said, I am going to bend a little so as to convince you without question of this, which should allow you to then concentrate your efforts in more promising areas...I'm going to show you the files on Mr. Brazier and Justice Poulson..."

Teller and Susanna looked at each other, not quite believing what they were hearing.

"Surprised, I see. Don't be. I wish to cooperate and indeed *help* you in a meaningful way. So I will show you the files but *not* allow you to *read* them. You'll see they exist. You'll see they're intact and therefore played no part in the death of my son."

Sutherland buzzed Vera Jones, said into the phone, "Please bring me the files on Dan Brazier and Jonathan Poulson." She obviously balked because he said in a firmer voice, "Just do it, Miss Jones. Thank you."

She entered the office carrying two thick file folders, her face mirroring her displeasure, handed them to Sutherland, turned around and left the room. Without a word.

Sutherland first took up Brazier's file. "Here." He removed sheets of typewritten paper and spread them on the coffee table. "All here, all my notes and observations, my comments about treatment and how it was progressing, copies of letters between myself and other physicians. Mr. Brazier was not a seriously ill person. Losing one's legs is, of course, traumatic, and he needed psychological support. Which is what I tried to give him, the support to accept his physical problems and to push ahead in spite of them, using, by the way, a quite intelligent and indeed creative mind."

"He isn't succeeding too well," Susanna said.

"I'm sorry to hear that. But of course that's only your opinion, Miss Pinscher. Well . . . so much for Dan Brazier's files. All here, intact, just as they were compiled. Nothing changed, nothing out of order. My son did not, on the evidence, ever remove them, nor did anyone else."

"Are his comments about Justice Childs in that file?" Susanna asked.

"Good question, that, after all, is at the core of your interest. Here, see for yourself." He took three sheets from the pile and turned them on the table so that they faced Teller and Susanna. On top of each was typed in capital letters: KOREA-CHILDS RELATIONSHIP. Just as Teller and Susanna leaned forward to get a better look, Sutherland shuffled the pages together and returned them to the folder. "Sorry," he said, "but I told you I would not go along with actually having these files read by you . . . All right, now for Justice Poulson." He opened the Chief Justice's file and almost casually spread its pages on the table. Teller and Susanna again came forward in their seats. Teller started to ask a question, when Sutherland's face suddenly tightened. He forced a smile, collected the pages from the table and put them back into the folder. "Satisfied?"

"I suppose we have to be," Teller said.

"I think I've demonstrated beyond any question not only my willingness but my desire to cooperate." He stood, the folders under his arm. "Now, I'm afraid I really must ask you to leave. The files you place such importance on are here, as you've seen. I must trust that even my showing them to you in the limited fashion I have will remain between us, and that you will appreciate the confidentiality of *our* relationship."

Teller and Susanna stood, shook hands with him and left

through Vera Jones's office. She did not acknowledge their good-byes, just sat at her desk, hands folded on it, eyes straight ahead. . . .

They'd driven to Chevy Chase in Teller's car. When they were on their way back to Washington he asked, "Did you notice what I noticed?"

"I did, or at least I think I did. When he started looking at the sheets in Poulson's file he seemed at least for a minute there upset. He recovered quickly, but it seemed he was surprised. I think it was because the sheets in Poulson's file didn't look like the ones in Brazier's. Right? . . ."

"Go ahead. I may make you a member of the force."

"The sheets in Poulson's file all looked the same, like they'd been typed in one sitting. Brazier's were different. Obviously, Sutherland's notes on Brazier were taken and typed over a long period of time. Not so Poulson's. Maybe Clarence cleaned out the file and the loyal, honorable Miss Jones made up a new one."

"I think you're right," Teller said. "And if you are, it was the first time the shrink knew about it. He was clearly surprised, even though, like you said, he put back the old professional suave double time. . . ."

Teller pulled up in front of the Department of Justice. Susanna started to open the door, paused. "And now?"

"Good question. I'll consult my magic wall chart and see if it yields the answer. Also, I'll call you later. Okay?"

"You'd better."

MEANWHILE, IN Chevy Chase, Dr. Chester Sutherland slowly got up from his couch and approached the door leading to his outer office. He'd been sitting there for ten minutes reading through Jonathan Poulson's file. Vera had come into his office the moment Teller and Susanna were gone, but Sutherland had waved her away. "Let me explain," she'd said. "Get out, Vera."

Vera now straightened at her desk as the door opened. She looked up at him. "I did what I had to do."

"Damn it," he said, flinging the files across the room in a highly unpsychiatric fashion. "Where is Poulson's original?"

"I don't know."

"You told me he gave it back to you."

"I lied . . ."

"Do you realize the position this puts us in?"

"Did they notice?"

"I don't think so, but I'm not sure."

"Why did you ever show the files to them? It was stupid."

"I wanted them off my back. Besides, I only *showed* the files to them. I didn't allow them to see anything specific—"

"Then there's really nothing to worry about."

Sutherland gathered up the papers from the floor and put them on her desk. "I hope you're right," he said. "I just wish—"

"Just wish it hadn't happened, doctor. Yes, how much we both wish that."

CHAPTER
32

Laurie Rawls sat at her desk in Justice Conover's chambers, the phone wedged between her shoulder and ear. "Yes, I understand," she said to the caller. "Yes, that's wonderful news. I'll let everyone know immediately. Thanks."

She hung up and doodled the outline of a frame house on a yellow legal pad. When she'd added a chimney from which a thin curl of smoke twisted up to the top of the page, she picked up the phone and dialed Chief Justice Poulson's extension. His secretary Carla answered.

"Laurie Rawls, Carla. I'd like to see the Chief right away."

"He's busy, Laurie. He left word not to be disturbed."

"I think he'll want to see me, Carla. I have something

very important to discuss with him concerning Justice Conover and the abortion vote."

"How is Justice Conover?" Carla asked. "Any news?"

"No change. Please, tell Justice Poulson that I need ten minutes with him, no more."

Moments later Carla came back on the line. "Come on over now, Laurie, but make it fast, for my sake."

POULSON SAT behind a desk piled high with legal briefs. The remains of an egg salad sandwich he had brought in for lunch topped one pile of folders, two stained paper coffee cups another. He was in shirt sleeves, his face was drawn. He did not get up when she entered, simply waved to an empty chair.

"I know you're busy, Mr. Chief Justice, but I was certain you'd want to hear what I have to say."

"Carla said it was about Justice Conover?"

"Yes. Marisa called from the hospital. He briefly came out of his coma. She said he slipped back into it, but the doctors are now optimistic that he will at least partially recover."

"That's good news. Have you told the others?"

"No, only you."

His smile was fatherly, concerned. He sat up, gestured at the materials on his desk. "I feel as though I'm drowning in paper..."

Laurie smiled. "We all feel that way at times, sir. Justice Poulson, there's something else I'd like to discuss with you."

"Oh? Well...how about another time, Miss Rawls? As you can see, I'm—"

"This is the time, I think," she said, her voice determinedly firm. "Justice Poulson, I know what Clarence knew..."

"I beg your pardon..."

"I have the files, sir."

"What *files*?"

"About you... and your stay in the place in Delaware... about how the White House has known this and used it ever since you became Chief Justice..."

Face flushed, he came half out of his chair. The half-eaten sandwich slid to the floor. "How *dare* you?"

"Please, Mr. Chief Justice, try to understand. There's no need for upset over this, provided we can talk about it. Sort of man to man, sir?..."

He slumped back in his chair. Blood seemed to drain from his face, leaving it with the appearance of having been dusted with gray powder. He looked toward the door leading to the outer offices.

"Don't worry, sir," said Laurie, "no one else knows about this. It can stay that way."

He looked at her, face expressionless. Eerie, she thought to herself. Well, press on... She stood up, picked up a pitcher and poured ice water into a glass. "Here you are, sir," she said, placing the glass on the desk. "Go ahead. Drink it."

Poulson did.

Laurie sat down again. "As I said, Mr. Chief Justice, there's really no need for any of this to leave this room. I admire you very much, I always have. I think people become, well, sort of victims of circumstance and just do their best under the circumstances... sir, you've done that, I respect people who can do that..."

"Do you?" Strength had returned to his voice, along with color to his cheeks.

"Yes, I do. So did Clarence, only he went too far, didn't he?"

"Did he, Miss Rawls?"

His new-found calm bothered her. Before, when it appeared that he might fall apart, she felt in control. Now her heart tripped as she said, "I have great compassion for your . . . dilemma, Justice Poulson. You must be under tremendous pressure from many quarters, especially with the abortion vote so imminent—"

"That too?"

"Well . . . yes, it's all there in the file Clarence took from his father's office, sir. How difficult it must be to be forced to make a decision on something as sensitive as abortion . . . when your own daughter has had one . . ."

He squinted at her as though she'd gone out of focus.

"I'm sure whatever decision she made was the right one, Mr. Chief Justice."

His silence was damned unnerving.

"I understand, sir, I really do . . ."

"Do you, Miss Rawls?"

"Yes, sir, I do. An entire life ruined over one indiscretion, one mistake. It just isn't fair."

"Since you've been so busy reading, I assume you know I encouraged it."

"Yes, sir . . . the guilt, I read about it in the files."

His mood changed. He was no longer the angry, grieving, guilty father. Now he sounded like a public person . . . "Miss Rawls, I know many people don't agree with my position, but I feel my daughter is also a symbol of what must not be allowed to go on in this nation. It's not just a matter of morals, of self-determination. The same *attitude* that got my daughter into such trouble—(and you too? Laurie thought)—has gotten this nation into trouble . . . live for the moment, forget the consequences, the future . . . it's *not* just a legal matter, this case, though it comes up in a legal forum. It is a question that transcends legalisms. Because of its implications it goes to the heart of the question of our own national survival. I *believe* that, Miss Rawls, we have a President who believes it, for which I'm grateful—(not to mention that he appointed you, she thought)—I am proud

251

of where I stand, Miss Rawls, and intend to use every power at my disposal to make that stand prevail."

She assured him she was touched by what he'd said. It surely was quite a speech. "That's why we can help each other, Justice Poulson," she said. "I too want to make a contribution. As you know, sir, Clarence was offered a job on President Jorgens's staff."

"Yes, matter of fact I tried to stop it."

"You did?"

"Of course. The notion of someone like Clarence Sutherland serving the President was anathema to me—"

"Why didn't you succeed?"

"Circumstances. I don't want to talk about it, Miss Rawls."

"I've been offered the same job."

His face showed authentic surprise.

"I'm not Clarence Sutherland, Mr. Chief Justice. I'm no saint, but I want to advance *and* contribute at the same time. I believe in the late Ayn Rand's theory of selfishness. It's *not* a negative word. By being selfish, self-interested, I can achieve the sort of personal freedom and power that will enable me to help others."

"Rather oversimplified, Miss Rawls, but I suppose there's a point there... Well, so the job is yours, with, I take it, the same conditions as applied to Sutherland."

"Yes... that the abortion vote goes the way the White House wants it to."

"As I said, I believe in the President's position in this matter. Do you?"

"My personal feelings are beside the point, sir."

He grunted, leaned on the desk. "What do you want, Miss Rawls?" (Of course knowing full well the answer.)

"Support for me in getting the job I want. And support inside the Court on the abortion vote."

"My position is well known, I've never wavered. I'm for Illinois in *Nidel v. Illinois*—"

"But what about Justice Childs? They say his commitment isn't so strong . . . that his vote was supposed to be for the state's position against abortion but now he's leaning the other way on strict constitutional grounds . . . I'm a law clerk here, sir, all us clerks know from the research we do for you justices how you're leaning on a particular case . . . or at least we have a good clue or two. I'm familiar with Justice Childs's research lately . . ."

"Yes, well, an effort is being made to convince him to hold to his original position in favor of Illinois."

"Yes, sir, and if he does that the vote will stay at four to four. If Justice Conover recovers he would vote for the plaintiff, which I gather is your reason for pushing for an early vote, but if Justice Childs shifts there's no question your position will lose."

And, Poulson thought, if Childs holds firm and Justice Smith changes to our side, we're home free . . . Damn Childs . . . can't he see this isn't just a matter of the state intervening in a private citizen's choice. It goes way *beyond* that . . . If Childs had a daughter like mine—

"Sir, with all due respect, isn't the one essential, the most immediate concern Justice Childs? His position has to be solidified . . . I do believe I—"

"You can do that, Miss Rawls?"

"With your help, sir . . ."

Poulson shook his head. This woman was a little terrifying . . . "My help? Such as, Miss Rawls?"

"Make a phone call and arrange a meeting."

"With whom?"

"Miss Jones . . . Dr. Sutherland's secretary."

He turned in his chair so that he faced the window. "I don't wish to have any contact with that office—"

"Just a phone call, Mr. Chief Justice. You certainly needn't meet with anyone, but the weight of a call from you will accomplish far more than one from me. All I need, sir, is a chance to talk to Miss Jones. Here, in these chambers."

"I'm not sure I understand, but in any case, why not go to her office?"

"Because here, in this building, in these chambers, matters take on a different, an added dimension, sir. Mr. Chief Justice, if you would call and ask her to meet you here in your chambers tonight, at seven, she will certainly not question you about reasons... You can be gone when she arrives, but I'll be here. I have a... a proposition for her, an exchange that I believe will benefit everyone... you, her, me, the White House, this Court, indeed, the nation..."

"And if I refuse?"

"Well, sir, then I suspect you jeopardize a great deal ... personally and professionally, including the outcome of *Nidel v. Illinois.*"

He wanted to strangle her. What he did was to nod and turn away.

"Good. I'll be going back to Justice Conover's office. Will you call and let me know about tonight? Sir?"

"Thank you for stopping in, Miss Rawls."

Twenty minutes later she received a call in Justice Conover's chambers.

"It is arranged for seven." And then the phone was hung up.

"Thank you, *sir*," she said to the dial tone.

CHAPTER
33

MARTIN TELLER LOOKED AT HIS WATCH. HE HAD BEEN parked near the Sutherland house in Chevy Chase for nearly three hours. He had decided to renew the tail on Dr. Sutherland and Vera Jones that afternoon, and elected to take one of the shifts himself. Sutherland had left the house an hour ago and had been picked up further down the road by one of Teller's men. He would wait for Vera.

His stomach growled with hunger. He was out of cigarettes. It had turned bitterly cold, and he started the engine from time to time to keep warm. He had just turned it off again and was watching a mongrel dog cross the road when Vera Jones came out of the Sutherland driveway and turned left, in the opposite direction from which he faced. He started the car, turned and drew close enough to keep her in view. It was quite dark.

She found a parking spot near Union Station, got out and walked down First Street in the direction of the Supreme Court. Teller parked illegally and walked behind her, always ready to turn away should she decide to look back. She did not.

He stood at the foot of the steps leading up to the Supreme Court's massive front doors and watched her go up to terrace level, then veer left to a visitor-and-staff entrance at the side of the building. He looked at his watch—6:50.

LAURIE RAWLS left Justice Conover's area and walked down the long, wide corridor toward Justice Poulson's chambers. As she came abreast of Justice Childs's chambers he came through the door. "Hello, Miss Rawls," Childs said. "Working late?"

"Yes," she replied pleasantly. "You too?"

"Afraid so. I've got some time to put in before the conference in the morning on *Bain v. Paley*."

"Well, not too late, Mr. Justice."

"I'll try not to. Have a nice night."

She headed toward Chief Justice Poulson's chambers.

MOMENTS EARLIER the Chief had left his chambers, carrying with him a set of legal briefs and a law book. A guard at the end of the hall greeted him.

"Hello, John," he said.

"Be here late, Mr. Chief Justice?"

"Not too late, I hope."

He continued walking until he reached the doors that led to the main courtroom. They were open; a guard who usually stood in front of them was at the far end of the corridor drinking from a public fountain. Poulson stepped into the courtroom. It was dark except for lights playing off the fountains in the courtyard that cast flickering, erratic flashes of white across the huge chamber.

LAURIE RAWLS saw Vera Jones standing outside the entrance to Poulson's office suite. She had never actually met her before but recognized her from descriptions Clarence had given her... "looks like a bird... Miss Prim... a hatchet face... not bad in the sack, though... Laurie's face, and stomach, tightened at the memory of these last words.

Vera turned at the sound of Laurie's shoes on the marble floor.

"Miss Jones?" Laurie asked.

"Yes... I have an appointment, with Chief Justice Poulson..."

"Yes, I know. I'm Laurie Rawls, a law clerk here."

Vera gave no sign that she knew about Laurie through Clarence. She stood stiffly, without expression, as Laurie offered her hand and said, "Actually, I'm afraid Justice Poulson won't be able to be here for your meeting. He was called away, but I can fill in, with his approval."

"I don't understand..."

"Please, come in." Laurie entered the outer office and flipped on the overhead lights.

Vera remained in the hallway. Laurie turned. "Come on in, Miss Jones, it's just like any other office. No dragons."

Vera still did not move.

"Miss Jones," Laurie said, hands on hips, "I really don't have all night. If you'll just come in I'll get to the point right away."

Vera looked to her left and right before moving across the threshold.

"Have a seat," Laurie said, pointing to a leather chair against the wall.

"I'll stand. I'm not sure I approve of this. Justice Poulson said nothing about you—"

"It's *okay*, Miss Jones, I assure you. Justice Poulson and I discussed it at length this afternoon. What I'm about to suggest, as I said, has his approval."

When Vera still didn't take the chair Laurie shrugged, leaned back against a desk and said, "I have something you need, and you have something we need."

"We?"

"Here, at the Court."

"What could I possibly have that—"

"The file on Dan Brazier."

"I don't know what you're talking about—"

"Oh, of course you do. Dan Brazier was a patient of your boss, Dr. Sutherland, just as Chief Justice Poulson was. I don't intend to beat about the bush, Miss Jones. The fact that you and Clarence had an affair . . . an amusing word for something between people of such different ages . . . is not my concern now, nor is your reason for allowing Clarence to take certain files from his father's office. What *is* important is that I've come into possession of Justice Poulson's file. I assume you'd like to have it back. At the same time, there are things in Mr. Brazier's file that are of interest to—"

"You are sick, Miss Rawls."

"Only of you and your posturing, Miss Jones. Let's get down to it . . . I'm offering you an even swap that will benefit everyone—"

"Everyone? You mean you."

"I mean everyone. I'm not at liberty to discuss Court business, but the importance to this Court of having Mr. Brazier's file, the importance to the administration itself and to the nation is substantial, I assure you. It is not just a matter of individuals. There's a greater good—"

"Greater good?" Vera said, shaking her head and now sitting on the edge of the chair. "My God, what would you

or Clarence know about a greater good, or any good? Those files represent a sacred trust—"

"You should have thought of that when you gave them to him."

"I didn't *give* Clarence anything. He *took* advantage of a situation—"

"Yes," —Laurie smiled— "he was very good at that, wasn't he? What did he do, Miss Jones, steal the keys while you lay next to him on the office couch—?"

"You're disgusting."

"Please, let us be ladies . . . now, back to business. You give me Brazier's files, or a true copy of them, and I'll return Justice Poulson's files."

"After you've copied them?"

"Trust me."

The laugh burst from her.

"What choice do you have, Miss Jones?"

". . . I'll have to think about it—"

"After consulting with your employer?"

"Leave Dr. Sutherland out of this. He was as much a victim of his son as I was."

"A convenient way to get off the hook."

"Think what you will—" Suddenly Vera felt an intense, enveloping heat. She took off her cap and unbuttoned the top of her coat.

"Are you all right?" Laurie said. "Would you like some water?"

"No, I feel fine . . . Is that all you have to say to me?"

"That's all. Brazier for Poulson. I need to know first thing tomorrow morning."

"Why?"

"Not your concern, Miss Jones."

Vera stood, touched the back of the chair for support. She felt light-headed, her legs were weak. She clenched her

259

cap at her side, squeezed it as hard as she could, her long, sinewy fingers pushing through the loosely knitted fabric.

"I'll walk you out," Laurie said.

Vera's body seemed to go rigid, as though the words had physically touched her. "No, stay away from me. You're no different than he was—"

"Oh, we're very different, Miss Jones. We're in the same business, of course, but Clarence is dead and I'm alive. Quite a difference, I'd say. I intend to carry on in Clarence's memory at the White House . . . I've been offered the position Clarence would have had . . . if he'd lived. Isn't that good news?"

"God, you are so vile—"

"Miss Jones, I'll be at my desk in Justice Conover's chambers by eight in the morning. Here's my extension." She scribbled a number on a slip of paper.

"Go to hell."

"Whatever you say, Miss Jones. Good night. . . ."

Laurie waited a few moments, then turned off the lights and stepped into the hall. Vera was gone. She returned to Conover's chambers, where a shaft of light came from beneath the door to the justice's private chambers. Laurie was sure she had turned off all the lights before meeting with Vera Jones. She thought of calling the security office, then decided to investigate for herself. She went to the door, listened, heard something slam shut. She opened the door.

Cecily Conover was hunched over her husband's desk. She jumped to attention, lost her balance and fell into her husband's large leather chair.

"What are you doing here?" Laurie demanded.

"I was . . . God, you scared me. I was looking for that file—"

"How dare you search through his desk."

Cecily got to her feet. "I called and asked you to help me find that file. It has nothing to do with the Court, with

260

government, with anything except my life . . . can't you understand that? I'm trying to survive, just like he is."

"And it looks like he will?"

"Yes, it does, enough to make sure of a divorce that will strip from me everything that's rightfully mine—"

"Since when does a wife who sleeps around deserve anything in a divorce?"

"Coming from *you*—"

"Get *out*."

"Please, Miss Rawls . . . I'll pay you. If I have that file at least the settlement will be decent for me. I'll share it with you, I promise . . . I'll do anything you want, only get it for me—"

Laurie snapped off the lights and went to the outer office, leaving Cecily standing in the dark next to the desk. Slowly Cecily crossed the carpeted room and joined Laurie. "Won't you listen to reason, Miss Rawls? Clarence told me you were the brightest female he'd ever met—"

Laurie, whose back had been to Cecily, quickly turned. "Clarence told you that?"

"Yes. I suppose it was his way of making me feel stupid. He used to tell me I was dumb—"

"I know," Laurie said, taking satisfaction in the look on Cecily's face. "Mrs. Conover . . . I suppose I can call you that a little while longer . . . the record your husband collected about you is very safe—"

"It is? Where is it?"

"I have it. Clarence gave it to me."

"Then for God's sake give it to me. What good is it to you?"

"Maybe we can work something out. Meanwhile, be assured that we share what's in it, just you and me and, of course, your husband. But it really isn't of much value to him unless he has it, now is it?"

"You're blackmailing me."

261

"It was your suggestion. Look, all you have to do is make sense with me from time to time ... We could have lunch, perhaps even dinner. Relax, Mrs. Conover, we can be good friends. We have quite a lot in common."

Yes ... we have Clarence—"

"*No*, we don't have him in common, Mrs. Conover. Clarence loved me. For him, you were just a temporary diversion. Good night, Mrs. Conover, you know the way out."

HE ENTERED the darkened courtroom and stood next to the bench, his fingertips resting lightly on it. Here was America's highest *concilium*, where in daylight eight men and one woman decided the various fates of millions of people. Their power was as great as the tons of lactescent marble used to create the arena. Greater.

Words. Millions of words spoken here on behalf of men condemned to die, the disenfranchised seeking justice, corporations in conflict with individuals, the issues always more important than the individuals bringing them for adjudication. For here, truly, was the court of last resort.

It was operatic, he thought, the room a slumbering giant, sated with that day's offerings and waiting for another sun to rise, for another case to be debated and decided in favor of plaintiff or defendant, hero or villain, Christian or lion.

Above him the justices' nine chairs, each a different height and shape, stood empty and facing in different directions. He smiled. The Court ran with precision, yet the chairs were never lined up. Appropriate. There were few unanimous, orderly decisions either.

He climbed the few steps leading to the bench and slowly walked behind the chairs until he reached the middle one. It faced to its left. He sat in it, not turning, simply accepting the direction in which it pointed him, toward the windows and fountains. The chair did not feel comfortable to him. . . .

She entered the courtroom and stood just inside the door. Light from the fountains played across pews and benches, off the long brass rail and silent microphones, occasionally reaching the ceiling.

There was one nearly constant pool of light that splashed across the lectern, causing its burnished finish to glisten. She felt calmer than she had minutes ago, although she knew it was misleading. Until her collapse, which thank God had occurred in private, she'd felt very much in control of herself. But then it had happened, as though plugs had been pulled from her body, allowing every drop of control and resolve to pour from her, leaving her drained and shaking, feeling as though she would break into a thousand pieces. Laurie Rawls . . . that horrible woman had been the catalyst to her coming undone . . . God, she was Clarence reincarnate—worse, if that was possible . . .

She fixed her attention on the lectern, something to lean on. She walked to it, touched its illuminated surface, then its dark part, as though there might be a tactile difference.

She heard something, looked up at the nine black leather chairs. Had the middle one moved? Darkness played tricks . . . sound was exaggerated, light created bizarre shapes.

Another sound, this time from behind. She turned slowly and peered into the section of the courtroom reserved for the press. Nothing. She started to tremble again and gripped the lectern, head lowered, legs threatening to collapse under her. This was where it had happened . . .

Another sound from the bench, metal against metal. "Is someone there?"

No response.

Her purse dropped to the floor. She did not pick it up. . . .

Teller, who sat in the shadows of the press section, wasn't sure for a moment whether to stand up and let her see him. He had followed her to the building, used his earlier security clearance, as detective in charge of the investigation of

Sutherland's murder, to gain access and note her being met by Laurie Rawls; noted too Chief Justice Poulson leave his chambers and walk to the courtroom. Teller had decided the best he could do was to trail the Chief Justice, which he had done, followed him to the courtroom, watched him take his accustomed seat at the bench. Did he expect to see the woman who now was behaving so erratically? No, actually he had intended to wait a few minutes, see what, if anything, Poulson was up to, and then go outside the courtroom to wait for the woman who had disappeared into Poulson's chambers with Laurie Rawls. Yet here they both were, and it was clear that the end of this bizarre, in so many ways unsavory, case was about to take place where it had begun — with the discovery of the chief clerk, dead from a gunshot wound in the chair of the highest judicial personage of the land.

Now Teller watched, with sadness and a shivery feeling that he was somehow invading the sanctity of a very troubled human being's innermost feelings. She struck the lectern's side with clenched fists, muttered, barely audibly, "And what was it for? Was it all for nothing?..."

As if in eerie answer, the leather chair at the center of the bench turned slowly to face the front. She could not make out the figure in the chair clearly, little more than a hand on the chair's arm was clear. But Teller knew who it was...the same man who regularly occupied that chair during the proceedings of the Court...the Chief Justice of the Supreme Court of the United States. Both he and the woman, for reasons that obviously compelled them, had returned to the scene of the crime, and in their separate but related fashions were principal players in the final act of this crime's resolution...Teller shook his head, reflected with some frustration but also with a sense of the appropriateness of it all, that when this murder, like so many others, was solved, it would be the principals rather than the police—whatever their contribution—that brought it to its finale. Well, at least he was here on the scene, which was more than he was able to be in most cases he'd worked on. At least he had, thanks in large part to Susanna's digging and smart evaluations, pretty much figured out who the guilty party was, and it was what he knew and suspected that had brought him here for the denouement . . .

"It was not for nothing." The voice came from the Chief Justice's chair. And now Chief Justice Jonathan Poulson leaned forward so that his face was illuminated by the light that came in through the windows. "But let me tell you, young lady, you have no obligation to say anything more—"

"I want to, though. I need to . . . It wasn't just that he was so cruel to me, and he was . . . but he was cruel to other people too, I know that. He was so damn clever, and more than that, unscrupulous. That was really what made it all possible, his willingness to do anything, say anything to get what he wanted—"

"I repeat," Poulson interrupted, "you really should not say anything more. You have your rights, and you will be well defended—"

Teller decided it was time to show himself. Leaving the shadows of the press section, he crossed halfway to the lectern, looked up at the bench. "Good evening, Mr. Chief Justice." Poulson did not reply, only nodded to him, clearly annoyed that there was a witness to this scene, one that he felt was uniquely private, one that he and the troubled woman at the lectern had a right to share alone, at least for now.

Teller turned to her. "Miss Jones, I'm sorry to break in on you like this. Believe that. But I'm also afraid that I have to tell you that you're under arrest." Feeling almost ridiculous, he proceeded to read her her rights, as he was obliged to do—after all, some judges in this very Court had prescribed them, or at least sanctioned them.

"Listen to him," Poulson said. "It's in your interest—"

But she was not yet through. Speaking slowly, as though not quite hearing either Teller or Poulson, she said, "I thought it was the right thing to do, he had hurt so many, and was threatening so many more. My God, he had things to hurt the Chief Justice of the Supreme Court, to ruin the reputation of another justice, a national hero even, to get to the President . . . he was going to use his rotten influence, influence based on filth, poking into other people's lives . . . to make laws about having babies . . . abortion . . . *he* was an abortion . . . even his father, his own father, a doctor, said so . . ."

Poulson came down from the bench, asked Teller to leave, that he would see that Vera Jones came to headquarters later, but Teller, much as he would have liked to go along with that, knew he could not properly do it. Sometimes Supreme Court judges, especially the Chief Justice, tended to forget the nitty-gritty of lowly police procedure. They could afford it. He couldn't.

As he began to lead Vera out of the courtroom, he asked her what she meant by saying, "Was it all for nothing?"

She shook her head. "I mean that terrible Laurie Rawls . . . I know people will say I hate her because we both had affairs with Clarence, but it's not just that." She looked at Teller now, seemed to come back from the remote state she'd been in. "Detective Teller . . . yes, you and Miss Pinscher were right to come to the office, to wonder about the Poulson file. God knows, I only wish I had it when you came, that I hadn't been such a damned miserable fool as to believe him about what he said he felt for me. Did I really believe him? I'm afraid I did . . . because I so much *wanted* to. You never knew him, but he could be the most charming, loving, even . . . yes, loving . . . At first it was the looks, some people said a Robert Redford look-alike. He could convince you that you were the only woman alive . . . yes, he convinced me of that, and of course I badly wanted to believe it, like I said. I'm not the most desirable woman to most

266

men, I was flattered, excited, felt like a real woman for the first time since I could remember . . . Oh, there are no excuses, not really . . ."

"Well, that's right, Vera, but there are explanations, and you've got them, if anybody in a case like this ever did. I don't know what will happen, but I'm damned if I'm not going to do what I can to see that those explanations aren't forgotten when it counts . . ." He was about to say "when you come to trial," but maybe that wouldn't happen, maybe they'd get her off on grounds of temporary insanity, which would be okay by him in one sense, but in another, damned unfair. What the lady had done was murder and nobody could say that was okay . . . but if ever there was a justification . . . and not saying there was . . . Vera Jones sure had it . . .

"Thank you," and she almost smiled, "but there's still Laurie Rawls. Now she has the file on the Chief Justice, just like Clarence did. She just now tried to get Justice Childs's file too, threatening me. Well, at least she won't get that. But Justice Poulson's file . . ."

"I wouldn't worry too much about that now," Teller said, although he was plenty worried. Whatever Vera Jones said would be discounted by Laurie. That tough little lady would deny everything, say Vera was cracked, had gone around the bend because Clarence gave her a tumble and then dumped her, and so forth. And some might be inclined to believe her. Well, by God, Clarence hadn't given him a tumble, and he hadn't gone round the bend . . . well, not yet anyway, but if he hung around this city much longer who could predict? Sooner or later it seemed to get to everybody, even to a wonderful opera-loving gourmet cop like Martin Teller . . .

"But I am worried," Vera was saying. "I know people won't believe me. I know what they'll say about me. And if that woman ever gets a job close to the President, like Clarence was going to do and like she says she's after—"

"We'll work on that, Vera... Tell me, what happened that night... I mean, if you can talk about it now, maybe it will help me to help you..."

She nodded, shrugged. "I'd called Clarence and pleaded with him to return the files on Justice Poulson that he'd gotten from me. My God, along with everything else, I'd betrayed his father, a man I've worked for and respected for years. Clarence told me to come to his office, we'd talk about it. When I got there he laughed at me, called me names... some of which I deserved... especially about being dumb. Anyway, after a while we came into this courtroom—"

"Why?"

"He liked it here, said he'd be sitting in one of the chairs up there one day, maybe even the chair in the Oval Office. God, isn't that scary?"

Teller nodded. "It surely is, Miss Jones... Well, what happened then?"

"I knew that there was more than idle threat in what he said. He had so much on so many people... I asked him for the file, for *my* sake... that will show you how dumb I was, all right..."

"Go back a moment, Miss Jones. That night with Clarence before you came to the courtroom. Did anything else happen there?" He was wondering about the gun.

"Yes, he had a file of material that Justice Conover had collected about his wife. Clarence had found it in Justice Conover's chambers and took it, along with a gun. He laughed about how he had found out about the file, that Mrs. Conover had told him about it, that she was sure her husband was keeping tabs on her... she and Clarence had been... intimate... too. And so Clarence went to the judge's office and found it, got into his locked files... and we know how he got the key, don't we? From Laurie Rawls. Clarence brought the gun with him into the courtroom. He told me not to worry, that he'd take good care of me, just as his father had done for years. Imagine, trying to compare himself with his father . . . He also laughed at Justice Conover, said how hypocritical it was for a great liberal and anti-gun-control man to keep a gun in his office. I didn't think much about it at the time, but now I wish I had said something, that maybe a man like Justice Conover had made enemies in his career by his courageous stands, maybe he had good reason to keep a gun. Clarence, though, said it was to scare away all the men sniffing around the old boy's . . . those were his words . . . wife. And I knew then what I'd known but never admitted to myself . . . that Clarence had been one of those men, that he'd had an affair with Mrs. Conover too. And then he started in about all the other stuff he had to keep other people in line . . . justices of this Court, his own father, even the President . . . Oh yes, he said, he'd be in the White House sooner than anybody thought . . ."

Teller stopped her just as they came to the courtroom door. He led her back, gently holding her arm, and up to the raised area of the bench. Poulson, as he expected, had gone. He followed now just behind her, letting go of her arm. He removed his .38 from its holster beneath his armpit, emptied the bullets into his pocket. He offered her the gun when she reached the middle chair, the Chief Justice's chair. "Vera, show me what happened. Was Clarence sitting here?"

She nodded.

Leave it to paranoid Clarence to pick the Chief Justice's chair. Crazy, but crazy like a fox . . . Teller sat in the chair. "Go ahead, Vera."

She resisted taking the gun at first, then did and quickly placed it on the bench in front of Teller. "He began one of his speeches about how grateful he was for all the stupid, corrupt people who made themselves so conveniently vulnerable to him. How in a way they were all working for him, and maybe someday he'd have a reunion, when he

269

made it to where he was going . . . He went on like that, until I just couldn't stand it. Oh yes, he included me in his group, but it was more than the awfulness of what he said, it was the way he said it so calmly, like it was already done, like nothing could stop him . . . it took hold of me then, my own part in what he had done and even worse what he would do . . . all because of my own stupidity and weakness . . . And then, you won't believe this, but then he actually tried to make love to me, grabbed hold of me and I picked up that gun"—she picked up the gun now—"and . . . I did it . . ." And as she said those last words she squeezed the trigger, and the only sound in that august courtroom was the sound of metal striking metal, a sound that the late Clarence Sutherland never heard.

Gently he took the gun from her hand, returned it to his holster, and led her out of the courtroom, out of the building and into the dark Washington night.

CHAPTER
34

THEY LEFT THE KENNEDY CENTER AFTER A PERFORMANCE of Puccini's *La Bohème*.

"It was great," Susanna said. "So much . . . passion."

"That's Puccini," Teller said as he let go of her hand and fumbled for his car keys. "Where to now?"

"Up to you. No, I take that back. You picked the entertainment, so far, now it's up to me." She looked straight ahead, and said, straight faced, "We go to your place."

And just as straight faced, he said, "The cleaning woman hasn't been in, joint's a mess—"

"You don't have a cleaning woman."

"I surrender."

* * *

IN HIS apartment, which was fully as much of a mess as he'd warned it would be, he took an old blanket off of the couch. "Keeps the cat hairs off. Sit, but watch out for the middle, a bad spring." He put on the stereo. "Drink?"

"Love one."

When they'd settled in with their drinks, he said, "Vera told me Clarence looked like Robert Redford. Not in the morgue he didn't. I didn't go into that. I'd already put her through enough in the courtroom. God, it was eerie, Poulson there, then her showing me how she shot Sutherland . . ."

They sat on one end of the couch, drinks in hand. One of the cats rubbed against her leg.

"Martin," she said, "do you think it's over?"

"Yes . . . well, our part in it anyway. Tell me about your scene with Laurie Rawls." After he had told Susanna what Vera had said about Laurie, Susanna had approached Laurie. To try to talk her out of what she intended to do . . .

"I went to her apartment. Of course she was very different from what she'd been the other times we'd been together. All self-assured and hard. Until I told her that you were ready to press blackmail charges against her."

"What did she say?"

"At first she hung tough, said I was bluffing. I told her that besides having enough evidence to make a solid case, a few leaks to the media would ruin her White House chances anyway."

"And?"

"She quickstepped into Miss Sugar again, even managed a few tears. Told me as a woman I ought to *under-stand* . . . she was only trying to look out for herself in a tough man's world."

"And?"

"I'm afraid I almost hit her. What I told her was to stuff it, that if she didn't resign from the Court, turn down the

272

White House job and get out of town I'd make it my career to make sure she went to jail. I think she believed me."

"Good deal. And of course the White House wouldn't touch her now anyway, and she knows it."

"Do you know what still bothers me, Martin? Jorgens is still President and Poulson is still Chief Justice."

"Susanna, we solved a murder. After that, it's life goes on. Speaking of which," and he reached for her.

"Hold it, detective. I'm still *talking* . . ."

"I know. All right, look, you could leak the story to some buddy reporter about Poulson having been in an institution and that President Jorgens knew about it when he nominated him for Chief Justice."

"I couldn't—"

"Of course you couldn't."

"Besides, there's Childs. He's still an inspiration to millions of people. His story would come out, and in the worst possible light." She sipped her drink. "Do you think Dr. Sutherland knew Vera Jones had killed his son?"

"I think so. Boy, what a rat he was, his own father wouldn't turn in his murderer."

"Did she say so to you? I mean that the doctor knew?"

"She as much as said it, and it was pretty clear anyway. But what do I do with that kind of information? I could bring charges against him for obstructing justice by withholding information about a murder investigation, but that's not in the cards. It's been billed as a crime of passion. That way nobody's boat gets rocked. And it's a better defense for Vera . . . God knows, she deserves all the breaks she can get. Besides I've got other things to worry about, like a pregnant daughter, my pension and two mangy cats . . . What about you, counselor?"

"I'm thinking of taking off."

"You just got here. And this was your idea, remember?"

"I mean to California, idiot. And I do remember—"

"No, damn it."

"I talked to my ex. It hasn't been so easy for him, trying to start over again, taking care of three kids. It's time I took them on, grew up. I think a new start might be good for all of us."

He didn't know what to say except, "Want another drink?"

"Please."

When he came back from the kitchen with the refills, she asked him more about what Vera Jones had told him before her formal interrogation.

"I really felt for her," he said. "Still do. She snapped in the courtroom when she was with Clarence that night, like she did at first the night she confessed. Funny, she lost control, shot him, then collected herself enough to return the gun to Conover's chambers, using keys Clarence had with him. More, she goes back to the courtroom and puts the keys in his pocket. It's ironic that Clarence had Poulson's file with him that night, only she didn't know it. She thought he only had the file Justice Conover had built on his wife. Vera returned it to Conover's chambers too, along with the gun and Poulson's file, which is now back in Dr. Sutherland's office where it belongs. She could have taken it that night but didn't have her wits about her enough for that. Or maybe she was scared to be stopped going out and having it found on her. I guess that was it . . .

"Well, after seeing the phony file Sutherland showed us. I thought so. He was surprised, you'll remember, so that left Vera as the only one who could have taken it, and then tried to cover her tracks with retyped stuff. That's why I decided to follow her myself. I got lucky."

"Not so lucky . . . for a cop you're pretty smart . . . By the way, what did you think about the decision in *Nidel v. Illinois*?"

"What did you think?"

"Well, you know my sentiments, but more than anything,

I think I was especially pleased to see Justice Conover get well enough to vote. He's a good man and has had a rough time."

"Must be a blow to the White House," he said.

"I guess, but like you say, there are more important things —like your kids, mine, our lives—speaking of which, detective, enough of this talk, let's get down to cases." She moved over close to him on the couch.

"Not here, the spring..."

"Doesn't a bachelor detective have a bedroom?"

He did, and after shoving the cats from their way, proceeded to show her, and to put thoughts of California, at least for the moment, far, far out of her mind.

ABOUT THE AUTHOR

Margaret Truman is the author of *Murder on Capitol Hill*, *Murder in the White House*, and *Murder in the Smithsonian*, as well as *Letters from Father: The Truman Family's Personal Correspondence*. Born in Independence, Missouri, she now makes her home in New York City.